DEAD ON ARRIVAL

BY: KYM ROBERTS

Cover Art by

Susan Coils of Custom Covers

www.coverkicks.com

Edited by

Pamela Dougherty

www.pameladougherty.com

To my husband, you will always be my addiction.

SPECIAL THANKS

There are so many people who took part in the creation of this book, The Lit Girls: Jessica Davidson, Mary Duncanson, Kimberly Quinton, Misa Ramirez, Rebekah Reed, Beatriz Terrazas, Marty Tidwell, Tracy Ward, and Wendy Watson who have helped me in countless ways, to the women of Chick Swagger who walked with me on this journey, to Jerrie Alexander who made this book possible, and to all the members of NTRWA for your continued support — Thank you!

But most of all thank you to my family, who sacrificed so much for me to catch the wave.

CHAPTER ONE

My brother says I'm vain.

I pretty much think he's an idiot, so we're even.

He's the oldest of the four of us, and he followed our dad's footsteps into law enforcement (that's not the idiotic part). But I found the uniforms boring, so I forged my own trail in the sands of paradise, where board shorts and bikinis rule. Favorite pastimes on Kaua'i consist of surfing the waves and catching some rays. Both of those activities require endurance and very little clothing, which is the reason why I run. A lot. Whether I'm narcissistic, or a masochist in denial, remains to be seen.

To avoid the tourists, I jog the beaches only the locals know about, in the dark, before the sun crests the inky line across the white-capped ocean. Those early morning hours when vacationers are asleep in their beds dreaming of island sex trophies. (Been there, done that. Big mistake.)

This morning's run was supposed to launch my day with the rejuvenating effects of nature. It should have been peaceful — the surf beating against the shore, my feet pounding the sand, my heart striking my ribs — while I convinced myself that I absolutely loved to work out, and that it had nothing to do with vanity.

But an unexpected intruder interrupted my routine. I would have missed it completely if I'd left my flashlight in the car. (Why didn't I leave the damn thing behind?) At the high tide water line — like he'd crawled his way up the smoothed surface of the beach.

A body. A body that didn't look very appealing. Youngish, maybe 30-something, it was kind of hard to tell. Bloated. Discolored, with parts missing. Fish bait or decomp, I don't really know. This was a first for me.

I apologize for sharing the creepy facts and gory details. The image of a body being a piece of discarded driftwood is the last thing anyone wants to see. When you live on an island, it's a well-known fact that when bodies wash up, they rarely look like the gorgeous models you see on television.

Maybe I reached down to roll it over because my brain expected to see the television image. You know, bulging pecs erupting from his shirt. A strong jaw accentuated by wet strands of wavy hair and a slightly grayish color to an intensely male mouth.

Nope, that's *not* reality. That's television. And this wasn't a TV show. What I got was worse than seeing an obese grandpa in a white Speedo. It was beyond revolting. It was DOA. And I was stupid enough to put my hands on it.

Trust me when I say the last thing you want to do is *touch* a floater. I made that stupid mistake. Just to make sure it was completely dead. Like the sand, seaweed and bugs weren't enough evidence for me? Even the light of my flashlight couldn't hide the dark holes filling the eye sockets as I rolled it over by its arm.

Help me.

The plea disappeared with the granules of sand in the outbound tide. A small utterance, tumbling into the depths. Never spoken. Never heard. At least not in any reality I cared to live in.

A hope that the scene I discovered was just a vivid nightmare, raced to the forefront of my thoughts. "Wake up," I whispered.

Nothing happened.

"WAKE UP!" I commanded.

But I wasn't asleep, and I couldn't escape the sight in front of me.

My body spasmed and my shoulders hitched. A juicy slurping noise followed with the immediate response of a bone-chilling crack. In horror, my reflexes froze, and I was left with an arm.

In. My. Hand.

Like, *totally* detached from the rest of the body. A cold squishy arm with jellyfish-like skin slipping from the bone. In terrorized awe, my

3

fingers refused to disconnect from the vile waste. Instead, they sank into the flesh, vanishing into the muck that once held human form.

A ten-foot wave of nausea built in my stomach, thrusting my body into action. I dropped the arm, my mini flashlight, any sense of reality I'd had two minutes earlier, and sprinted for the rocks. My momentary brain fart cost me the contents of my stomach. Last night's dinner no longer came close to resembling my dad's sumptuous Saimin recipe. Life turned into piles of discarded refuse. No longer appealing. No longer the rare lovable form it once held.

I lost the weight in my stomach the hard way. Bulimics might say it was the easy way, but they'd be lying. When my stomach could give no more, I stumbled for the ocean, determined to rid my hand of the contagions I'd contacted.

I should have been able to stop there…right?

Wrong.

I saturated my entire body while imaginary insects skittered up my arms and legs. I knew they weren't real, but they trailed across my stomach and onto the back of my neck anyway.

The creeping just *would not* stop.

Too afraid to venture out any further, I immersed myself in shallow water. My wobbly legs, however, were no match for the beating surf and I collapsed. My knees sank into the earth as the tide retrieved the sand — pulling and pulling, in what I imagined to be an attempt to swallow me whole.

Depthless eye sockets flashed in my mind, forcing me to crawl closer toward shore. I would not end up like that mushy thing on the beach.

Sightless. Lifeless. And now *almost* armless...thanks to me.

The water should have been cool and refreshing. It should have soothed my violently quivering body as I used the sand like a loofah pad. Instead, the ocean did absolutely nothing to calm my panic.

I rubbed and scrubbed beyond the point of pain, but I still couldn't shake the sense of contamination. I'd been exposed to the worst possible toxin.

Death.

No matter how hard I tried, nothing worked. Nothing made the corpse on the beach jump up, laughing hysterically. Nor did a camera crew pop up from behind the rocks to say I'd been punked.

I hadn't considered myself naïve until a few minutes ago. Now, I knew. My blissful innocence was gone.

Finally, the crawling sensation across my body eased. I left the water with skin that felt, and undoubtedly looked, like the raw bright flaky meat of red salmon. Forcing myself back on the beach, I refused to let my eyes stray toward the body, now lit up from the beam of my flashlight like a retail display window.

Why hadn't I looked closer before turning it over?

Thoughts of approaching it to retrieve my flashlight had my already hung-over digestive tract threatening to explode. It didn't help that the earth no longer absorbed death's odors like a sponge. Instead, a mocking swirl of wind carried the stench through the air to meet its final resting place — permanently attached to the inside of my nose.

Help me.

I ignored it. Again. I couldn't help *myself*, let alone the lost soul of a dead guy who I imagined was talking to me.

Instead, I retched again, making a frat boy on spring break look like a professional yakker. The decision to abandon my hundred dollar Mag-lite the size of my palm was simple. I'd rather risk the jagged path to the road in total darkness than approach that thing again.

However, as I passed its final resting place, I couldn't stop myself from apologizing. "Oh, God, I'm sorry. I'm *so* sorry."

The slight incline to the road, covered with the roots and branches of a variety of coastal plants and bushes, became as difficult as scaling the Napali Coast. Slipping to my knees, I clawed my way to the top and collapsed at the finish line — exhausted, wet, whipped and warped. I pulled myself to my feet and frantically waved at the few passing vehicles, but none of them stopped.

Frustrated and exhausted, I gave up and staggered down the side of the road. My only option was to run back to my car and get my phone. An option I really didn't want to take, and wouldn't *have* to take, if only I'd listened to my parents and carried my phone with me while I ran.

What they didn't know wouldn't hurt them. It might kill me, but they'd be asleep and oblivious to my predicament.

That mile to my car was the longest, stupidest run of my life.

CHAPTER TWO

The police finally arrived, and I was ever so grateful to punt the case in their direction. Rid myself of the questions that plagued my mind like the death cooties that contaminated my body. I'd hoped to get back in my car and head home to take a nice hot shower. Instead, I was stuck standing outside my car with a yellow plastic crime scene blanket wrapped around me for warmth while we waited for the detectives. Shaking and trembling, I bounced back and forth from one foot to the other in my disposable blanket.

A dark colored Dodge Charger with tinted windows pulled to a stop in front of my car and I cringed, half-expecting, half-hoping it wouldn't be him. But I knew better. Pulling the blanket tighter, I waited for the moment our eyes met, for him to actually see who had stumbled upon the body.

I expected him to be emotional. Angry. Concerned. Something.

I got none of that. Beyond an eye roll, he refused to acknowledge our relationship. No hug. No questions about my health. Nothing. He just ignored me, until it was time to issue orders.

"Have a seat in my car before you freeze your ass off." He turned toward the uniform.

For a moment, I just stared at his back. Then I gathered my pride and said, "Sure thing, *detective sergeant*." I think I may have spat out his title in anger.

I stomped my way to his car and ignored the conversation I couldn't hear between Detective Sergeant John Kumu and the young officer who'd already taken my information.

A lot of my friends thought John was hot. The strong silent type. I didn't see it, nor would I ever see it, because John was my older brother.

Remember? The idiot.

I slammed his car door shut and waited, staring out the windshield into the dark blue sky. John slipped into the driver's seat a few minutes later and sniffed. "What's that smell?"

"The man's arm…" I was unable to finish, unable to fathom the actions of my brother, as he got comfortable in his police car.

John opened a bag on the seat between us and raised a soft glazed pastry in front of my face. "Want one?" His tone was innocent as a child. A *devil* child.

My innards seized. I shook my head, afraid to say anything as my stomach searched for something to throw at him. Acting oblivious to my discomfort, John tilted back his head, closed his eyes and moaned in an act of savoring every bite. His fingers sank into the sugary casing.

Like mine had indented the shell of the corpse.

Red jelly filling oozed from the side of his pastry.

Like the fatty tissue on the arm that had separated from the body.

I stared in horror as the jelly plopped on his napkin.

Like...

I would never eat a donut again.

John had the nerve to snicker, his lips drawing back in defective cop humor as a strangled laugh escaped his lips.

Strong silent type, my ass.

I laid into him. "You jerk. You've never t*ouched* a body. Your hands have never come in contact with cold flesh. No. You study bodies with your *eyes*. When the time comes to get dirty, you leave that job to the body snatchers."

"The men and women of the Medical Examiner's Office don't particularly like being called 'body snatchers,'" he lectured.

Ignoring his correction, I focused on the obvious. "You couldn't pay me to do that job."

"Yeah, just call Malia Fern, part-time go-fer for Private Kaua'EYE's Investigations; she'll do it for free," he countered before taking another bite of his donut. "Why couldn't you just call the cops like a normal person without tearing up the crime scene? Do you think you're a private detective now?"

I glared at him as he chewed and looked back at me. We were reduced to our old staring contests. The ones we'd mastered when I was four and he was ten. He always won, but I was determined not to lose this time. I wrapped myself in anger and self-pity. My legs irritated me with involuntarily twitching. The sand in my shorts was driving me crazy, but I refused to show any more discomfort for John to use as props for his sick sense of humor. I would win this contest if it killed me.

His phone rang and John looked away. He was using work as an excuse for losing. I smiled. Chalk one up for Mal.

I turned to stare out the window, flexing the muscles in my legs and concentrated on getting the feeling back in all of my extremities. I ignored his conversation, until something in his voice caught my attention.

Was it the inflection? The words? The slight lowering of his voice when he said, "Missing tourist." Whatever it was, it snagged my curiosity and awakened the part of my brain the detectives at my job were always trying to engage — the private investigating part. The voice I'd been trying to silence. Until now.

I listened. My ears pricked as the officer on the other end of the phone reeled me in. "…wife said he was a recovering addict." John moved the phone to his other hand, making the conversation mumbled to my ears.

The garble grated under my skin almost as badly as the sand chafing my ass. Who was the man I'd found? That body hadn't look like that of an addict's. Although the clothes were dirty, I didn't believe the cause was from poor hygiene, at least not before the time of death. No, the clothes had appeared business-like, professional. I'd seen my fair share of addicts. If this guy had been an addict, he'd been into the expensive shit.

Before I could obtain any more information, John ended the conversation. "See you in a bit, Officer Natua."

Natua. My brow furrowed as I tried to stretch my over-extended brain. I knew the name, but how?

Casually, I pulled down the visor and looked at my yellowed reflection in the mirror. I tried to smooth my mangled hair before calmly asking, "Do I know Officer Natua?"

"No, he…" John stopped and turned to give me a serious big-brother warning. "You won't get to know him either, if you know what's good for you." John's sentence ended like the beak of a heron grasping a fish. Smack — end of story. Yet his response piqued my curiosity. Did he swallow the words whole, out of jealousy of Natua, or chomp them up with irritation?

Officer Natua.

Dawning struck me like the slow rising sun in the Eastern sky. Sluggishly, it seeped into my weary brain.

"Ohhhh, *that* Officer Natua."

"He's out of your league, Mal." John's voice was back to the ordering-me-around-tone.

Someday he'd learn that tone didn't work well on me. "I was merely asking who he was, not for his phone number. If I want a guy's number, I'll ask him for it."

"Is that what you were doing with the dead guy on the beach, putting your phone number in his hand?" John pulled out his notebook and began jotting down information.

"Your brotherly concern is heartwarming."

That earned a long, drawn out sigh from John. "Do you know how long it took me to calm Dad down when your name came over my radio?"

"Dad knows?" *Hua*. The last thing I wanted was to worry my parents. "Does Mom?"

"No, Dad and I agreed the less she knew the better. So tell me what happened."

For a few moments, we got down to business. Me telling him all the yucky details, and John taking my statement while asking questions here and there. Then John went to talk to the officers for a few minutes, while I thought about the officer who was 'out of my league.'

I hadn't met Officer Makaio Natua, but I'd heard about him from Lani. Trouble had earned him a transfer from the Big Island to working dogwatch on Kaua'i, and after Lani's intel, I'd quickly put Natua in the low-life category. Wrote him off as pariah. He may be a god to look at, but a woman would have to be *lō.lō* — crazy stupid to get involved with him.

John, the smartass, interrupted my thoughts. "Could you give me a hand?" He asked as he got back in the car. His face was blank, expressionless, waiting for me to bite, like I didn't know he was making fun of the hand I'd recently held.

He glanced down at my lap, and brought my attention to the fact that I'd been rubbing my palms against my shorts. A pathetic attempt to remove excrement cooties I'd subconsciously felt lingering on my abused skin. I stopped, crossed my arms over my chest and resisted the impulse to strike out. I bit my tongue and refused to respond. Tapping my foot, I waited for him to explain what kind of help he needed.

Two could play this game.

He gave in first. Again. I was getting better at it.

"Could you talk to some of the surfers and see if they've heard anything about this guy?" He flipped through his notebook, as if his favor was just a teeny thing he needed done.

"No longer trusted like *ohana,* John?" A smile of satisfaction creased my face for the second time in what had started out to be a very bad day. Once John donned the uniform, he'd been expelled from the family of beach dwellers, and now he needed my help.

John ignored my jab. "Just let me know if you hear something. Anything. If this was robbery, drugs or gang related, I'd really like to know."

I asked what he wasn't giving. "What's this about a missing tourist? I haven't heard anything about it. Is he a user or a dealer? Did someone see him go into the ocean? Because that thing's fully dressed, and most people don't swim in slacks."

"Malia, you know I can't tell you about the investigation. The command staff would be all over my ass, but if you hear *anything* about this guy, you tell me. Understand?" Looking down at his notepad, John dismissed my questions like those of a nosey little sister butting in where she didn't belong.

I understood his point of view, I really did. I'd been ready to join the academy after college, until I changed career paths from police officer to…I don't have a clue. Understanding John's position, however, didn't stop my voice from raising an octave.

"Do I look like a C.I. working for a get-out-of-jail-free card? I'm not some washed up, drug using, beach bum who *lives* to be your lackey."

John's eyes traveled the length of my body. Starting at the tip of my head and progressing to the tips of my toes. He studied me. Nothing creepy or anything like that, but in the same way he would the body on the beach. Adding up the details one by one — hair a tangled mess, the puking-my-guts-up hue on my face, my arms, legs and chest looking like tenderized meat seasoned with sand, and my still sodden clothes, all wrapped up in a yellow blanket normally used to cover dead bodies.

His silence answered for him. I looked like shit. Like a worn out, burnt out, strung out streetwalker. His assessment pissed me off without his uttering a word.

"I'm a college student holding down two jobs and I get *paid* by the hour." The corner of John's mouth rose in victory. Hourly wages for my services weren't exactly a winning argument. My fists clenched, but I refrained from punching the sarcastic smile off his face before grinding out, "If I'm going to work pro-bono for a *defective*, I want my answers and a piece of the action."

Again, my words attacked my credibility, but there was no way in hell I'd blindly ask questions of my fellow surf and sun worshipers. Nope. Not without knowing a little history about this case.

John, on the other hand, didn't liked me pushing, his impatience visible in the erratic beat of his pen tapping against the steering wheel.

"You do some digging with the locals, then we'll see what I can share."

Go run in circles, jump through hoops, roll over, and then, maybe, he'd toss me a bone. Right.

I wanted to throw his answer back in his face, but I kept my mouth shut and decided to judge the tide for a better wave to catch. One with a better angle and a back door. One outside John's rules.

Natua's voice popped in my head. Smooth as the water in a koi pond, it caressed my memory.

"…wife…"

Natua had information about the dead guy's wife and he was going to be here any minute, but if I stayed with my brother, he would nix any attempt I made to get more information. If I wanted to question Natua, I'd have to corner him away from John, and away from the body.

16

"Do you need me for anything else?" I asked, hiding my eagerness to get started on the case without KPD's directives.

John stared at me, trying to get inside my head, like the bugs crawling out of the sunken pits formerly known as eye sockets on the — well, *you* know. I could tell the detective sergeant desperately wanted to read my thoughts, but was afraid to ask. Afraid he'd have to stop me…as a cop.

I gave him one of those annoyingly innocent looks he'd given me earlier. "I'd really like to go home, take a shower and call Mom and Dad," I explained.

I was rewarded with a don't-do-something-to-make-me-put-you-in-jail eye squint before he replied, "Let me know if you hear anything."

"Okay. *Mahalo.*" I bolted from the car before he could offer to have someone give me a babysitting ride home.

My vision, however, snagged on the latest addition to the law enforcement personnel gathering at the scene. A sculpted body stood next to the last car in a slew of police cars parked along the roadway, and I immediately knew it was him. Even in the flashing strobes from all the emergency lights, he looked *deelish*.

I walked past the trunk of my Mini-Cooper and scurried toward Mr. Yummy, who was eyeing my yellow blanket with interest.

"Malia!"

Damn. Disappointed I'd been caught before I did anything, I made a 180, smiled, laughed and waved at my brother. "I can't believe I walked right by my car!"

John wasn't fooled for a minute. He waited with his arms crossed over his chest as I climbed into the driver's seat.

I glanced in the rearview mirror in time to see Natua check out my car before he turned all business and headed toward John, who of course, continued to stare at me until I started the car and pulled out onto the road. The last thing I could make out was the silhouettes of my brother and a much larger Natua heading down the hill toward the body, carefully threading their way through the low growing plants that protected the beach from erosion. Then I forced myself to concentrate — what's the best location to accidentally-on-purpose run into a police officer at five o'clock in the morning?

Decision made, I prayed my shot in the dark actually hit its target.

CHAPTER THREE

Sitting in the local pastry shop, waiting for a cop to pee — okay, it may not have been the brightest idea I've ever had. Waiting on the off chance Natua would see my car on his way to headquarters and stop for a break was probably a waste of time. So there was a spark of interest in his eyes, but what are the chances of a drop-dead gorgeous body (without an ounce of I-eat-junk-food fat) stopping at an all-night donut boutique? Even I knew that was a lousy investigative technique.

I chewed on my lip and watched the empty streets. He probably hadn't breathed the heavenly scent of a donut since childhood. What was I thinking?

I glanced at my watch, but never saw the time. Inflamed red welts covered my forearm. That's when I realized my other hand was scratching even bigger welts and lumps on my thigh. Then a few private areas of my body, those I really didn't want to have sand fleas, became very uncomfortable.

Thoughts of bugs anywhere near my crotch, drove me out of my seat. The small bamboo table I occupied crashed to the floor. My empty styrofoam cup rolled across clean red clay tiles, and the middle-aged woman behind the counter jumped and looked at me as if I'd grown horns.

Her big Texas hair didn't budge. "Darlin' you look like you've been attacked by those damn fire ants I came here to escape." Her slow southern drawl *tsking* my stupidity.

I tried to remain calm, but failed. "Pearl, I need the key to the restroom. I'm having an allergic reaction."

She flipped a page on the gossip magazine spread out in front of her on the glass display case. "Sorry, child, the ladies' room is closed. There's a leak in the pipes, and we had to shut off the water in there. You can use the men's restroom, but there's no lock on the door." Her voice held about as much sympathy as an over-worked clerk at the local department store when it's out of the one thing you need.

Panic chilled my brain to a level of freezing. What if the fleas got inside me? What if they laid eggs? What if—? I had to cleanse my body, and it couldn't wait until I reached the sanctity of my apartment. I had to get my clothes off...*now.*

Damn, why hadn't I just gone home?

Faintly aware of Pearl smacking her gum and turning another page in her magazine, I ran for the men's room and yelled, "Please keep everyone out for me!"

My clothes were off before I was even aware of my surroundings. Sports bra, running shorts and thong flung over a hook as I desperately sought to make sure I did not get impregnated with an entire population of sand fleas. I grabbed for paper towels and started scrubbing my body with what looked like round brown towelettes in the shape of coconuts. Definitely a sign of Pearl's '*haole*' ancestry from the mainland. No self-respecting Hawaiian business owner would be caught dead with coconut-shaped paper towels in the crapper. They looked more like brown turds than coconuts.

I stood there, buck-naked, scrubbing my body as goose bumps covered every inch of me. My feet practically screamed with the desire to kick off my shoes and scratch the skin off, but my wet, sandy running shoes were staying right where they were. I wasn't risking naked feet in a public men's restroom, no matter how clean the floor appeared. My reproductive organs were in danger, not my feet.

Instead, I stomped them for relief as cold water splashed across the floor and I desperately scrubbed my raw skin with mango scented soap.

Do men really want to smell like fruit? I wondered as my gaze nervously traveled to the door for the umpteenth time.

The itching lessened with the splash of cold water, but was replaced with the prickle of naked unease, and the fact that I was pushing my luck with a lockless door. As if just thinking about it set my fate in motion, I heard Pearl's pathetic idea of a doorbell ring throughout the store — the long, drawn-out song of a whale calling to its mate — announced the arrival of another customer. The bell of a *haole* business owner, coupled with the deep resonance of a male voice calling out a greeting to Pearl, stopped my scrubbing.

"*Aloha*, Pearl. I'm going to use your facilities."

I froze. Oh, shit.

My heart no longer pitter-pattered with anxiety, it boom-ba-boomed on the walls of my chest with panic. Pearl wasn't watching the door. She wasn't anywhere near it, and one of her regulars was coming in...here.

Hua!

I scrambled for the entrance, but my fast moving peds turned into my enemy on the wet floor. My feet slipped. My arms flailed. I struggled to keep my balance and took a nosedive into the door, just as he pushed from the other side. Luckily, I maintained my footing and our force was evenly matched — the door stayed closed.

The stalemate wouldn't last. I forced the hysteria down, out of sight, as I looked at my clothing on the hook, across the room, just beyond my reach. My arms splayed wide across the expanse of the door with my feet braced against the slippery floor.

Frantically, I looked around for something to cover myself. Only my flea-ridden clothes stood between humiliation and me. I lifted my eyes to the heavens. *Please let him be courteous.*

"Just a moment! Please." If I could make it to the stall...

He pushed again. Harder, causing my feet to slip with his decision not to be a gentleman. A little girly yelp escaped my mouth, something I don't normally do. Considering I was *naked* in a men's restroom, I'd let it slide. I don't normally do that, either.

I had to stop him before he tried again, or I was going to die of mortification. Desperately, I grabbed at the round, coconut paper towels, the tips of my fingers barely able to clamp onto my only source of modesty. The last three came out of the dispenser.

I know what you're thinking. Oh sure. The perfect number to cover all the pertinent areas of your body, but I can tell you those three little towels did very little to cover *any* part of my body. As I positioned the coconuts in the obvious places, I tried again.

"Excuse me, sir. I'm not..." I groaned as a paper towel slid from my hand. Cat-like, I tracked it, "...decent."

I pawed it and missed. "...If you'll wait..." Clawed it. Missed. "...just a few minutes...I'm allergic..." The coconut's journey of flight ended on the floor, and out of my reach. "...sand fleas."

I knew I was rambling. I'm sure, he recognized it as well.

"Ma'am, you need to step outside." His voice demanded to be heard. Ordered to be obeyed.

My heart stopped mid-beat. My chilled body heated.

Hua.

He sounded like a...cop.

"I..." I bent forward, reaching with one hand and holding the door with the other, precariously teetering in the balancing act of my life.

Whop!

The door smacked me on the ass. I flew forward, suspended in mid-air, desperately twisting and turning to cover anything and everything. The brute force sent my naked butt skidding across the very floor I refused to allow my feet to touch.

Are you kidding me? Could this day get any worse? I mean really.

CHAPTER FOUR

He forced the door open, causing it to strike the wall, rebound and close behind him as he entered the restroom. His fists clenched around his baton as he snapped it open with a flick of his wrist and made the twelve inches of the expandable black polycarbonate weapon twice as long.

Holy shit!

I yelped. A really pathetic girly noise slipped through my lips as my bare ass screeched to a halt against the stall. In my defense, it looked like he was going to hit me, but then his eyes flicked to my chest and I glared through my fear, determined not to cower to a man who wouldn't wait for a woman to make herself decent. Cop or no cop.

"Nice coconuts."

I don't know why he said it. It was totally inappropriate. Maybe he just realized the novelty towels were fruit, and not turds. Before I could respond, he tuned me out, dismissed my presence like little old me couldn't possibly be a threat (or that a twenty-something *wahine* wasn't naked in front of him) as he glanced under the stall. What was he expecting, a gang to come pouring out of the tiny space?

I scrambled across the floor holding my paper coconuts across my chest and one a little lower. It would be nice to know that he was at least tempted to glance my way. I scooted up the wall of the stall, inching closer to my clothing hanging on the hook.

He glowered at me. "Don't move," he ordered, and then kicked the empty stall open.

His angered brow smoothed, and I could have sworn there was desire written across his face as he gazed at the toilet.

WTH? A naked woman gets a scowl and a toilet gets a happy glow?

His attention turned back to me, and his face registered a seven-story wave at Pipeline crashing down on top of him. He'd screwed up, and he knew it. Whatever he'd been expecting, it wasn't an innocent college student trying to ease the pain of an allergic reaction...while wearing coconut pasties.

He maintained eye contact and returned his baton to its holder on his gun belt. "Ma'am, can you tell me just exactly what you're doing naked in the men's room?"

I thought he'd move away from the stall, but he didn't. My voice somehow got lost in my throat and my words came out as a whisper. "I...the pipes are broken in the women's restroom, and I had an allergic reaction....Pearl was supposed to watch the door for me."

The flare of his nostrils was the only indication he was having an *Oh, shit*, moment.

"You need to get dressed and leave," he ordered.

My body stiffened with indignation. I couldn't put those clothes back on, and even if I could, there was no way I'd get dressed in front of him. "I can't put my clothes on." I scooted toward the stall.

"Excuse me?" His eyebrow lifted, his voice a bit incredulous.

"Sand fleas," I explained. "My clothes have sand fleas in them."

"And what exactly did you plan to put on when you took them off in the first place?" His voice dripped with sarcasm.

It was at that moment I reached my limit. I had dealt with enough crap from enough men for one day. From a dead man falling apart in my hand and begging for help, to my overbearing brother treating me like an annoying eight year old, to Mr. Hot and Sexy acting like I was a common criminal. It was all too much.

I blinked back the tears that wanted to spill and bit my quivering lip to stop its unwanted tremble.

Officer Natua dropped his head and let out an exasperated sigh. Then he surprised me by stepping back and holding the stall door open.

"I...I didn't have a plan," I explained. "I...panicked when I realized there were bugs in my shorts. I'm not some stupid..."

"I would argue that point, since I found you naked in the men's room, but I *really* gotta go. So, to expedite things I'm going to see if Pearl has something for you to wear."

He cut me off before I could finish, and that insult dried up my tears faster than if he'd been kind enough to offer me a handkerchief.

"Don't look," I ordered. "I don't have enough paper towels to cover the back of me."

He turned and walked away without a backward glance and I locked the door to the stall.

I heard him call, "Pearl," from the other side of the bathroom door, as I stood naked in the stall. What the hell was I going to do, stay in the stall all day until someone was kind enough to give me their clothes? What if Natua called my brother? Oh, God, please don't let him call this in.

He returned a moment later and tossed a white apron over the top of the stall. "This was all I could find. Try it." His voice was all business, tight and commanding. Then he was gone again.

The front door opened with that awful moaning whale again, echoing through the empty store. I suffered a moment of panic as I slipped the apron over my neck. My boobs hung out above the bib. I adjusted the strap and found all my girly parts exposed below. It wasn't going to work.

"You decent?" He opened the door wide enough to poke his head inside.

"This isn't going to work." I pulled the apron off and tossed it over the side. The silence seemed electrified with anger and I wondered if he was just going to cuff me and stuff me in the back of his patrol car.

He yelled for the storeowner. "Pearl!"

Where the hell was she?

The whale moaned again and I began to think I'd pushed him over the edge. Driven him into insanity. Then what would I do?

I stomped my itchy feet and scratched my red arms. The whale groaned again, but this time, it brought a smile to my face. He hadn't deserted me. The door opened a moment later and he yelled, "Incoming!"

I looked up, expecting clothes to come flying over the top of the stall. A bag smacked the metal wall and bounced to the floor, out of my reach.

"I can't reach that."

Muttered, exasperated sounds came from the other side of the stall as he picked up the bag. A zipper tore open and I heard him digging through the contents of the bag. A muscle shirt and shorts flipped over the top of the stall without another word, followed by the whale call from the lobby.

Pearl, thank God.

"Just ask her out. The most she can do is say no." A deep male voice chilled my bare skin. I quickly pulled Natua's shirt over my head and began stepping into his shorts.

"There's no way her brother would allow that," another man replied.

29

"Um, ma'am, are you dressed?" Natua whispered.

"My name's Malia. Malia Fern." I stepped out of the stall, and extended my hand in a professional greeting.

His eyes flew to my chest in horror. He ignored my hand and I hid the sting his expression caused me as I dropped my hand to my side.

"We have a problem," Natua whispered.

"What?" What could possibly be worse than what I had just gone through? "If the cops out there— find me in here — with you, I'm going to lose my job," he explained.

"But we didn't do anything." I filed his comment away in my ridiculous file and started for the door.

He blocked my path, stepping between me and the end of this nightmare.

"I'm new here," He pleaded. "Trust me, I can't be found with a prostitute in the men's room."

"Excuse me?" My voice rose well above his whisper.

"Shhhhhh!" He raised his finger to my lips to hush me.

I smacked his hand away. Hands on hips, no doubt a pruney look covering my face as I pursed my lips together. "What did you call me?"

"A prostitute." He said it like he was giving me the definition from the dictionary. Ma·li·a Fern. [Mah-lee-a furn] **Noun**. Definition: A woman who engages in sexual intercourse for money; prostitute.

My temper flared. "Where the hell did you get the idea that I was a prostitute?"

Again, he looked tired of dealing with me. "Look, I'm sorry. Could you keep it down? I didn't mean to insult you. Next time, I'll say escort, sex therapist, lady of the evening, or whatever you want, but please don't expose us."

"I am not a prostitute, a hooker, an escort or even a...a sex therapist!"

Shushing me with his hands, he agreed, "Okay. Fine. Whatever. Just please, please keep quiet."

I remained quiet for a whole thirty seconds as he put his ear to the door and listened to the two cops in the lobby ordering donuts and coffee from Pearl, who had finally decided to show up. The half-minute mark turned out to be my limit for letting the topic go.

"Who told you I was a whore?" I demanded.

"Detective Kumu told me that you were the one who found the body. When I asked what you were doing on the beach, he said you were a prostitute," he explained over his shoulder in a hushed voice.

My teeth ground together involuntarily. "I'm going to kill him," I declared.

"That's really not something you should be confessing to a cop," he countered.

"You'll be the hero who solves the case." I inhaled and slowly let the burn extinguish as I exhaled.

"How about you just not kill him." His matter-of-fact tone said what he failed to say. If the shoe fits — wear it.

"He's my brother! Of course, I'm going to kill him!" And maybe Natua next.

He swung around and covered my mouth with his hand.

"What was that?" Asked one of the men in the lobby.

I yanked his hand from my mouth and stepped back.

"Who's out there?" I demanded.

"Officer Kāne and Chun." His response sounded desperate.

"Biagio Kāne and his partner?" I asked.

He nodded and relief swept through me. "I went to school with Biagio. Tell him you have to take a dump and he won't come in; he's got a weak stomach."

Natua cringed as if I'd insulted him. "First off, I don't have to take a dump, I have to urinate."

What island was he born on? Nobody says urinate.

"Badly," he emphasized and I suddenly understood his attraction to the john. He had to pee. I felt a little bit of my spine soften with sympathy.

"...and by now, I would be out there with Kāne and Chun with an empty bladder if a naked hooker hadn't been standing in the men's bathroom."

My sympathy disappeared quicker than it could form. "I. Am. Not. A. Hooker."

"Secondly," he continued as if I hadn't said a word, "Kāne and Chun were just standing over a decomposed body. I hardly think the idea of me taking a dump will keep Kāne out of the bathroom if he needs to go." He paused, searching for another answer. "You could tell him about your allergic reaction and that you're washing up so he can't come in, then we'll wait for them to leave."

He waited for my response as I gnawed on my lower lip. It was either that or lay into him and let Biagio and Chun storm the bathroom. To be honest, the last thing I wanted was to be caught wearing Mr. Sex-on-a-Surfboard's clothing.

"Fine." I moved toward the door, and then stopped. "What about your police car? They know you're here somewhere." A solution hit me. "If they ask, I'll say you walked across the street to pee since I was using the restroom."

Without waiting for permission, I grabbed the handle on the door and met his eyes. He didn't want to step back. Didn't want to lay his future in my hands. But he had no choice, he relinquished his position in front of the door and I slowly pulled it open to see the two cops in the lobby.

"Where's Natua? Wasn't that his car in the lot?" Chun asked Pearl.

Where the hell had she been when I needed her?

"He went…" Pearl started.

I interrupted. "Biagio?" With my head hanging out the doorway, I curled my finger toward my chest, motioning Kāne to come forward.

Kāne smiled and headed toward me, his tennis shoes squeaking on the tile. At that moment, Natua decided I couldn't handle it, and started forward like he'd handle the situation himself. I stopped him with my palm on his chest. My fingers splayed across his stiff bulletproof vest stilled him.

"Hey, Mal, what are you doing in the men's room?"

"Arguing with my brother on the phone and trying to relieve an allergic reaction to sand fleas. The women's restroom is closed for repair." I held my arm out for him to see.

Biagio cringed at the lovely sight of my welts.

"Were you asking about the other cop parked out front?" I asked. Kāne nodded, and I continued, "He really had to go to the bathroom, but he let me use the restroom first because of my bites. I think he went across the street to pee. Please don't get him in trouble. He was really nice."

"I'll bet he was." Sarcasm dripped from Kāne's voice. Obviously, I wasn't the only one aware of Natua's reputation for being less than what my parents would want for me.

"Look, I've had a really bad morning and I should have known better than to scrub with sand after I found that body. Please. I don't want anyone else getting in trouble because I couldn't make it home before I washed off."

"I won't say anything, Mal. Not even to your brother. You want me to watch the door?" Kāne's voice softened and took on a brotherly tone that my own brother was incapable of showing.

"No, I don't want Chun or anybody else to see me looking like this. If you could just get your food and leave?" I hoped he took my question as more of an instruction on how to handle the situation properly. He didn't disappoint me.

"Sure, but it's going to take me a little bit to convince my partner to leave. He was going to ask you out."

"Really?" That was the first nice thing that had happened to me all day. I smoothed back my hair, flattered that despite all I'd been through, someone found me attractive.

"Yeah, but I'll convince him today's not the day."

I put my hand on his wrist and thanked him, "*Mahalo,*" then closed the door. Natua and I stood with our backs to the door waiting for the officers to leave. He suddenly crossed his legs while his face tightened with pain. A vein on his forehead appeared.

Not looking at each other, we listened to the low voices talking on the other side of the door, waiting for our moment of escape.

Chun's voice interrupted our wait. "There isn't even any water running in there."

I looked to Natua, knowing the sound of water rushing down the drain was the last thing anyone wanted to hear when they had to pee as badly as he did. He nodded his permission and I went to the sink and turned on the faucet. In the mirror, I saw him bite his lip as water drizzled into the sink. His eyes closed as he reached his breaking point.

"I'm sorry, Ms. Fern, I can't wait. I have to go." His voice barely audible, he didn't look at me as he entered the stall and locked the door.

I heard his zipper unzip and I turned the faucet on full blast. His apology had been cute. Surprising me in a nice way. His polite manner in complete contrast to his reputation. Not only had he given me his clothes, he'd maintained a sense of professionalism most cops wouldn't. Yeah, he said I had 'nice coconuts' and called me a prostitute, but could I really expect a guy *not* to comment on fruit molded to my breasts? Nor could I blame him for believing my lying brother when he found me naked in the men's room. I also couldn't fault him for getting irritated about me not thinking two minutes ahead in regard to my lack of clothing options. If he hadn't barged in, I would have been cussing up a storm while desperately trying to wash out my clothes.

Splashing the cool water on my arms, I tried not to think about what he was doing in the stall. I turn on the water harder, strictly for my benefit, not his. I didn't want any images popping in my head. Images like his hand around his short leg.

I adjusted his shirt, which was still damp from his body. The alluring scent of Cool Water Cologne mixed with his pheromones lingered in the weave of the cotton. The image in the mirror told more of my current mood than I wanted to admit. My nipples pointed through the damp cotton clinging to my breasts, daring me to deny his effect, and the armholes extending to my waist didn't help conceal my chest, either.

Whoosh!

The roar of the toilet flushing signaled his imminent departure from the barrier between us. There was no way he was going to see me like this. If he looked at me and saw my boobs, which he couldn't miss, he'd know what I was thinking.

He'd know I was daydreaming about jumping his bones.

And if he reacted in a positive way?

I'd be on him like the manic surfers flocking to Pipeline during January.

Standing on my tiptoes, I grabbed the stall door before he could open it. My hand clamped down on the cold metal of the side panel and the door, effectively keeping the door from moving.

"Uh…what are you doing?" The door rattled gently as he tried to open it.

"You can't come out." Please don't ask me why.

"Excuse me?" His voice was incredulous. Again, he shook the door. Any moment we'd be repeating our pushing contest. The one I'd lost and would no doubt lose again.

The whale call hummed throughout the store signaling Biagio and Chun's departure. I could just run out the door.

"Listen, I helped you out and I gave you privacy. Now, you need to give me a little consideration…because your shirt isn't doing the trick."

"Are you trying to rob me of my underwear?"

"No!" I was trying to stay *out* of his underwear. Irritated he had been so close to the truth, I couldn't stop the bite in my retort. "That is so typical of a man who thinks with his short leg. Listen, di…"

The sound of him clearing his throat stopped my tongue before I finished 'dick for brains.' That would have ruined everything. I wasn't sure if his non-verbal communication was from irritation or amusement. I took a deep breath, closed my eyes and soothed my over-active tongue before it got me in more trouble.

"I'm trying to reason with your common decency. In return for me giving you privacy, I'm asking you for a little compassion. This t-shirt is a little… revealing." I was embarrassed even to say the word. I knew a man who noticed my coconuts, would look as soon as I opened the door.

"Pull the bottom of the shirt up through the neck, then I'll walk out in front of you." His voice was stiff, irritated.

Like he couldn't wait to be rid of me. Damn. I ignored the damage to my ego and accepted his proposal.

"Okay, but you need to give me a minute to fix the shirt."

"Let me know when you're done." Again, the sound of his desire to throw me out with the trash reverberated through his voice.

Tentatively I released the door, and waited for him to renege on our deal, but the door remained closed.

Quickly, I followed his instructions, effectively giving me a double layer of coverage across my chest and closing off the gap under my arms while baring my middle. A perfectly good trade off as far as I was concerned. Although, it'd look a lot better if I didn't have welts encompassing my stomach. I looked in the mirror and tried to convince myself my nipples could pass for two of the many welts on my body. Deep down, I knew I couldn't persuade anyone into that line of thinking.

Especially not Officer Natua, so I gave up.

"You can come out now." He came out and we both tried to maintain eye contact.

We failed miserably. His gaze traveled the length of my body in his clothes. Mine was drawn to the uniform concealing his short leg.

"And by the way, I can assure you, the women who have taken a stroll with me…have *never* complained about my *stride* being too short."

I rolled my eyes but held my tongue. He *would* focus on the short leg comment. Yet at the same time, I couldn't deny the increase in my heart rate or the slight moisture between my legs.

I could also see he was telling the truth. His short leg was definitely not short.

CHAPTER FIVE

"I came to Pearl's hoping to talk to you about the body on the beach," I confessed.

He cleared his throat for the zillionth time since we met. "How did you know I'd come here?"

"I didn't. But a lot of cops stop in on their way to HQ."

His eyebrow rose and a humorous twinkle sparkled in his eye.

"My *brother* is a cop and my *dad* is a retired cop," I explained before he drew the conclusion the cops I knew were all in Vice.

"John Kumu really is your brother?" He sounded incredulous.

"We have the same mother. His father died before he was born and our mom remarried."

Despite giving him more information than he deserved, Natua still questioned my story. "Why would your brother tell me you were a prostitute?"

"Because he didn't want you anywhere near me."

For whatever reason, that made sense to him. Natua nodded and moved forward like he'd never accused me of being a whore. "Why don't we go get a cup of coffee? Then you can tell me about it."

He reached for my flea-ridden clothes and shoved them in his gym bag. I wasn't sure if I should protest or be thankful he was carrying them for me.

He turned toward the door, but being a typical guy, I caught him peek at my boobs one last time.

Whump!

The door smacked him on the forehead, catching him off guard. It was fairly reminiscent of the hit my ass took, except his head was a lot harder. He staggered back with his arm spread wide, groping for something to hang onto as he swayed. He found the very thing that got him in trouble in the first place. My boob.

As soon as he touched me, I sucked in a whole lot of air and he yanked his hand back before I could smack it away. He swayed and I moved behind him to steady his balance, lest he fall on top of me.

Pearl stood in the doorway chomping on a piece of gum — one hand on her hip with her elbow holding the door open and her free hand grasping a spoon, full of batter. She glared past Natua, directly at me as the smell of cigarette smoke drifted into the room. If looks could kill, or spoons full of batter could pierce a woman's heart, I'd be dead before I reached the door.

Natua raised his hand to his wounded forehead while I hid behind his giant frame, pretending to keep him on his feet.

"Looks like I caught cha with yer pants down, darlin'." She popped her gum waiting for a reply.

Rubbing his head, Natua glanced over his shoulder, then moved forward and held the door open. I hesitated until his body completely blocked Pearl's path. "I was helping Ms. Fern, but I knew Kāne and Chun wouldn't see it that way."

It was the truth. It just felt like a lie.

It must have sounded like a lie to Pearl, because her eyes traveled from his crotch to my too-exposed boobs.

"Un-huh. I knew ya were quick on yer feet, but hell, yer downright dangerous. I may have to re-think this relationship of ours. I don't need anuther brokun' heart." Pearl stepped back on the opposite side of the door with the pinched look of a pious preacher's wife, waiting for me to exit the restroom and proceed with my walk of shame.

Natua scowled, the big goose egg forming in the middle of his forehead drawing Pearl's attention. I, however, was too grossed out by the thought of the two of them being involved. A shutter of revulsion traveled through my body as I snuck by.

Pearl attacked, catching us both off guard. Natua raised his arm to block the shot that wasn't actually directed at him. Pearl's spoon aimed over his shoulder directly at me. I made a run for the exit.

Wet goo smacked the back of my head and slid down my shoulders. For a moment, I imagined I'd been impaled by a spoon, brain matter seeping down across Natua's shirt. Someone screamed as I grabbed my head and made it through the door. The call of the whale followed me outside and I realized the goo dripping down my back was donut batter.

Unbelievable.

I made it to my car door, thankful I hadn't locked it before going into Pearl's and sank down into the seat, not caring what happened to the upholstery and watched Natua lecture Pearl. She still had the gall to glare at me through the glass. I returned the favor.

The whale bellowed one last time as Natua exited the store.

Angrily yanking batter from my hair, I demanded, "I want her arrested. Your little late night snack — and she is late night if you hadn't noticed — attacked me for no reason."

A self-satisfied smile spread across his face. One that spoke volumes to what he thought of my reaction.

I sounded jealous. Jealous of an old woman who was not in his league. Not that I was in his league or wanted to be in his league.

I growled.

"Malia."

I liked the way my name played with his

tongue, but squinted angrily at him anyway.

"Pearl is not my 'late night snack.' I haven't had any 'snacks' since I've been on Kaua'i. Although why I'm confessing that to you, I have no idea. She's a lonely middle-aged woman who lost her husband to a younger woman. Surely, you have some compassion for a divorcee in her position?"

No snacks? Really? My shoulders slumped and my hands fell from the mess in my hair. My anger slipped away as I looked past him into the store. I shouldn't believe him. About the snacks or about Pearl, but looking at the middle-aged woman standing alone inside her shop did something to me.

"Officer Natua—" I started.

"Makaio."

I ignored him and went back to mistrusting the womanizer in front of me. "Officer Natua, I need to speak with you about the missing person's report you took a few days ago."

Pearl moved toward the door, her spoon raised in the air. I sunk down in my seat again.

Natua came to my rescue, or his, I'm not sure which. "Why don't you follow me to the construction site across the street? There's a big parking lot and we'll be able to talk without being interrupted."

"Okay," I agreed before another scene erupted.

Natua winked and turned toward his patrol car.

He definitely spelled T-R-O-U-B-L-E.

CHAPTER SIX

Makaio.

I gave myself a mental head thump. Officer Natua was not drawing me in with his hot sexy looks. I have three brothers, so I've seen and heard every cheap move a guy will make to get into a girl's pants.

Yeah, sure, I was in Makaio's shorts at the moment, but he wasn't getting in them. Period.

Maybe.

I filled my nose with the salty air and exhaled, loudly. I tried to slow my racing heart as I followed Natua's patrol car to the construction site. By the time I passed the empty guard shack in the parking lot of *The Garden of the Gods*, my palms were sweating, and the all-over body itching had returned. I stopped and waited for Officer Natua to swing his vehicle around.

Vying for more time to control my emotions,

I ignored his approach and reached over to pull a small spiral notebook from the glove box. By the time I turned to roll down my window, he was patiently waiting with his car pulled up within inches of my window. His sexy smile dared me to make a move.

I got right down to business. "You know I'm helping my brother with this case, right?"

"He said his C.I. was going to ask around for him."

I rolled my eyes and continued, "When did you take the report on the missing tourist?"

"Monday around 0300 hours."

"Why would someone report a missing person at three o'clock in the morning?"

"That's when the victim's business partner flew back from Oahu and realized the victim hadn't been to their condo since he left three days earlier."

He was answering my questions as if he had the script in front of him. I was glad one of us did. Coming up with questions was harder than I thought. "Sooo… he's not just a tourist?"

"The witness said he wasn't here on business. He was just here to have a good time. A mini-vacation from the wife."

I hid the smile wanting to spread across my face. Despite the fact that we were talking about a guy looking for an island sex toy, Makaio was giving up all the information John wouldn't. "What's your victim's name?" I reveled in my ability to obtain information.

"What does that have to do with the body?"

He asked.

I scoffed, unsure why he was playing coy. "You're the one who told John you thought it might be your missing person."

"We won't know that until we get a positive ID."

"But...but that's the direction John was taking the investigation," I argued.

"Yes, to identify the body, but my missing person may not be the guy you mutilated."

My pen stopped in mid-sentence. Natua had the same sick sense of humor my brother did, and both of them delivered at the expense of my ego. "Give me a frickin' break. About sixty thousand people live on Kaua'i. Even with the million and a half tourists visiting annually, everyone knows when there's a death, or a missing person. So why didn't your report make the local news? What's different about this case?"

I waited for him to answer my questions. They were good questions if I did say so myself.

"Why didn't your brother give you this information?" He countered.

"We got in an argument. He wanted to boss me around and I..."

Hand in the air, he stopped me before I could explain any further. "I get it. He wants a little bit of information from the surfers you hang out with, and you were being nosey."

"I wasn't being nosey!"

"Okay, fine, if you weren't being nosey, why the third degree? Once the vic's ID hits the news, you ask your buddies if they know anything about him. Some say no, others say, 'I saw some *haole* businessman scoring some ice at Joe Brah's. It's as simple as that. End of story."

He suddenly sounded *a lot* like my brother. "You knew what I wanted, and that my brother wasn't going to share any information with me."

His smile was no less than glorious. "Not until there was distance between us and I was in my car. Then my brain was able to function a little better."

I might have lashed out at him if he wasn't so damn attractive. But then he did the unthinkable. He talked.

"The missing guy was a business man who was also a recovering addict. His family didn't want his addiction exposed in the media because his partner believed he was on a drug binge. Since there was no sign of foul play at the condo, his partner assumed the guy fell off the wagon, which it looks like he did, and ended up getting washed off some rocks. Or he walked too far into the surf and lost his footing."

Wow, I didn't expect that much info, but I wasn't buying it either. "He had on socks."

"So he fell off the rocks and drowned." His skepticism was evident as he yawned. He wasn't going to jump on my band wagon.

"And wasn't found for several days?" I waited for an explanation.

"The tide carried him out and finally brought him back in."

Oh, please. "Nope, the surf's been puny and there haven't been any riptides on this end of the island for almost a week. He would have been found sooner if he started on shore. What condo was he staying at?"

"It's a private condo in KaPa'a. What did you say you did for a living?"

We had graduated to a serious conversation about what could have happened to the body. A body I didn't want to keep visualizing or study in my mind any longer, yet there it was, face-to-face staring at me with real-life gore every time I so much as blinked. It wasn't the scene of a natural death or an accidental death. I was convinced of it. It was a homicide.

I don't know how I knew it, I just felt it. In that split moment when its arm was still attached to the body, it whispered in my ear.

Help me.

Obviously, the body didn't really whisper in my ear, but if I admit it whispered in my *mind*, I might have to commit myself to the funny farm.

"I'm a surf instructor." He didn't need to know my other job. "And no, the guy didn't drown. He was killed."

"Okay." His fingers tapped on the steering wheel.

We were on the same page. Brainstorming about the case and somehow I found myself more intrigued by the moment. I suddenly understood my brother's drive, and my dad's thirty years of what he called working 'the dark side.'

Nevertheless, I still had no desire to be caught dead in that ugly uniform.

"And what makes you think the Menehune

aren't up to their old tricks?" Natua asked, his mouth twitched with humor while his eyes twinkled. The man was a first class flirt if he could make a move while talking about a dead guy.

"How the hell did we get on the Menehune people?" I asked.

"Maybe, this was their ploy to bring us together." He licked his lips again.

I couldn't stop the happy dance in my heart, yet wondered where my resolve to resist him had gone. Slapping up emotional reinforcements against him, I delivered the kiss of death, to a great pickup line, with my favorite tactic. A history lesson. "The Menehune aren't mythical elves who live in the forest, nor are they cupids or leprechauns. They were the first occupants of Kaua'i who were turned into workers and slaves by the Tahitians. Cold hard facts supported by the 1820 census which listed sixty Menehune people as residents on Kaua'i."

I knew my Hawaiian history. Elves my ass.

"Mock me if you want, but the Menehune have pierced your heart with their arrows. Arrows tipped with magic to make you fall in love. With me." He was relentless in his flirtation. "The census doesn't give the story behind the numbers."

Was he kidding? I couldn't tell if he was serious. Part of me wanted to jump on the seductive bandwagon. Makaio was serious eye candy. And he'd been better than I could possibly imagine up to this point, but I didn't want to go down that road. Yet.

Or did I?

If he was teasing me, I wouldn't be able to face any of the cops at KPD. If he used me and spit me out, I wouldn't be able to face my brother or anyone else for that matter. I'm not a woman who falls for guys like him.

"No sane person really believes the Menehune are capable of shooting love arrows like cupid. I don't believe in Menehune elves, and I don't believe the body I found belonged to a user, either. What's the name?" I wasn't leaving without a name.

He capitulated. "Peter R. Johnson, white male, thirty four years of age from New Mexico. He left behind a wife and a baby boy."

To say I was elated when Natua gave in easier than I expected, would be incorrect. In fact, my stomach bottomed out, but it was from a combination of things. One — my soul was inexplicably repentant when I denied the Menehune. Two — I wanted Makaio to chase harder. And three — *It* had an identity.

It was no longer just a body. *It* was a *he*. *He* had a name. Peter. Peter Johnson, who had a baby robbed of his father and a grieving wife made into a widow. They deserved better than for me to refer to their loved one as *it*.

CHAPTER SEVEN

Officer Natua and I went our separate ways. I had no doubt he was going in search of action he didn't get from me. I raced home to take my overdue shower, wondering what the hell was happening between me and a guy I knew was a man-whore. He didn't come across like that, but weren't the real players deceiving? Didn't they make you feel like you were the only woman in the world who could possibly affect them so deeply?

I pulled into the gravel parking lot behind the russet colored strip mall and Private Kaua'EYE's Investigations, spraying gravel in my haste to get inside. I ran up the outdoor steps to my small studio apartment, grabbing the newly painted off-white railing to help me take the steps two and three at a time.

I didn't wait to get in the bathroom before I kicked off my shoes and socks, but paused before stripping off Natua's clothes. Part of me was reluctant to take off his t-shirt and shorts, something the other side of my psyche — the part that desperately needed cleaning — found disturbing. Yet it couldn't be denied.

Even his shorts smelled good.

Not that I sniffed his shorts. That would *so* be crossing a line. But his essence drifted from them as I folded them in a neat pile.

Essence?

I did a mental headshake and rolled my eyes at the dreamy thoughts sneaking into my head. The man reeked of sex. Period. He was a walking temptation to the female gender. Hell, men would want to get close to him, even if they didn't swing that way.

A sex god.

A sigh escaped my lips. Okay, my imagination was officially out of control. He probably sucked in the sack.

Shoving his pile of clothes in my hamper, I slammed the lid closed, then headed toward the bathroom. Angry with myself, I turned on the massaging shower head full blast, stepped into the intensely hot water and basked in the simple pleasure of cleansing water. I had been dying for this moment ever since I stumbled upon Mr. Johnson's body. I lathered the washcloth, soaped myself all over, and tried to rinse all the morning's anxiety down the drain. But whenever I closed my eyes, Mr. Johnson's empty eye sockets haunted me — followed me the moment I let my eyelids drift closed.

Images of Natua's broad chest finally took away the nightmare. His smile and appreciative look as those deep brown eyes traveled the length of my practically nude body, assaulted my memory. My mind begged for a distraction and my body begged to be touched. My massaging showerhead was too much temptation.

I can't remember the last time I had a real date. A *real date*, with *real sex*. Hot and wild sex. With a guy. I'm not a one-night-stand kind of *wahine* and after seeing death, I needed to feel alive. On top of that, Natua didn't help me quell those latent urges demanding to be satisfied after a long dry spell. So between the *no-sex-god-needed* shower head and thoughts of one hot cop, I managed to release all the tension built up in my body.

What can I say? I'm self-reliant. I take care of myself.

After a shower that satisfied me on several levels, I applied my *kapuna wahine's* special lotion to the ugly welts covering my body. My grandmother's ancient blend of kukui nut oil, aloe, jojoba oil, papaya and some secret ingredient she said she'd give me from her deathbed, was the best thing for any skin breakout.

After a quick call to my dad to let him know I was in one piece — yes, I shouldn't have been running at that hour of the day, no, I wouldn't do it again (until tomorrow) and no, we definitely weren't going to tell Mom — I went through the mundane tasks of vacuuming and cleaning my apartment (all 390 square feet of it). I found my day off filled with the smell of cleaning products and thoughts of Peter Johnson's family. The search for their missing loved one was over. They never got the opportunity to be with him on his deathbed, or hear family secrets he promised to share. I could only imagine the torture they endured not knowing the *what* or the *why* of it all.

By late afternoon, I was more than ready to go to work. The wait put me on edge and made me fidgety. I needed to find out just exactly why Mr. Johnson had disappeared and washed up on the beach a few days later, wearing socks.

I changed into a sport bra tank and board shorts. My usual bikini wouldn't hide the lingering welts, and the last thing I wanted was to distract the surfers I was going to question. I needed answers, not exclamations of how gross my skin looked.

Grabbing my exceptionally pretty pink and purple, custom-made board, I headed out the door. I'm not a beginner surfer by any means, but I'll never get to the big wave level either. I prefer fast zippy rides with water spraying my face and the breeze whipping the hair out of my eyes. It's like being on the edge of the world waiting to go over. Exhilarating? Yeah. A little scary? Yeah. Do I love it more than my life? YEAH.

I always get this deep, grounded, satisfied feeling when I put Paradise in the back of my little convertible. (If you haven't figured it out, I name my boards like other people name their pets.

Paradise is the best companion a girl could ask for.) That board, that six foot long, pink and purple fiberglass platform tells you everything you need to know about me. Paradise tells you I love nature and spending time outdoors. She defines my independence, despite my occasional reliance on family for secret recipes and college tuition (that I'm not using at the moment). She hints at the fact that I'm a *wahine* who likes to accessorize bikinis to her tropical theme. And she likes to ride in style in my MINI Cooper, telling everyone to get out of my way. I may not be big, but I'm quick and won't let anyone or anything define the road I take.

The beach was going through its daily afternoon transition when I arrived. Families packing up their gear and abandoning the shady spots they'd laid claim to for the day while dragging screaming kids away from the salty water (the same salty water they'd complained about all day because it burned their eyes and got in their mouths). Surfers headed out into the waves to catch the adrenaline rush they'd been anticipating all day. Everyone wanted to feed that part of the brain that drives humanity to take risks and do the unthinkable.

We all have our addictions in life.

Like a symphony warming up for a performance, each instrument playing to its own tune, the surfers scattered in different directions, ready to hit the water and put their toes to the nose. I wanted to join the lineup going out to boost the lip in a perfectly orchestrated concert. All of us ready to entrance the onlookers by ripping through the waves like a rock guitarist shreds his metal strings. Since it also happens to be feeding time for sharks, some people secretly hope our performance will crescendo into screams of agony, as we become dinner for the bottom dwellers, but that doesn't stop us.

The homicide case did, however redirect me when I saw a group of friends walking toward the water. I ran to catch up.

"*Aloha*," I greeted them casually, as if it was just another day.

"Brah, where you been? Did you hear they found a body on the beach this morning? Right down there." Moa crowded me and pointed toward remnants of yellow crime scene tape waved in the breeze like a silent vigil for Peter Johnson.

Help Me. A shudder ran through my body with the memory.

This was going to be easier than I thought. "Yeah, I'm the one who found him." Again, I wore a casualness I didn't feel.

"No way! Gnarly, dude."

I'm not sure who said it, as the group of the regulars began to circle around me. Some of the surfers were native to the island, some were transplants. Others were working stiffs or college students taking a much needed break from it all, like me. Then there were the few lost souls who only follow the direction of the next wave, like Moa.

I told the group my story, leaving out the fact that I was too stupid to keep my hands off the body, which left the tale without much gusto. But believe it or not, that was my plan. If I made it too interesting then no one else would make it *more* fascinating. I needed someone to amp my story and make it totally rad. I needed to find a missing link.

I'm smarter than you thought, huh?

Moa asserted himself in the crowd, pushing to maintain his position next to me, which I thought was interesting since his nickname meant 'chicken.' He wasn't the brightest bulb, but he survived on shore just like he did when catching a wave. In other words, if things got a little out of control, he disappeared. He avoided fights and dropped off the backside of the big waves. In my book, he wasn't chicken, he just played it safe.

"Yo, brah, I heard it on the news that he was a business man with a habit. Liked the local flavor of meth too much and drowned."

Now how in the hell could the news report that? Wasn't it a little slanderous?

"Brah, I saw him doing a hand-to-hand with some of the construction workers at the new condos in Poipu," chirped in Mutt, a guy with a permanent buzz and the shaggiest hair you've ever seen. Seriously, his hair isn't long, but it's a mess and it smells like a wet dog most of the time. Whoever nicknamed him wiped out his real name a long time ago. I'm not sure anyone knew him by anything but Mutt.

"No way. Did you score at the site?" Moa's eyes lit up like a shark with its meal within striking distance. Maybe that's why he called himself shark — it had nothing to do with his talent on the water and everything to do with his ability to smell out new dealers.

"Nah, brah. I just saw 'em last week. I was running late, so I took a short cut through the lot. There was definitely an exchange of cash." Then Mutt's eyes began to roam the crowd suspiciously, like maybe he'd given up too much information. Or wanted to buy his next high.

"Maybe I should check it out." Moa's eyes lit up with the prospect of scoring new dope, which left me compelled to point out the flaw in his plan.

"Moa, the guy Mutt saw making the buy, ended up dead."

"Ohhhh, riiight." He drug out the two words like a kid learning phonetics. "Thanks for watching my back, salty sis." He gave me a solid appreciative smack in the middle of my shoulder blades, and sent me forward a few steps.

The group began to break up, giving me the perfect opportunity to pull Mutt aside.

"Mutt, can I talk to you a minute?" I asked while lightly touching his arm to stop his progress toward the water.

Mutt's gaze traveled from my breasts to my toes and back again, as if my wanting to talk to him meant I was ready to get busy. Geez, can't a *wahine* just talk to a guy without him thinking she wants to get in his pants?

We walked up the beach, our feet sinking in the lush white sand and stopped under a couple of palm trees. As I turned toward him, I noticed he'd already stood his board in the sand and was coming at me like an octopus. Somehow, in the past ten seconds, he'd grown more hands than the average guy. I hastily shoved my board in the sand between us.

"I need to talk to you about the guys at *The Garden of the Gods*."

"Oh." His light bulb turned on and his octopus arms disappeared.

"I think my little brother is working at the condo complex you were talking about. He's been in some trouble lately and I really hope he's not mixed up in this." My lie wasn't too big, since my younger brother Kionni was a construction worker, but I had no idea what site he was working at, and I was pretty sure the only trouble he'd been in was for being late for dinner at my parent's house. "Can you describe the guys to me? I really need to know if he needs my help."

"Dude, anything for *Ohana*. It was two guys, one a local. Big guy. Pro wrestler type, well over six-foot and close to three hundred pounds. But this guy wasn't fat. He was pure muscle, and the way he walked, dude, he could break you in half. He was definitely there to show force. If his size didn't make him stand out, he had this trim goatee and a ponytail hanging down to his waist... so, wow, y'know?

"The other guy had short brown hair, a full goatee, and a tattoo on his forearm. It was big and red. Maybe a lizard?" Mutt was fairly certain of what he'd seen, and basically, it pointed toward a drug buy.

Still, I couldn't accept it as a dope deal. Lizard tattoos were a dime a dozen on the islands. Everyone had one, including my boss. So finding a brown haired guy with goatee and a lizard tattoo wasn't exactly the best description to launch a manhunt.

The big guy was the best place to start.

"Surely, one of those guys ain't your brah?" Mutt looked me up and down, using the lack of resemblance between the two dopers and me as an excuse to check me out again.

I think the closer inspection of my body was making Mutt change his mind, because once he started seeing all of my flea bites, he took a step back like he might catch something from me.

"No, they don't sound like my brother. You're sure no one else was there?" I wasn't letting him get away yet.

"Nope just those two guys and the dead guy."

Mutt's mention of Peter Johnson was all it took for me to be sure that he knew much more than he was saying.

"How do you know it was the dead guy with them?" I watched Mutt shut down on me. His eyes completely glazed over in what appeared to be fear. He'd given me more information than he wanted to and Mr. Helpful no longer felt the need to assist a fellow surfer. Or get laid.

"Ah…Moa said it was the dead guy. Look I gotta go catch some waves. They're totally righteous." Mutt hastily pulled his board out of the sand, spraying sand all over my legs and ran for the surf before I could even finish thanking him.

I stood there for a few moments thinking about the case, wondering what Mutt was hiding. This morning when John asked me to 'give him a hand' on the case, I didn't hesitate. Sure, my brother was a smartass, and I wasn't getting paid, but I had the inside track when it came to information on this beach — it was definitely *my* beach — and John needed my help to solve this case whether he believed it or not. In addition, I was starting to believe Peter Johnson's *"Help me"* plea was the real thing. That he somehow chose to communicate with me long after his death.

Needing to clear my head with a couple of good waves, I grabbed Paradise headed out into the surf in Mutt's wake. I couldn't help the grin spreading across my face. Not only was I heading out to hang ten in the most glorious place on earth, I'd gotten some good information on the case that the police couldn't possibly obtain.

Eat your heart out, Officer Smarty Pants.

And, no. I was not thinking of Officer Natua.

CHAPTER EIGHT

Catching a wave and feeling its power build under your feet as you ride the mounting surge is comparable to, well, really good sex. Getting lost in the passion while you focus on nothing but the climax. Then gliding down the slope into a foamy aftermath of joy. Your toes tingling with the pleasure of an orgasmic achievement. It definitely ranks up there with the best ride of your life.

Bless the Duke for making this sport what it is today. No, I'm not talking about John Wayne. I'm talking about the father of surfing, Hawaiian native Duke Kahanamoku, an Olympic swimmer who popularized modern day surfing in the early 1900s.

Rolling comfortably in the hills of water while straddling my board, I watched over my shoulder for that last perfect wave of the day.

Waiting, watching — is that it? No. I let several smaller ones pass me by.

Don't let anyone tell you size doesn't matter. It does.

Finally, I spotted Mr. Right among the crowd of waves heading my way. Watched him build and back build, my body humming with anticipation. Timing was everything. I laid flat on my stomach and paddled for all I was worth as the surge caught up with me. My hands palmed the surface of my board and I hopped to my feet, joining a slew of other surfers determined to put their autograph on this particular wave. It was heavenly. The swell built higher and higher — bigger than I should try, but I was on the top of the world without a care. There were warning signs alerting me to exit — but I ignored them. The sheer power building under my board as I weaved back and forth across the roaring surface beckoned me to follow, and I couldn't let go. Normally, I would have fallen off the backside, or at best, rode out its length, never tipping over the precipice. Played it safe like Moa did with a wave this size.

Not today. Today, I *needed* the surge of life to flow through me. My body demanded the adrenaline only an experience outside my comfort zone could bring. I had to prove I was worthy to continue on...when Peter Johnson could not.

I crested the swell and began riding the biggest wave of my life. Other surfers appeared in front of me, dotting the surface like barriers on an obstacle course. Riding low with my weight toward the back of the board, the fingertips of my left hand skimmed the wall as I grasped my board with my right and pulled inward, zigzagging around my buddies. My balance was shaky, but I hung on for dear life as the wave began to enclose over me. Crouching even lower, I leaned forward to gain speed inside the curl. I looked down the tube, and my heart skittered as it started to close.

The pure roar of noise left me alone in the universe, encapsulated within the wave. Just me — the ocean — and God.

This wasn't just your average four footer. This was a double overhead and then some. Concentrating on survival, I squatted down so low my butt touched the surface of the board. My left arm now fully extended, as I balanced my board against the crashing wave. The exit funneled tighter, leaving the smallest door of escape.

In that instant, I knew I wasn't going to make it, but I wasn't giving up either. My adrenaline stoked and I headed for the exit. Where I got the guts…or the stupidity, I have no idea. I just followed the rush, which was leading me to certain doom.

Water crashed down on my head, making my legs wobble, but I refused to give in. Too late, I realized the door ahead of me had closed. I caught a glimpse of Paradise flipping up in the air before being swallowed up whole. The velcro strap around my ankle tugged, and then released under the pressure as I went down. Nature crushed and rolled my body, flipping me over and over till I didn't know what was up or down.

This was it. The end, I thought, before my back scraped across coral reef, identifying where the bottom was. The nerves along my spine woke up with pain. I'd pay the price for that hit, but it gave me hope. I continued to relax and go with the flow, my lungs feeling smaller and smaller. Tighter and tighter they squeezed. Thoughts of a riptide entered my mind — I pushed them away, along with the panic trying to catch me.

Finally, a rainbow of color splashed in front of me. The sun filtering through the water, leading me toward the light. Fighting my way to break the surface, I sputtered for air. Desperately, I caught a breath and dove back in as another wave crashed down. This time, better prepared, I body surfed with it at an angle and let the swell break in front of me. Again, I surfaced.

Turning around to look in the general direction where I lost my board, I spotted it dipping in the waves a short distance away. Moa was almost alongside it.

That's what it's like in the surfing community. No matter how different you are on shore — when you're out catching waves, your brah's got your back. Grinning, I swam toward him, enjoying the rush of water across my body with the afterglow of success.

"Dude, that was awesome! You *gotta* go for it!" To say I was totally stoked was an understatement.

Moa's eyes orbed like saucers as I approached. Moa's eyes never open wide. He's one of those sleepy looking dudes. He wasn't looking at my face. He was looking...lower...where I was feeling incredibly free in the water as the waves splashed against my chest. My bare chest.

"Ay!" The water swallowed my yelp as I went under. More panicked now than when the force of the ocean tumbled my limp body to an uncertain destiny, I swam underneath Moa and came up behind him.

"Don't turn around!" I blurted as I surfaced.

He turned around.

"Moa!" I splashed water in his face and he turned away.

"Sorry, brah. I can't help it. When there are boobs in front of me...I look."

"They're behind you!" I practically screamed.

"Right. I look there too." The grin in his voice was evident by his tone, but I chose to ignore it.

"Do you see my suit?" I grabbed my board, ready to splash him again if he dared to take another peek. Another swell pushed us closer toward shore. Anticipating the surge, I repositioned my board before Moa made a fatal error of looking a third time.

"No..." To his credit, he was looking for my top in the water. "Wait, I see it!"

"Where?" Frantically, I spun around looking for it, wondering how a sports bra could come off without my knowledge. The abrasive scraping across my back had left it raw, but still...

"Uh…5-0's standing on the beach holding it up."

My stomach sunk deeper into the depths of my embarrassment. I didn't have to *see* the officer to know who the officer was holding up my top. I looked anyway, hoping against hope…but there he stood. Officer Natua. My pink top swayed in the breeze like a sign of my surrender next to his chiseled mocha face.

"No frickin' way!"

It's bad enough to expose oneself twice in a twenty-four hour period, but to the same guy? I bobbed in the ocean, hiding my naked breasts from my fellow surfers and stared at model white teeth reflecting the sun. Bag of Toys' song *Smile So Wide* played in my mind.

"I'll tell him about a stash of weed down by the water breaker if you want to make a run for it." Moa's voice was resigned in solemn sacrifice.

"You'd give up your weed for me?" Touched by his loyalty, I couldn't believe he would give up the stash he valued like gold.

"You saved me from making a fatal error by chasing the wrong dealer. It's the least I can do."

At that moment, I debated letting Moa distract Natua. His gallantry was selfless, and he definitely needed help with those delusional ideas about me saving his life.

"Thanks, Moa, but I can handle Natua." My voice carried more confidence than I felt as I held my board in a death-grip against my chest.

"No problemo, brah." His shoulders slumped with relief, Moa shrugged off his knightly armor. "How you going to get your top back?"

"I'm going to walk up to him and take it." Moa was looking at me skeptically. It sounded delusional to me, too.

"Won't he arrest you for like indecent exposure or something?"

"No, we go way back." Way back to this morning when he tried to push me out of the men's restroom only wearing paper coconut pasties. Surely, my board counted as more clothing than wet paper towels molded to my breasts.

I slid onto my board, scrunching my chest against the rough surface, not sure if the abrasive contact felt good on my bites, or hurt like hell.

"Brah, I need to surf with you more often." Moa's eyes were wide open again, and he wasn't making eye contact.

"Thanks, Moa." I felt my face heat up but tried to act carefree.

Would I surf this beach tomorrow? Hell no! It'd be months before I recovered my dignity. But no one, except me, was going to know the extent of my humiliation.

I rode the waves in on my stomach, catching a few looks and whistles as I passed the guys. My hands cut through the surf with more strength than I thought possible while I plastered my chest to my board and kept a steady gaze on Officer Natua's ear-to-ear grin. Reaching the shoreline, my hands grasped the sand and stopped my advance. Steadying the board against the waves is easy if you're lying on your back basking in the sun, but this wasn't a nude beach, and there were little kids everywhere. My boobs stayed plastered to Paradise.

Natua smiled. Arms folded across his chest, eyes hidden behind aviator sunglasses, he waited for me to get up and walk out of the water. I bit my tongue, thinking the good manners his mother had surely taught him, would defeat his gloating male mind.

"What happened to your coconuts?"

So much for manners. Maybe he wasn't born. Maybe he was spawned.

My bravado began to slip. "Are you going to arrest me?"

"Why would I arrest you? Did you kill Peter Johnson?"

I ignored that and shot him full of bullets with my eyes.

Fine.

I started to stand up, and his etiquette finally kicked in. Head tilted down and cocked to the side, like he wasn't peeking over the top of his sunglasses, he raised his hand to halt my entrance onto the sandy shore.

Do cops direct boob traffic at nude beaches?

I stopped and smooshed my chest to the board again, wondering what his next stunt would be. He turned and walked toward a woman and her kids playing in the sand. I don't know what he said, but she looked at me, tossed him a hotel towel, then scurried her kids away in the other direction.

Natua came back to the water's edge, still sporting that toothy grin, and bent over to take off what looked like expensive combat boots. His eyes didn't leave me as he rolled up his uniform pant legs, showing off muscular calves. Then he actually walked into the surf and stood in front of me, holding up the towel like a dad ready to wrap up his little girl in a warm embrace.

There was nothing fatherly about the look in his eyes.

I took a deep breath — which wasn't easy since my breathing almost stopped when he looked at me like that — and went for it. His arms curved the towel so no one else had a view, but boy did he make sure he got an eyeful. He turned his head to the side, his mirror sunglasses hiding a sly look no one else could see. To the average beach dweller, Natua appeared to be my knight in shining armor.

"Hah..."

My mouth was so dry, I nearly gagged on my attempted laugh, then figured I was better off keeping quiet, since I couldn't trust myself not to blurt out breathlessly, "Take me now, big boy," as his arms enveloped me. I craned my head back to meet his gaze, now openly directed toward me. Hunger. Pure unadulterated need reflected in his sunglasses.

Unfortunately, that look was coming from the reflection of my eyes, not his. He appeared calm, cool and collected, though the pulse pounding on the side of his forehead told me otherwise.

Once the towel was wrapped around me, he handed me my top, torn down the backside from my brush with nature and stepped back, leaving me longing for more.

Geesh. Get a grip, I admonished myself. Moa had seen my boobs, but Moa…wasn't Natua.

Aw, hua.

The familiarity between us was growing. A closeness that was bringing me one step nearer to his bed, which was probably not going to happen.

Officer Natua picked up my board and held it in front of him. I wasn't going to speculate why he held it at his waist, covering the front of his uniform pants.

Nope, not going there. I can say I was a little jealous of Paradise, though.

He grabbed his socks and boots, and we walked in silence toward my car, parked under the trees. He was the first to speak, once he finished putting my board in the MINI Cooper's backseat. The sun's last golden glow burst through the trees and across the ocean surface, making Officer Natua's expression dark and unreadable as he faced me.

"A young woman told me there was a girl surfing topless. I never dreamed it would be you."

"Oh, please. Who would say…?" I stopped as my anger started to form. Only one person would say that. "Was she a surfer?"

"Yeah, long blonde hair, large….." he cleared his throat. I knew what he was going to say before he realized he shouldn't. Only guys who considered me a friend would talk so casually about another woman's *attributes,* which meant Natua didn't see me in the same way I saw him. I swallowed the hurt and filled in his sentence for him, just to prove it didn't bother me.

"Boobs?"

"I was going to say board, but yeah, now that I think about it, she did have pretty large breasts."

The slightest rise of his left eyebrow and the quirk of the corner of his mouth were the only signs he was teasing about Windy Trapp's double D cup boobs. Then again, I didn't know him very well. Maybe he was enjoying the memory of her.

"Was her name Windy?" I couldn't hide the animosity in my voice. It had to be *her.* She's a walking billboard for a boob job. Of course, her ass was already huge pre-boob surgery, so now the guys just thought of her as *curvaceous.* In my book — the book I reserved just for Windy — it meant something entirely not-so-nice to say.

Natua recognized he'd pushed a button and decided to take advantage of the situation. His face turned innocent. "I believe she said her name was Windy when she handed me your top. She thought a little girl lost it. Wait, I've got her number here somewhere."

While he dug through his pockets for her number, I gritted my teeth and held my breath as I called up the image of the Tiki God of Happiness in my mind. It was better than ripping off Windy's head and shoving it down her throat. For that deed, I'd need to concentrate on the Tiki God of Strength.

I began to wonder if Natua was one of those guys who wanted to see women fight over him. Not going to happen, brah.

"Forget the number. I don't think it was meant for me."

"Do you know her?"

Did I know her? Only my entire life. Best friends as kids, until she graduated past the training bra, and by that I mean a whole different universe past a training bra. Her taunts about my sports bra being too big for my itty-bitty boobies destroyed our friendship. She'd been flaunting her rack in my face ever since and when she got the boob job...well, from there it just got worse.

Again, I thought of the Tiki God of Happiness, unable to respond to Natua's question during my meditation.

"Did you find out anything about our victim?" Luckily, Natua wasn't as brainless as I'd started to think and changed the subject.

"Yeah, Peter Johnson was at *The Garden of the Gods* one morning last week meeting two guys. One of the guys looked like a professional wrestler, with long black hair in a ponytail down to his waist and a goatee. Probably a local. The other was a mainlander. Brown hair with a fuller goatee and a predominantly red tattoo on his forearm."

"That sounds like his business partner, Mr. Raines."

I nodded and then it suddenly occurred to me. Natua worked midnights but was standing on the beach in uniform before sunset, shaded by the Ironwood trees, aptly named for their bark that appeared as colorful as aged iron with a patina finish. "What are you doing here so early? Don't you work dogwatch?"

"They were short-handed so I'm working a double. Besides, your brother wanted to talk to me."

My stomach flipped but I kept my tone casual. "Did John learn anything about the cause of death?"

"That would be privileged information for the investigators on this case, not a part-time surf instructor who works for a private investigator." His voice was business-like.

Mine was pissed. "That's bullshit. You wouldn't have a case if it weren't for me. You shared with me this morning. What's changed?"

The towel slipped a little as I got excited and started moving my arms around. Although I couldn't see his eyes, I knew he was staring at the top of my exposed breasts. My mouth clamped shut and I turned for my car.

"Is there something you're not telling me?" His tone sounded like we should be sitting in an interrogation room.

In the best innocent, Southern belle voice I could muster, I responded, "Now offisuh. I would ne'vah hold back information. Y'all such big, strong lawmen. Someone like lil' 'ol helpless me could ne'vah solve a murdah."

Natua pulled off his sunglasses, his eyes narrowing. Well, screw him — and John both. Let them find out on their own about the hand-to-hand exchange between the victim and the other two guys. Let them find out that Mutt somehow knew the dead guy on sight. Let them just try to solve this murder without me.

I grabbed a t-shirt out of the back seat of my car, slid it over my head and reached for my keys. Then I tossed the towel on Natua's patrol car, turned on a dime, and with sand spitting up behind me, left the beach without a backward glance.

Three could play this game.

CHAPTER NINE

After leaving the tree-lined beach, I called my little brother Kionni several times hoping he could add to the story about the construction site. I wasn't sure where he was working, but I thought maybe he'd heard some gossip through the construction workers' network. Unfortunately, all I got was his annoying voicemail. No doubt he was out for the night and wasn't about to answer his sister's phone call.

Determined to investigate a murder case I had no clue how to solve, of a man I'd never met, should have made me wonder what the hell was wrong with me. Instead, the more I learned, the more connected I felt to the case. As if a grand plan was in the works, and I had no control over it.

Not one to dwell on the meaning of life, or the choices we make that alter our destiny (remember I'm just taking a break before my senior year of college), I jumped into the case with both feet. Back in the peace and quiet of my apartment, I documented everything I knew on my laptop. When my (yes, I know) amateur reports were complete, I wrote the names of the major players on the dry-erase board that normally lived a blank existence on my kitchen wall. Now, it looked a bit like a family tree. Peter Johnson was the trunk, his wife and son branched to the left, his business partner with the dragon tattoo sprouted to the right and the location of his body became the roots.

Then on another side of the board I started a separate list of individuals who may or may not play a role — kind of like a surrounding forest. The big wrestler definitely hit the top of the list and then... I tapped the marker on the board, hesitating. As much as I didn't want to write the name, Mutt needed to join the ranks of loose ends. I scrawled his name and felt guilty for even thinking someone I knew could be involved in something this bad.

I'm not sure how long I stared at the stick tree on the board before sitting down on my couch and getting lost in the words. I laid my head down on the arm and before I knew it, dreams of hooking up with Natua filled my mind and body with desire. The scene was hot, and sexy as hell. Sun setting on the beach, clothes flying, muscles glowing and his tongue doing unimaginable things...until I grabbed his sculpted bicep to pull him closer. But what should have been rock-hard muscle turned out to be squishy flesh ripping from his body.

I shot off the couch, panting, and shaking my hands free of the goo as I looked around for the missing appendage. Nothing.

Hua.

My body itched, repeating the creepy crawly attack of the day before. The only good thing — my stomach remained intact. Without hesitation, I shook my mind clear of Natua, headed straight for the bathroom and took a fast, coldish shower, then for the second time in less than 24 hours, applied my grandmother's ancestral lotion.

To my disappointment, the sun still wasn't up, but there was no way I was going back to sleep. I put on my bathing suit, covered it with a tank top and shorts, and sat down to put on my running shoes. Pulling my hair back in its usual ponytail, I left my small apartment above the now quiet office of Private Kaua'EYE's Investigations.

I'd gotten the job as a Runner (not a go-fer) for the business after moving in. Turned out my landlord owns Private Kaua'EYES, and his people did a background check on me before he offered the lease. My daily contact with the employees coming and going in the parking lot turned into friendship and a beer here and there with the lead investigator, named Lani.

One particularly drunk night, I complained about the possibility of having to move back home. A large surf company had moved in next to our stand, making *Aaron's Surf Zone* ragtag group nearly invisible with their flashy boards, hot guys and bikini babes. Business had dropped so dramatically that I was going to have to make some serious changes in my life.

Lani graciously stepped in and said I could help her with deliveries, police reports, and other odds and ends. Helping her out began a natural progression to assisting the other detectives when they got in a pinch, and the money slowly but surely became a steady supplement that kept me afloat. So my little studio, with its private entrance and a view of Koloa's small, quaint downtown, had saved my sanity. The last thing I was ready to do was decide on a real career. I wasn't even sure about finishing my degree.

Normally, I'd hop in my car and drive to the beach to run, but after yesterday and the ever present dream of Natua's detached arm, I decided to risk the roads.

I hit the pavement and all my troubled thoughts disappeared. I didn't love my daily run, but it always took my mind off everything else. And today, I definitely needed that. My feet created a steady beat on the pavement, lulling me into a steady rhythm. The sights, scents and sounds of waving Eucalyptus trees and grasses filled my senses and soothed my mind. All was peacefully quiet.

The hum of a car engine behind me broke my reverie. With no flashlight to warn of my existence, I ran off into the grass to avoid being hit as headlights silhouetted my body. I could see my shadowed form jogging as I glanced back a couple times, aware of the vehicle slowing down. The bright glare of the headlights made it difficult to see anything until the car drew closer, and I could make out the outline of a Jeep.

My nerves now skittering like my uneven steps, I wondered if I should give up jogging all together or at least take my dad's advice — get a treadmill or join a gym. Maybe then I could avoid dead bodies on the beach and creeps on the road.

The Jeep pulled up next to me, permanently sealing my decision to get a treadmill if I actually made it out of this encounter alive. It slowed to match my pace as my pulse attempted to outrun us both, and I warily tried to see the occupant. As if reading my thoughts, the driver turned on the interior lights of the vehicle.

"Baby Doll, it's dangerous to be driving on the road at this hour, let along running it."

Shit. I stumbled.

There was no doubt in my mind as to the identity of the man lecturing me. It was Mutt's 'pro-wrestler' staring at me from the driver's seat. His body was so large, I was pretty sure if the canvas roof had been attached, he would have had his head bent forward in an awkward position. His hands made the steering wheel look like a child-size toy in his grasp, and his chest sat wider than the seat could accommodate. His hair, longer than mine, was held back in a ponytail that disappeared behind his back. I couldn't see his legs, but if they were anything like the rest of him, they had to be tree trunks.

My heart stopped. Slammed into an invisible wall. I couldn't breathe. My rhythm — lost.

KYM ROBERTS

"Ayyy!" I yelped as I tripped over some imaginary tree root and found myself eating grass, seasoned with dirt.

The Jeep stopped and before I could get up, the pro-wrestling dope dealer was standing above me. Tilting my head, I looked up at his Red Dirt cargo shorts and gray tank top. I couldn't crane my head back far enough to see his face. Then he picked me up under my armpits, no doubt to break me in half for asking too many questions.

No longer in shock, my blood pounded in my ears. The headlights of his vehicle illuminated his frame but kept his face hidden from my view as he turned into the light to get a better look at me. My feet dangled a couple feet above the ground, adding to my sense of alarm.

I wasn't ready to die.

I started fighting the dope-dealing killer, refused to allow him to kill me and throw me to the fishes. I felt like a two year old throwing a tantrum in his arms as he held me out in front of him, my feet and arms swinging wildly. A couple times, I connected with his head and body, but not once did he flinch.

I was in deep shit.

I'm not sure how long I struggled, but it was long enough for exhaustion to set in. I'd fought for my life...and lost. My kicking and squirming came to an abrupt stop, but my chest continued to heave. I hung limp in his hands, waiting for the fatal blow.

"Are you done, because I don't want to set you down if you're not?" His voice sounded...cheerful?

Then he turned, revealing the biggest, bluest eyes lined with long curly lashes most women would kill to possess. As startling as it was to see blue eyes in his native face, I was caught more off guard by the realization that there wasn't a mean bone in this guy's body. Yes, he was big enough to break me in half, but he wouldn't. He had *happy* eyes to match his voice, and a crooked smile with a dimple that came off sexy as hell.

"Yeah..." panting, I tried to finish my sentence, "...I'm done." was all I could manage.

Slowly, he set me down on the ground and began brushing bits of dirt out of the strands of hair escaping my ponytail. There was no way he was a dope dealer. Dope dealers don't pick people *off* the ground, they put them *in* the ground.

"Thanks..." I felt like I should know his name, like I'd known him for a lifetime. Nevertheless, I didn't know him at all, which left me feeling a little confused.

"Alapai. Alapai Lincoln. My friends call me Pai."

In the Hawaiian language, Alapai means Elf Council. Pai means to encourage, rouse, hold up, exalt. As a culture, we choose the names of our children with great care for their meaning. Did Alapai's family believe in the Menehune, the mythical elfin people of Hawai'i?

I don't normally give my name to strangers, but Pai exuded faith in humanity and somehow, I wanted to return that faith. Why, I had no idea, I was still suffering from the shock of how quickly my fear turned into trust.

"I'm Malia...Fern," I nearly gasped. I'm not sure the delay in catching my breath was from my little fit or from his pure male scent blending in with the eucalyptus to create an incredible aphrodisiac. My hand shook as I held it out.

He engulfed it with an intimate, two-handed grasp.

"Well, Malia, I'm sorry I distracted you and caused you to trip."

"No, really. Thanks for stopping to help me. Can I...can I buy you a cup of coffee?" There was no way I was going to let our chance encounter go to waste. This man was a lead that I needed to follow. He might have been the last person to see Peter Johnson alive.

"I'm on my way to work, but I'll take a rain check."

He reached for his wallet and pulled out a business card. The headlights clearly lit up the bold script of *Lincoln Security Firm,* 66 Fern Rd. Kailua-Kona, HI (808) 555-1325. His cell phone number was listed below the office number.

He was from the Big Island. The name of the street where his business was situated did not escape my notice. If he recognized the irony of my last name being the same as the street location for his security company, he didn't comment.

"I'm opening an office on Kaua'i so I'm staying with a friend. Call my cell and we'll have that cup of Kona."

Before I could respond, another car turned down the road. The roar of the engine obvious as the car sped up. Just when I began to worry about another dangerous encounter, red and blue lights ricocheted off the foliage and a police car pulled up behind Pai's Jeep.

I knew it was him, before I actually saw him. Who else would it be, other than the guy who had a knack for showing up at the most inopportune times?

Son of a...

Officer Natua got out of the car with his body stiff and his chest puffed up like a silverback gorilla. His nightstick was cocked close to his side, as if he was going to beat the shit out of someone. I glanced at Pai thinking he'd get humor out of this situation, but those happy eyes, weren't so happy when they looked at Natua. In fact, they looked pretty damn mean.

So much for my judgment of character.

Natua walked over to the Jeep and Pai pushed me behind him, placing the two of them face-to-face. Pai was taller than Natua by a couple inches and broader by a couple muscles, if that was possible, but Natua looked a hell of a lot more street wise and very capable with his night stick. I wasn't sure who would win or why this scene had turned into one with so much aggression.

"I should have known it was you, when she described a wrestler with a long ponytail."

My heart sank. Natua knew how to expose every inch of me. My deception revealed, I wasn't sure Pai would ever take a call from me once he realized I had actually been looking for him. I had stumbled upon some good luck, and Natua ruined it.

Obviously, the two were previously acquainted…and they weren't particularly fond of each other.

"Malia and I were just leaving. Is there something we can do for you, *Officer*?"

I flinched at the snide way Pai said officer. I also didn't remember making plans to leave with him, nor was I feeling very trustful of a guy whose emotions changed so dramatically. In fact, just looking at these large men eyeing each other like they were ready to launch fists…well, I seriously thought about running away. But, no matter how much I wanted to, I knew it wouldn't be the right thing to do.

As they both gritted their jaws to the point I thought they would break before either one threw a punch, I took a deep breath and stepped between them. Looking up from one man to the other, I began to see similarities in their features, if not their eyes, and realized they could be brothers staring at each other in a fierce sibling rivalry.

Neither one seemed to realize I was there. Well below their line of sight, their bodies began closing in on me as they leaned in, posturing for the upper hand.

"Excuse me…" a tiny little whispered plea escaped my mouth as their chests crushed against my shoulders. I should have run away. Any woman who thinks dying, sandwiched between two mega hunks, is a great fantasy, should be locked up in an asylum.

Pai seemed to notice me first. His expression softened as he backed up and caught me before I crumpled to the ground. Then Natua grabbed my other arm trying to pull me toward him, and I became the rope in a tug of war contest between them. Was this really my life?

"Enough!"

Both men stopped pulling and actually looked at me instead of each other. I shook them both off.

"What is it with you two?" I didn't expect an answer, which was good since neither one offered one.

"How do you know Pai?" I asked the one in uniform.

Natua's jaw tightened again before he muttered under his breath. "He's my cousin."

That explained some of it. They were both from the Big Island, they were cousins and they had a rift between them. Well, *too* bad. I had other business to attend and I wasn't going to wait. To hell with my polite invitation for coffee.

"Is there a reason you stopped, Officer Natua?"

"I thought you might need my help."

"Well, I don't. Is there anything else?" My words were short and clipped even to my ears.

"Well no…" Natua stumbled.

"Then thank you for stopping, but Pai and I are leaving."

"Pai needs to come with me and talk to Detective Sergeant Kumu."

"Don't be ridiculous. Pai has done nothing wrong, and John won't be in the office for another couple hours. Pai, give Natua your business card. Detective Sergeant John Kumu will be calling you in regard to a dead body found on the beach."

Pai obediently gave his card to Natua who muttered something about knowing the damn number. I thought I was beginning to sound like my mother scolding my brothers and I resented these two gorgeous men turning me into my worst nightmare.

"Pai, let's go. Goodbye, Officer Natua."

I stalked toward Pai's Jeep and was surprised when he beat me to the door and opened it for me. I looked up to see him triumphantly grinning back at Natua. An eye roll escaped me.

Men.

Pai stopped grinning when he caught sight of my lips pressed tightly together and my arms folded across my chest while sitting in his front seat. He gently closed the door. Unable to resist a last minute jab at Natua, he waved good-bye before getting in the vehicle.

"Sorry, Malia. As you can see we tend to compete at everything." Pai's shoulder brushed mine as he put on his seatbelt.

"Competing doesn't involve tearing apart innocent women."

He glanced my way as he pulled away from Natua's car. "How innocent are you when you were manipulating me to get information? Are you a cop?"

"No, and it wasn't like that. I was looking for a very large man with a long ponytail in regard to a…a body that washed ashore and then you stopped me. How the hell could I plan that? Did I plan the falling on my face part when a dope dealer pulled up next to me?"

"Dope dealer?"

So much for me interrogating him, I think he successfully turned the tables around. "A witness saw you with the victim and he thought it was a drug buy."

"Ahhhh."

"'Ahhhh? That's all you have to say when I accuse you of dealing? Don't do this, Pai. The detective on this case is working with your cousin and the two of them have already shut me out of this investigation. I don't need you holding back as well." He didn't need to know John was my brother.

"Makaio won't give you information?" A grin spread across his face and a light bulb turned on in my head. If John and Natua didn't want to share information, I could team up with Pai and solve the case before them.

"No, he won't, but I'm the one who found the body. I need to be involved in the outcome of the case." That got Pai's attention. "The detective asked me to snoop around the beach crowd and see if I could learn anything, but he won't give me any information in return. I don't know how to explain it to you other than to say, the victim deserves justice and I feel like I'm the one who owes it to him."

Pai's eyebrows rose with my last disclosure, but he remained silent. He was a good interrogator, waiting for me to fill up the awkward silence, and so far, I'd obliged him because I wanted his help.

"Did you know the victim?" When I shook my head no, he asked, "What's his name?"

"Peter R. Johnson. He was from New Mexico."

It was Pai's turn to be surprised. Although he wasn't very demonstrative, I caught the small hitch in his breath and the widening of his eyes as they appeared to sadden. His hand grasped my thigh just above the knee. I didn't get the impression he was making a play. It seemed more like he was grasping onto life for strength.

"So, you want me to help you solve this case before this detective and my shit-for-brains cousin do?"

"Yes."

His fingers began doing swirls on my thigh as he stared out the windshield. And something shifted. His touch no longer felt needy. Wanting maybe, but definitely not needy.

I must seriously need a real sex partner. Pai was the second guy in twenty-four hours that made my pulse pound in areas I shouldn't be aware of while discussing a dead body.

"Partner, you have a deal." Pai gave me that happy smile.

Partner. He drew the line in the sand for me. I don't get sexually involved with co-workers. I picked up his hand and returned it to the steering wheel.

Pai grinned. "I love a challenge."

As if I couldn't tell from the way he and Makaio went toe-to-toe. So now, I had a partner who loved a challenge, but what did that make Makaio?

"Where can I drop you off? I really have to go to work, but I'll call you later if you give me your number."

"Down the street about a half mile is the turn off to a private drive of a friend of mine. I was headed over there to take a swim."

"Lani's place?" His grin was infectious.

"Do you know her?"

"We've…worked together in the past. I'm renting out the in-law's quarters at her place."

"What? You're the tenant she wanted me to check up on?" I slapped my hand over my mouth. I suck at interrogations.

His eyes crinkled. "Do you check up on all of her tenants?"

"She doesn't have that many, but normally, no. She does her own background checks."

Pai actually threw his head back and laughed. I've never understood when people say that, but watching him, totally explained the expression.

"Lani told me a pool girl would be stopping by today."

Pool girl? I sat there dumb-founded. Why would she say I was a pool girl? Had I blown it by telling Pai I was supposed to spy on him?

"She said you were cute…and available." Pai's teeth gleamed in the low light.

"Oh," I managed. His grin did things to me. Lani knew I wasn't looking for a relationship, yet she'd lied to both of us and threw me temptation in a deliciously masculine form.

Pai pulled down the drive and up to the security gate to put in the code. Suddenly I didn't want to swim. I'd only run a couple miles. I wasn't sweating. I just wanted to get the information I needed and head back home. The sooner the better.

"I don't think I need a swim today, but I really do want to talk to you about Peter Johnson."

"Let me shower and change real quick. Then we can talk for a few minutes before I go to the office."

Images of soap on that broad chest and the rest of his body were the last thing I needed to think about. "Sure." I managed to squeak out.

Pai pulled to the rear of Lani's colonial two story house with a wraparound porch and parked in front of the cute bungalow that matched the main house. Originally built in the early 1900's by a sea captain, the estate became a sugar cane plantation, one of the few still in operation.

We both exited the Jeep, Pai stepped out like it felt good to get out of a small box, while I jumped down to the ground. He waited for me like a gentleman at the front of the vehicle and I suddenly had this image of him taking me home, like on a real date.

That's when I began to sweat.

We approached the quaint little house with his large hand on the small of my back. He took it away to unlock the door, but it returned when he swung open the door and allowed me to pass in front of him. My heartbeat was definitely working overtime, and not because I was afraid.

I took a deep breath for courage and ignored the twitch of his lips as I brushed past him. He knew damn well both of us couldn't fit in any doorway without touching.

I scurried into the modern décor, defined by a custom surfboard rack just inside the door. White shag throw rugs scattered across bamboo floors, and two plush green couches sat at an angle facing a plasma TV and stereo system. An abundance of plants graced the room, and photographs of beach scenes in black frames adorned the walls.

"There's water and tea in the fridge, or if you'd like to make some Kona Coffee, there's some in the cupboard. Make yourself at home and I'll be out in a second."

I nodded and watched him walk into the bedroom. He closed the door behind him, sort of, and I dry-gulped the desire rising in my body. Determined to ignore the sexual tension in the air, I went to the kitchen and poured a couple glasses of iced tea.

The colors and textures of the house should have helped soothe my tense body with the island atmosphere coming indoors. The blue glass breakfast bar had custom barstools, which appeared to be molded surfboards matching the blonde stain of the kitchen cabinets. Each stool held a spiritual symbol with its own unique inlay of mahogany wood showcasing images of a sea turtle, a whale, a shark and an owl on the back.

But none of that helped my tension dissipate — I could hear the shower, smell his scent throughout the small home, and I needed to escape, immediately.

I grabbed our drinks and went out on the patio, where I plopped down on a bamboo lounge chair facing the pool. A private Jacuzzi for the in-law's quarters sat toward the back of the patio, but I ignored that scene. It was way too intimate.

As I gazed out over the water, the floral garden's soothing scents filled my lungs, the ultra-soft cushions lulled my tired muscles, and I leaned back and closed my eyes. I had loved Lani's place since the very first time I walked in a year ago. She'd been looking for someone she trusted to teach her son to surf, and once she knew I'd been giving lessons since I was seventeen, she signed him up. We've been best friends ever since.

Lani had never mentioned Pai. In fact, I'd never seen him around the office. He was a guy you'd have a hard time forgetting once you'd seen him. Images of the two of us swimming in the pool began to creep into my thoughts.

"Are you dreaming about someone?"

I jumped and nearly fell off the chair. "No!" Of course, I was.

A blush ran across my face and chest and Pai grinned with mischief before taking the seat next to me. He looked good, (who am I kidding, he looked great) in a tan suit and cream shirt that were expertly tailored to his form. His ponytail and goatee added to the raw masculinity of him, which I didn't think was possible. I like my men in board shorts, but I was beginning to see the appeal of a suit. He was a modern day businessman in an athletic-cut suit that made you appreciate everything underneath.

Hell, he could wear a sack and I'd appreciate his body.

Our eyes locked as he took a sip of tea. His were still happy with a hint of desire. Mine probably looked like I was going to tackle him and have wild *Menehune* sex with him.

My shirt felt damp.

"Need a swim to cool down after all?"

Yes. "No." I was getting good at saying no. A real conversationalist. My face heated with embarrassment. This guy could read me better than any Madame Freak-a-zoid at a psychic fair. Makaio…Officer Natua, couldn't read an erupting volcano, but Pai knew my thoughts before I knew them myself.

"I think I'll skip it," I lied and I was pretty sure by the slant of his smile, he knew I'd jump into the refreshing water to cool the jets of my rocketing libido as soon as he left.

Pai took another drink from his tea. "Thanks, by the way, for the drink," he said, tipping the glass in my direction.

I nodded. I couldn't help but fantasize about the way his lips pressed against the azure goblet. I shifted and crossed my legs to cover the shiver that shook my entire body and quickly got down to business. "How do you know Peter Johnson?"

"Two weeks ago, Mr. Johnson and his wife hired my firm to provide security for his building site after he halted construction. As it turns out, a sacred *Heiau* Temple is located on the grounds and his partner was going to destroy it. When Mr. Johnson found out about it, he stopped the work in that area of the property and hired my firm to protect it. He thought his partner would bulldoze the temple by 'accident.'

"Then last week, he introduced me to his partner Daven Raines. We expected Raines to be resistant, but he actually caught us both off-guard. He wanted to extend the contract coverage to include the entire site since there had been some recent vandalism, thefts and a small arson fire. That's why Raines wanted to meet at such a weird hour. He wanted us to understand how vulnerable the buildings were after hours." Pai's jaw tightened and I wondered if he felt responsible for Peter Johnson's death. Then again, maybe it was something else entirely.

"But still, isn't it a little odd to meet before the sun comes up?" I asked.

Pai's right eye twitched with my question. This time, I knew he was going to lie before he even uttered a word. Call it woman's intuition or whatever you want to call it, but I felt the lie deep down in my bones, before he uttered a word.

"Mr. Raines was adamant about the time, and since Peter and I were trying to make him understand the implications of destroying a *Heiau*, we agreed, but Peter wasn't really happy about the additional security."

"Why would that make your client unhappy? It sounds like you won." Again, I waited for his story to skirt the edges of the truth.

"Peter believed that adding more guards wasn't the issue, especially since the budget was tight. He wanted Raines to stick to the construction timetable. He thought their biggest problems were personnel related. Then Mr. Raines stepped in and paid me cash to set up immediate security for the site. That's not a deal that I was going to turn down. I flew in a couple of my people from the Big Island later that day and I contacted an off-duty coordinator on the police department to have officers fill in the holes."

"Did you know Peter Johnson was missing?"

"A few days ago, I got a call from Raines telling me Johnson disappeared. He claimed Mr. Johnson was a recovering dope addict and had apparently gone off on a binge. He told me to keep providing the security with the retainer I received, but he wasn't sure what would happen after that."

"So what will happen after next week?"

"Our agreement ends. Until then, I'm going to provide the services…and at least try to figure out a way to ensure the *Heiau* is preserved after that."

I understood Pai's concern. Raines wouldn't be the first businessman to destroy our sacred ground and apologize after the deed was done. The truth had returned to his story. So what was he hiding?

"Have you been in contact with Peter's wife?"

"No, I left several messages for Mr. Johnson on his cell phone, but now that I know he won't be returning my calls, I'll have to call his attorney and go from there."

"I'm sorry I was the bearer of bad news. Can you tell me the name of the condos you're guarding for him?"

"*The Garden of the Gods.*" He answered in a reverent voice.

The same place my car had 'sixty-nined' with Makaio's police cruiser after we met at the pastry shop.

Even in my mind, that sounded bad.

"The condos across the street from Pearl's Hawaiian Pastries?" I asked, ignoring the guilt creeping up my neck in a deep shade of red.

"That's them." Pai followed the path of my guilt, straight up to my eyes. The man could make me seriously uncomfortable. I ignored the impulse to squirm in my seat.

"But I was there yesterday morning, and there weren't any guards working."

Pai frowned. "At what time?"

"It was around six in the morning. I was in the lot with…" somehow I didn't think Pai needed to know who I'd been with, "…a friend for a good twenty minutes. I didn't see a soul."

Pai rubbed his hand across his jaw and looked out over the pool. Without warning he said, "Baby Doll, I'd like to hire you."

"For what? I don't work security."

"I want to hire you to keep an eye on my security guards at the site during the night. All you need to do is make sure they show up for work and stay on the job. I don't need guards working for me that damage my business' reputation."

As I began to squirm in my seat at the prospect of babysitting his employees, Pai continued to explain the job he had in mind.

"Someone skipped out on their shift the other night. I can follow the paper trail and time sheets, but at this point, I won't have enough to fire anyone. I need to know if Raines is paying my guys off, or if this was a one-time thing. Maybe I just have one bad guard, but if it's going on every night on both shifts, I need to reimburse Raines and Mrs. Johnson for what they've paid me. If it's just one individual, then I need to fire his ass."

I'm all for people doing their job. You do the work, you get paid, right? But I also didn't want to be responsible for someone losing his job because he fell asleep during those awful hours between four a.m. and daylight. I've studied during those hours. They suck, and I certainly didn't want to work them.

"Pai…I really don't want to be responsible…"

"Baby Doll, a man lost his life. His family is grieving and I'm trying to protect the sacred ground that Mr. Johnson was trying to save. Do you know how rare it is for a company to see our culture as more than just a profit margin?"

Actually, I did, and Pai's guilt trip was pushing me into taking the job.

"And in the meantime, you'll be able to see if something isn't right at *The Garden of the Gods*. Maybe something the police and I are both missing will give you a head start in your investigation. I promise to come to you first with any information I learn about Mr. Johnson." Pai smiled at me as he reached across the table and grabbed my hand.

It was like one of those scenes from a girly flick, or at least that's how it seemed. His fingers wrapped around mine, and in slow motion while staring into my eyes with those depthless blue eyes of his, he pulled my hand up to his mouth. His lips pressed the back of my hand as he maintained a deep and meaningful gaze. He winked and my heart melted.

On a scale of one to ten, Pai's charm was about a twenty.

"Okay." I was in trouble.

CHAPTER TEN

Pai offered me a ride back to town, but I declined and took that swim after all. I was hot, over-heated and desperate for distance from Pai. A cold shower would've done wonders, but I wasn't getting naked until I reached my apartment. Alone. Besides, my jogs had been interrupted two days in a row. At this rate I'd get out of the routine and the next one would kill me.

With part of my workout complete, I used Lani's phone to check my messages before hitting the road back into town. (Yes, I'd left my phone on the counter in my apartment). Bad habits die hard.

Maybe I should just tell people to put that on my tombstone.

I had two messages from Lani begging me to file some papers with the courts that afternoon so she could go watch her son play baseball, and one from my boss telling me I had four surf classes lined up for the next day. Not exactly a full day's work, which meant more begging at Private Kaua'EYES for work, or working dogwatch for Pai. Since I'd already agreed to do it, the point was mute, but my excuses for not being able to make it were dwindling.

A message from my mom who wondered if I was coming home for dinner and nothing from my brother, Kionni. Figures.

I called Lani first, but she was with a client, so I left a message that I'd be in around one o'clock to get the documents. Then I called my mom to tell her I wouldn't be able to make it today, and left another message for Kionni. By the time I headed for home, it was almost eight. Traffic was light since it was the weekend, and half the islanders were staying in their own neck of the woods instead of heading out to work. I got the typical catcalls from guys, thinking they were all I needed in my life for the next twenty-four hours, but I ignored them all. In fact, I was pretty proud I hadn't flipped even one of them the bird, when a familiar car approached.

It wasn't a car I wanted to see, nor was it a car I could miss. It was a hot pink Camaro SS convertible with black racing stripes and matching pink wheels. It was hideous, and it belonged to Windy Trapp, my ex-best friend, the one who told Makaio I was a little girl surfing topless.

Two birds flew before I could stop them. (Not that I would have stopped myself from flipping her off, but you get the point — the feelings between us run strong and deep.) Windy returned the favor, her blonde hair blowing in the wind as her car swerved in my direction. She didn't intend to hit me. It was just an attempt to scare the crap out of me, literally, and it nearly succeeded.

I ran off the road at full speed, jumping into the ditch. I heard her cackle in the wind as my ankle gave underneath me, and I fell for the third time in two days. This time, pain was involved. I sat in the weeds among some trash from careless travelers and rubbed my sore ankle. I didn't think it was broken, but it wasn't a hundred percent either. The swelling started immediately. I stood up, tested my weight, and winced.

I was so stupid for not running with my phone. If I made it home in one piece, I swore I'd change that bad habit and buy an armband to hold it. I didn't even try to wave down a car. It was daylight, I was alive and I was in no mood to deal with anyone. So when the motorcycle approached me, I didn't even look in that direction, until it completed a U-turn and pulled up next to me.

Seriously, can't a woman suffer in peace?

I tried not to glare as I glanced his way and kept walking.

Yes, it was a man. And yes, he had killer biceps under a taut t-shirt. I didn't need any more biceps in my life. I had enough.

He killed the engine. "Malia."

I turned to find Makaio Natua approaching me on foot with his helmet at his hip. Cargo shorts teamed with his muscular body made him look like a warrior on a mission.

"What happened?" Concern covered his words.

"Nothing," I bit out and turned to stomp away. It was more of a pathetic limp, but I'm sure my attitude more than made up for it.

"Malia, stop. I can see you're hurt. Let me help you." His voice still dripped with concern, but I wasn't capable of handling it. If I softened, I just might cry.

"Thanks for stopping, but I'm fine. I only have a short distance to go."

Rough calluses, probably from lifting weights, wrapped around my upper arm and I stopped. If I tried to resist, I'd just end up on my face again, so what was the point of fighting it?

"Why didn't you call someone for help?"

"I left my cell at home."

"You went jogging without your cell?" He sounded incredulous.

"Don't lecture me, Makaio." My voice cracked as I said his name, the anger breaking way to a much deeper emotion. Afraid I'd break down on the spot, I demanded, "Are you going to give me a ride or not?"

"Well, I'm not going to leave you on the side of the road. You can wear my helmet, but you're going to have to wear my backpack, too."

I nodded, afraid anything else would lead to sobs, and without asking for permission, he placed his hand around my waist and practically carried me back to his Ducati before slipping his helmet on my head. The chinstrap snapped together leaving his thumbs too close to my mouth.

After carefully placing his backpack over my shoulders, Makaio straddled the bike and held out his hand to help me mount behind him. I pressed against his backside and the heat of our bodies mixed. The Ducati purred between our legs. I wrapped my arms around his chest, letting my fingers splay across his pecs and every muscle in his body constricted.

"You okay?" He asked.

I managed to respond with, "Yeah," and told myself I was breathless because I was about to cry.

"Hold on tight and I'll have you home in no time. You live in Koloa?"

Again my voice sounded soft and throaty, "Yeah, above Private Kaua'EYE's Investigations."

As we took off, my grip tightened, my breasts pushed against his back and a heavenly warmth spread between my legs as I practically ground myself into his ass.

This was not what the doctor would have ordered. In fact, it wasn't what I would have ordered a couple days ago, but in the last day-and-a-half, I'd turned into a raging slut.

I mean seriously. First Makaio, and then this morning, Pai, who I'd just met. Both of them had my hormones raging from the moment we met. Now Makaio. Again.

Only a loose woman lusts after two different men in that short a time frame. I mean, sure, if you're window shopping, you say, "Ooo, nice shirt," or, "Wow, look at those pants."

I wanted to try on both outfits at the same time. My character was slipping.

Makaio was the bad boy of the two cousins. He was a clean-cut cop, but he oozed a wild, dangerous sex appeal despite the close haircut and freshly shaven jaw. Pai held a different attraction for me. He made me feel precious. Taken care of…like a princess. I've never been a princess before, and the feeling was kind of nice. Of course, I've never been bad either, and *that* feeling was downright dirty. In a good way.

See my dilemma?

At the moment, my sluttiness was plastered to Makaio's backside wanting him to turn around while my hands wandered his chest. Damn, I wanted him. I wanted to move my hands down to his abs and explore the tight six-pack I knew was there. The draw of his muscles was incredible as the breeze whipped across my legs cinched tightly to his hips. With a little movement, I could have them wrapped around his waist. Hmmm.

The wistful feeling of being right where you belong in life saturated my psyche until the lack of vibration between my legs popped my dream like a bubble. That's when I noticed my hands had betrayed my desire and wandered to Makaio's muscled midsection.

Son of a ...

I jumped off the motorcycle. Forgetting my swollen cankle, I ended up face first in the dirt. Again. His helmet was the only thing that kept me from eating dirt for the second time in a couple hours.

Lying flat on my stomach, I looked up to see Makaio squatting in front of me. He actually looked worried instead of lustful, as he reached out and slowly removed my helmet. His concern revealed a side of him I didn't expect to see, and one I kind of liked.

In an attempt to regain any shred of dignity I had left, I pulled myself into a sitting position and smoothed out my hair, as my heart flip-flopped with Makaio's proximity. Unable to resist, I looked up and our eyes locked. His hand rose toward my hair, and my heart stopped mid-leap with the magnetic pull of his touch. I leaned into his palm as he pulled the rubber band from my hair. My eyes drifted closed in surrender to his fingers massaging my scalp. I should have flinched, should have stopped him when his hand trailed down my neck and brushed the dirt from my shoulders before proceeding to my chest. Instead, my breath turned shallow and his palm rested over my breast. I'm not sure how long it stayed there. I'm not sure if I leaned into his large strong fingers or if he began massaging me without any provocation on my part. Maybe it was all a figment of a mind that needed to escape reality for just a short time. Whatever it was, I would have let it continue for eternity.

Then it was gone.

Makaio reached out and picked me up in his arms, squelching any resistance from me with a kiss on my nose. That small peck held so much promise, I couldn't stand it. It didn't matter that I'd known him little more than a day. It didn't matter that there was no promise of tomorrow. All that mattered was now.

He carried me up the rear steps of my apartment like Tarzan whisking Jane off into the jungle. A new adventure waiting to rock my world. On the landing, he stopped and stared at me. This was it.

"Do you have a key?"

My mind was blank. His lips were moving. I heard the words, but the only thing I could comprehend was lust demanding to be sated. "Excuse me?"

His lips turned up in a devilish grin.

"Unless you want me to bust down your door, I need a key to get in your apartment."

"Oh, it's above the door."

His smile disappeared. "That's not a very safe place to put your key."

"I know." I could hear how stupid I sounded, but I was so caught off guard by the animalistic attraction I had for him, I couldn't think straight. Hell, at this point, I wouldn't have cared if he kicked down my door.

He reached up and grabbed the key with ease as I held onto his neck. Once he got the door unlocked, he pushed inside with his backside, then kicked the door closed behind us. His visual perusal of my small living space didn't faze me as he carried me across the sparsely furnished studio and laid me down on the couch, but his moves struck me at my core. You know that sexy way a guy lays a girl down on the bed in the movies and then lays down on top of her? And you think, 'Man, he's gotta be crushing her.'

Makaio had perfected the move. There was no crushing involved, just pure sensual enticement in all the right places. Our eyes still locked, my head sinking in the throw pillows, his mouth mere inches from mine, and I couldn't seem to breathe.

Damn he was good.

In the deep recesses of my brain, I heard my conscience shout, 'This isn't real!' and 'You don't know him!' But I didn't care.

I expected him to go for it, wanted him to go for it, needed him to go for it. Instead, he broke our intimate contact and rose from the couch. No scooting or smooshing, just one fluid move before he disappeared into the kitchenette. Fear of breaking the magical spell of what I just *knew* was a mutual sexual desire, I didn't move. The icemaker's chatter created mental images of cubes melting wet trails across my breasts. My body screamed to be touched, so to hell with the ranting of my conscience.

He was that good.

Okay, look, this stuff never happens to me. This only happens in romantic novels. You know, like the books stacked under your bed or hidden in your closet? Surely, I'd died and gone to heaven.

I guess I expected him to return buck naked with a hard-on from here to eternity but instead, I saw a towel full of ice, a glass of water and some ibuprofen.

The demands of my body shrieked in protest. Like a spoiled child, I wanted to pound my fists on

109

the floor and cry how unfair life was. I didn't expect pampering. Didn't want pampering. And I sure as hell didn't need pampering!

Hua. He sucked.

Makaio placed the towel on my now blue-green cankle and held out the glass of water and the medication. I took the pills, still looking up at him, waiting for him to do something…anything.

He took the glass, took a drink himself and set it on the table. I was a deer in the headlights the whole time. He stacked pillows under my foot and sat down on the edge of the couch, spreading his body alongside me, careful not to bump my foot. Without a word, he pulled me under his arm and closed his eyes. As I laid there with every nerve ending in my body ready for sex, his breathing evened out, and he fell asleep holding me in his arms.

I was cuddling with an incredibly hot guy who I thought was a bad boy, but I was the only one having dirty thoughts. Every fiber of my being demanded sex. And he was asleep. Was this real?

CHAPTER ELEVEN

I'm not sure how much time passed before I woke up. Wiping the little pool of drool from the corner of my mouth, I looked up and realized I was lying on top of Makaio, my legs straddling him. His breathing was still low and even, his face smooth and angelic in his repose.

His hand, however, was cupping my ass and driving it into the part of his body I had thought would be meeting mine…without clothes.

Slowly, I pulled his hand off while watching his face for a flicker of consciousness. With each breath I took, I inched his hand away from my body. Makaio shifted, stopping my escape and freeing his hand to grab my ass even lower. My heart stopped as his fingertips caressed the spot I had been dying for him to touch. I stared at his serene expression. Even peacefully asleep, the man knew where to find it. I forgot all about my attempted getaway and let him weave his magic.

My eyes closed with submission as I came up the backside of a wave of pleasure. My body shuttered with release as I crested and tumbled down the other side of an orgasmic swell.

Holy shit!

I laid the side of my face back on his chest and listened to the even beat of his heart. My own hammered erratically against his, and I debated with myself about the costs I'd pay if I took total advantage of him while he slept. So far, he'd been the giver. I was innocent of any crime and his sleep walking hands had freed my body from the prison he and Pai had sentenced it to. Yet even asleep, he still dangled the keys in my face. The beast within me demanded freedom.

I had to get out of there before I did something I really regretted. Yeah, the orgasms would be even better if he was awake, but after experiencing a little relief, my conscience had returned and I wasn't sure I wanted to pay the price. It wasn't the thought of prison that stopped me, it was the possibility of rejection. His constant state of arousal told me he was up for action, but he'd had the opportunity, and he'd chosen to sleep.

I'm no angel. I'd checked out every inch of his body before I fell asleep and right now, I was feeling it pressed hard against me. If he had woken up and said, "Sorry, I shouldn't have done that," I would be devastated. I shouldn't have let his hands wander, but I did, and I wasn't about to regret the experience.

It was a '*Wham, bam, thank you Sam*!' moment. Every woman deserves one in a lifetime. This was mine.

The phone rang, forcing me into action. I rolled off Makaio and onto the floor, grabbed the phone from the coffee table and whispered, "Hello?"

"*Me ke aloha pumehana*, Baby Doll. I have a few hours this afternoon and I'd like to show you a map of *The Garden of the Gods* so you know the layout before you start your surveillance tonight. Can I stop by and show you?"

Guilt flooded my body as Pai wished me a warm-hearted hello. I felt like a cheating spouse caught in mid-act. I looked back at Makaio who, with a soft snore, rolled over on his side, away from me, and I scurried across the floor toward the bathroom. Was I cheating on Makaio? Or Pai? Or both? I honestly wasn't sure. I crawled on all fours as I held the phone between my head and shoulder, scared to say anything until I got behind the only door in the apartment.

"Hello?"

"Ah…sorry. My…my brother is asleep on the couch and I…I didn't want to wake him up."

I'm a terrible liar, and I was so going to hell. Brother? In the broader sense, Makaio was my 'Hawaiian brother,' but the implication of him being any kind of relative after my state of arousal made a spasm trail down my spine from pure ick factor.

"Since your *brother*'s sleeping, do you want me to pick you up?"

"No!" I said louder than I meant to. "I mean no," I whispered. "I need to stop by Private Kaua'EYE's and pick up some documents to file at the courthouse. How about I meet you at your office?"

Pai agreed and gave me the address in Lihue. I quickly said good-bye before my guilty conscience caused me to confess.

Peeking out the bathroom door, I looked at Makaio's delicious backside, still relaxed in slumber, and I snuck out to grab a pair of slacks and blouse from the only closet in my apartment. With my cankle creating a duck-like hobble, I prayed Makaio wouldn't wake up to see me waddling across the room.

I chose my clothing and slunk back to the bathroom. Consciously avoiding everything sexy, I went for the comfortable cotton bikini underwear with a matching bra, a pair of loose fitting capris and an over-sized printed blouse. I did *not* want to feel sexual. My libido had been out of control for almost two days now, and I wasn't about to let it continue this afternoon.

My showers usually deplete every last ounce of hot water in the tank, but today, I took a Navy shower. In and out can have other meanings besides sex, so after a quick, cold rinse, I dressed without a second thought about the showerhead. I mean, Makaio had done the job for me, right?

I put my hair up in a clip, brushed on some mascara and lipstick, and slipped out of the bathroom to get my shoes. Lying on his back, Makaio's wonderful package stood at attention. I groaned before I realized how loud it would be and slapped my hand across my mouth while continuing to hobble across the room.

"Where are you going?" Makaio was looking at me with very sexy hooded eyes in his half-wakened state.

"I have some work to do. I'll be back later." I watched him closely to see if he knew what he'd done for me. To me. And if he knew who I was going to meet. But his eyes closed without giving me a hint. Totally comfortable in his masculinity. Totally comfortable on my couch. Totally comfortable with me.

"Okay."

I sat on the built-in bench at my front door wanting to touch him so badly my fingers tingled as I fumbled with the buckle of my sandals. Resisting the temptation, I grabbed my purse, keys, and my phone (see I'm learning) and slipped out the door, locking it behind me. I sighed and leaned back against it, realizing I should've written him a note.

But what would it say? Thanks for the good time? Lock the door on your way out?

This was so not my style.

I looked down at my cankle, wishing I had slacks on that actually covered its ugliness. There was no sign of an anklebone, just a bloated stump, a weird appendage with the blue hue of bruising starting to take over. And of course, that view brought my thoughts back to Peter Johnson's bloated body.

My sex drive completely cooled off with those images. I leaped — well, limped into action, carefully taking the steps down to the back door of Private Kaua'EYE's Investigations. The cool breezes flowed through the office clearing out all thoughts of the men in my life, dead or alive. Almost. I still had a bone to pick with Lani about the '*pool girl*' incident.

Lani sat at her desk talking on the phone with Scotty, her eight-year-old son. In her late twenties, Lani was the big sister I never had. I waved and got an eye roll as she pointed to the phone. I knew the drill. Tossing her thick, wavy hair across trim shoulders, she listened to an endless account of how the Teutons had just defeated the Pagans of Lithuania in her son's computer game. The kid was obsessed with it. I know because he'd cornered me on several occasions while teaching him to surf. The first couple times the stories were fairly interesting. About the hundredth time, I turned into a brainless zombie. How his mom was able to follow his babbling was beyond my comprehension.

I sat down and scrolled through my phone messages. Not one from Kionni. I sent another text. "Call me. It's important."

Several minutes passed, and he still hadn't replied. I was going to have to hunt him down. (I may have growled at that point.)

Lani tapped her desk and I looked up to see her holding out a couple envelopes. I limped my way to her desk and she leaned over to see what caused me to wobble. Her lips pursed in a silent, "Oooo," at the site of my cankle.

"It's nothing, but we need to talk." I did the finger-pointing thing at her, then me and back at her. She grinned and that's all I needed for a confession of guilt. I grabbed the folders, instructions written on the outside, and looked them over.

"Thank you," she whispered with her hand over the receiver.

"Un-huh." I waved goodbye and headed out the door as she grinned some more. It was going to be a long day.

The document filing took an hour and forty-five minutes at the courthouse. Twenty minutes to find a parking place within walking distance for my now throbbing cankle. Fifteen minutes to walk there, with several short breaks along the way that I used to cuss myself for not having iced it longer. Another thirty minutes in line, twenty-five more minutes for the clerk to quiz me about the orders of protection (she was more clueless than me) and fifteen more to get back to my car.

I was ready for a nap and a painkiller by the time I got behind the wheel. Instead, I drove across town and pulled up in front of a small office building raised on lava rock pillars for protection against hurricanes and tsunamis. The roof was thatched and the door had ancient symbols of feather standards known as *kahili* covering the glass. *Kahili* is like a royal crest found on ancient *kappa* cloth adorning the entrances of the homes of our noble descendants.

The question remained, was Pai *ali'i* (royalty), or was his office building *pulo'ulo'u*, (a royal house)? The third possibility could be that he just used it to show his Hawaiian ancestry and didn't have a clue as to what it meant. Somehow, I didn't see that as a possibility.

I stepped inside and found the décor to be masculine — dark teak wood softened by an abundance of local fauna. Past mixed with the present between heavy wooden furniture and modern art design. I heard Pai's voice coming from a side office and turned to see him sitting in a high back leather chair. Intricate carvings of the gods encompassed the front of his massive desk, and…

Pai's image blended into the surroundings; he looked like a king from long ago at 'Iolani Palace. My blood froze, my feet halted. Mesmerized by his unadulterated regal appearance, I couldn't help but wonder who he really was. I imagined I was in a time gone by when rulers made decisions for the people.

Pai looked up from his papers, his smile reflecting a joy for life so many other people would never find. "*Aloha*, Baby Doll."

He stood up to greet me, and my brain and feet thawed enough to meet him halfway across the room. My heart skipped as Pai watched me cross the room. His eyes looked past the façade I tried to wear. Unable to break eye contact, I swallowed the dry lump that somehow formed in my throat. Pai bent over and kissed my check, as if we had been dating forever. His warm breath tickled my ear. His masculine scent aroused my senses as I leaned into a kiss that sent goose bumps down my spine.

What was wrong with me? Makaio just gave me an incredible orgasm, and now I was lusting after Pai.

"What happened since I left you this morning?"

Shame ran through my body. I looked away and fidgeted with my purse. What happened? What happened? "Nothing happened. Why?"

My question was met with silence. He had an odd look on his face as he analyzed my lie. Finally, unable to endure it, I tore my eyes away from his hold.

"You're limping."

"Oh...," Standing in front of him full of guilt, I'd nearly forgotten about my altercation with the ditch, no thanks to Windy. "I twisted my ankle during my run back to Koloa. It's a little sore, but it will be alright in a few days." If I was going to attempt to lie, I had to reestablish eye contact. Unable to, I glued my eyes to his forehead.

"You walked home after spraining it?" His voice held no emotion.

"Ah...no, I got a ride." Geez, did I get a ride. A ride I wasn't about to tell Pai about, so I diverted my eyes again and quickly changed the subject to business. "Do you have a map of the complex to show me?"

I could have sworn by the look I glimpsed on his face, he disapproved of my morning activities. I chose to ignore it and chalked it up to my own paranoia about lying. How could he possibly know what a bad girl I'd been?

My face heated as our eyes finally met.

He knew.

The perfect gentleman let the subject drop, leaving me unsure how to act. I wanted to confess my deception, but I held it together and followed him over to rustic table covered with maps. His posture was regal, in control. Mine was full of shame.

So much for my '*Wham bam thank you, Sam*' moment.

CHAPTER TWELVE

The Garden of the Gods had a fairly easy layout. One large U-shaped building facing the ocean, which gave the interior rooms great beachfront or *makai* views, and the exterior rooms varied from beachfront to ocean view. At the base of the 'U,' the building attached to another U-shaped structure that faced the mountains — a *mauka* view. It also wrapped around the *Heiau* that Pai's guards were protecting. From an aerial view, the entire complex looked a little like the UnderArmour logo, underlined with a tall stone wall at the road.

The sides of the property were currently protected with orange plastic fencing that didn't do much except keep law-abiding citizens from wandering into the construction zone. The empty guard shack was still there, and the whole property was surrounded by mature shrubs that blocked the noise from the roadway, and my ability to spy on the occupants. There were only two entrances to the parking lot. The one I hadn't used was currently closed off with a gate.

From the roadway, there was only one stretch on the hill where I could see into the parking lot and watch the guard shack. Otherwise, I was going to have to be on foot.

Pai gave me a gym bag full of supplies, which included files on the different guards: photos and personal data such as names, date of births, marital status and addresses. He also gave me a pair of binoculars, a really nice digital camera that took low light photos, and he downloaded the coolest App on my phone that gave me night-vision. I'd checked it out in the bathroom in his office and couldn't wait to try it for real.

But once the business conversation ended, we both seemed desperate to escape each other's company. My excuse arrived as a text from my brother Kionni saying he'd be at my apartment in twenty minutes. It nearly sent me into panic mode — Makaio was sleeping on my bed. Technically, it was a couch, but my family wouldn't see it that way. My sleeper sofa was the only bed in the place.

With a promise to be on site tonight, I said goodbye to Pai, who again kissed me on the cheek with reverence, and I raced to my apartment. Makaio's fast and sexy Ducati was still outside, dominating the small parking lot with its mere presence. The Streetfighter with its low, deep growl personified the man occupying my bed/couch and made my body twitch with anticipation.

I was definitely going to hell.

With my pulse in my throat, I pulled into one of several open parking spots in front of Private Kaua'EYE's Investigations, and waited for my brother to drive by. Leaning against the trunk, I breathed a sigh of relief. I'd escaped a major scene with Kionni and my bed partner by a mere two minutes.

My little brother spotted me immediately and parked next to my car.

"*Aloha*, Sis," he said as exited his pickup. "So what's got your panties in such a bunch?"

Kionni looked more like John than me, taking on our mother's Asian heritage instead of our father's island genes. He wore his hair like John, he smiled like John, and he thought he was funny like John, but he was sweeter than our older brother. Moreover, he tended to bail me out of trouble when I needed his help.

"Since when do you ignore messages?"

"Since my adorable big sis is always asking for favors." He chucked me under the chin as if I was the younger sibling and I smacked his hand away.

"This is important, Kionni."

"What? You need to borrow my truck to move home?"

"No, that's not going to happen." I'd live in a box before I moved back home.

"Don't even ask to borrow my bike again." He shook his head to make sure I knew he wasn't going to change his mind on that one.

"I taught you how to ride a motorcycle, little brah, but that's not what I called about. I need to talk to you about your job."

He looked at me skeptically. "Don't tell me you want me to get you a job."

My ego bristled. "No." I ignored the ugly indignation rearing its head, and decided not to put Kionni in the middle of a contest between John and I — he might vote against me. "Are you working at *The Garden of the Gods*?"

"Yeah, I got promoted to Foreman."

Shocked by his announcement, I congratulated him with a hug. "That's awesome."

"Thanks, I think it will be. Why did you want to know if I worked there?"

"I need some information about Peter Johnson."

Kionni leaned up against the trunk of the car next to me and folded his arms. We watched the traffic go by like a tennis match before he noticed my injury. "What's up with the puffer fish attached to your ankle?"

"It's nothing. I twisted it when I was running."

"You didn't have your phone with you, did you?" Kionni accused.

I rolled my eyes and ignored the truth. "What can you tell me about your boss?"

"I haven't seen him in about a week. Are you looking to get a surf instructor job when the place opens?"

Well, now, that wasn't a bad idea. Everyone knew my job at *Aaron's Surf Zone* was on the rocks. My whole family was waiting for me to grow up and get a real job, or move home and go back to school. I wasn't ready to do any of it.

"Are they planning to offer surfing lessons?" I asked, wondering if that was a possible solution for me.

"Nah, the plan got nixed this past week when we had to rearrange the layout."

I nodded. If there was anything I understood, job opportunities came and went quickly on the island, and by the sound of it, my brother didn't know his boss was dead. Otherwise, he'd be fretting over his future.

I broke the news to Kionni. "I found Peter Johnson's body on the beach."

His arms dropped and my little brother turned toward me giving me his undivided attention. "Are you shittin' me? Are you okay?"

That was Kionni, more concerned about me, than his future. "I'm fine," I lied.

"Do Mom and Dad know you found a body?" He eyed me as if he knew I wasn't okay with my discovery.

"Dad does, but we're not telling Mom. We think it's best if she doesn't know."

He nodded. I knew he didn't agree, but he wasn't going to go against Dad. We all knew if Mom found out, in no time flat she'd be setting me up for grief counseling and moving me back home where she would hover over me until I died a lonely old woman.

"You know I don't believe in, don't ask, don't tell. Lying by omission is just as...."

"I know, Kionni."

At the tender age of twenty-two, Kionni's one of those type A personalities wrapped tighter than a fishing line pulling in a great white. Whereas, I drifted into my jobs, he chose his path and scaled the obstacles without looking back. A blown knee in college football ruined his future in ROTC and the military, but Kionni never complained. Instead, he changed his major to business, began working for our uncle's construction company as soon as he graduate college (before me), and he was already primed to take over the business. Better him than me, I wasn't ready to grow up.

"I need your help with this investigation," I told him.

"What investigation?"

"I found him, Kionni. I can't forget the images in my head. I have to know what happened to him." My patience was beginning to wear thin with my closed-mouthed brothers. "Can you tell me what you know about Peter Johnson, please?"

"Mal, you need to leave this for the police. Murder investigations are what they do. Call John, tell him your concerns and he'll take it from there."

The realization that my little brother didn't take me seriously was like a slap in the face. I wanted to lash back. Instead, I swallowed the pain and continued like a professional investigator.

"Was Peter involved in the business or was he just the investor type?"

Kionni turned and walked toward his truck without saying a word, forcing me to follow him.

"Please, Kionni," I pleaded.

He turned around at his truck door. "Mr. Johnson only became active in the project about six weeks ago. Mostly by phone conference, but he seemed to have a picture of where he wanted the project to go."

Finally, someone was giving me answers. "Did you meet with Mr. Johnson once he came to the island?"

Kionni looked away and ran his fingers through his hair, behavior that was completely out of character for him. "I actually met him in New Mexico."

My mind blanked. I couldn't believe it. My brother had gone to the mainland without me knowing? Did my parents know?

"Why?"

Again, he squirmed. "Some of the workers found the ruins of an ancient *Heiau* on the property. Originally, it was in a wooded area next to the old hotel, but with the current layout, it was going to be in the direct path of the bulldozers. I showed Daven Raines, who's been in charge of the project from the beginning. But he couldn't grasp its importance. He called it "a pile of rock with a wooden shack." Kionni actually made quotation marks in the air when he said it. "He scheduled it to be demolished. I couldn't just let that happen and if I tried to go through the courts, it was going to take too long. So I flew to New Mexico to meet with Mr. Johnson."

For a moment, I was at a loss for words. My brother had never shown an interest in Hawaiian heritage, let alone a passion to preserve our history. He'd flown to the mainland to protect it. Really? It was mind-boggling.

"What did Mr. Johnson say?" I asked.

"I knew I was taking a big chance and I wasn't sure how he'd react, but he actually knew more about *Heiau*s than I did. He called Raines while I was there. Even though he didn't understand the problem, Raines was pleasant and said he'd already stopped the demolition. He'd already thought about moving the spa, which was allocated for the area where we found the *Heiau*, to the beach. And he did away with a hut for beach rentals since there was already one next door. Finding the *Heiau* was the perfect answer for him, so they went ahead with the plans with the architect to have the *Heiau* restored and a garden area surrounding it. The plans are set. We're just waiting for zoning approval."

"So you over-reacted."

"No. When I got back, the demolition was almost to the *Heiau.* I called Johnson, and he tried to get in contact with Raines, but couldn't reach him. So he ordered me to stop the construction around the area and hired Lincoln Security Firm to protect it."

"Wow, that's a little drastic, don't you think?"

"No, when Raines finally surfaced, he apologized and said there was a miscommunication between him and his assistant. He was really sincere, but Johnson didn't want to take a chance on any more miscommunications, so the guards' presence acted as our safety net."

"So there was no problem between the developers?"

"None. They got along very well."

My shoulders slumped with disappointment. I really wanted there to be some dirt between these two guys.

John would tell me that's the point of an investigation. You can't 'want' something. You have to let the evidence lead you to the right person, not your desires. So maybe I was wrong. Maybe Peter Johnson did fall off the rocks in a drunken stupor.

"Did you ever meet with Johnson while he was on the island?"

"Once at the office last week. He was looking for Raines, but he was nowhere to be found. Although Raines was in charge of the project, he island hops frequently working on other projects, which can cause him to be forgetful."

"What was Johnson's mood like when you saw him at the office?" I was beginning to think I was up a totem pole with no way to get down. This was going nowhere.

"Johnson seemed surprised by the slow progress of the construction. He kept asking about when we started contract negotiations, building plans and the date we actually started working at the site. He seemed confused about the details, but that was it."

The one question I didn't want to ask, had to be asked. "Were you aware of Johnson ever using drugs or partying?"

"There were rumors, but the guy's dead. Why drag his name through the mud now?"

Again, my disappointment tried to surface. I wanted Kionni to clear Johnson, but he didn't. He left the uncertainty floating around in my head.

"Who chose the Lincoln Security Firm?" I asked, trying to change my mood.

"I asked Dad what company was good and had reasonable rates. He said Lincoln Security Firm was the best and since Dad knows the owner, I recommended them to Johnson and Raines."

Oh, shit.

CHAPTER THIRTEEN

Despite the trade winds blowing my blouse in the breeze, I felt the world closing in on me, constricting my chest like a boa constrictor going in for the kill.

My dad knew Pai. My dad brought Pai to Kaua'i. Then my best friend tried to set me up with Pai. Were they working together to plan my future?

After Kionni left, I went inside Private Kaua'EYE's and dropped off the receipts for the orders of protection Lani had served. She was gone for the day, but that didn't stop me from calling her and quizzing her up this side of the island, and down the other while sounds of her son's baseball game bled through her answers.

"How do you know Pai?"

"We've worked a few cases together." A parent booed in the background.

"Did you know my dad brought him to the island?"

"Pai may have mentioned something about a favor for a friend." I could hear the smile in her voice.

"Did my dad ask you to set me up with him?"

"Why would he do that?" Another deflect, another smile. She was definitely laughing at me.

"Did you know he's related to a cop on the PD?"

"Really? Who?" She asked.

The cop sleeping on my sofa bed. "I don't know, just some cop," I lied.

"Well most of us are," she replied.

She denied everything, and I wanted to believe her, but sometimes the truth will bite you in the ass when you least expect it.

I gave up when Scotty came up to bat, and left the office feeling no better. Every bit of me wanted to return to my apartment and beg Makaio for sex. At least then, I'd be choosing my own partner. That would probably be a huge mistake, but it'd be *my* mistake. I wasn't ready to have a partner for life, and that's exactly what Pai represented.

I tried deep breaths to calm my sense of panic as I drove through my favorite tunnel of trees on the road to Poipu. For the first time in my life, I had island fever. Five hundred and fifty two point three square miles was not enough room for me to escape the possibility of a committed relationship. Nope. I had to get out. Now.

But I had a job to do. The sun had set and I had a date with a security guard. I went through the drive-thru of my favorite hamburger joint and ordered a plain double cheeseburger with no bun, fries and a double chocolate shake before I went to my spot on the hill and pulled out my fork to dig into my burger. Then I reached over and pulled the bag of supplies Pai had given to me from the floorboard.

I was halfway through the guards' files when I spotted a green minivan pulling into the lot. It disappeared along the hedge but then reappeared at the guard shack where it made a U-turn and parked directly behind the small wooden building.

The driver got out and approached the female working the day shift. They were dressed in the typical khaki shorts and Hawaiian shirt uniforms for a beachfront condo unit. However, what caught my eye was his height, or rather his lack of height. He looked a lot shorter than the five foot eight inches my file said he should be. I'd have to get close to take a picture and make sure of his identity.

He carried what appeared to be a lunch box as he patted the woman on the shoulder and she got on a bicycle and rode away. I ducked down when she appeared on the road and peddled past me on her bike. She was definitely Maggie Chu, Asian female born in 1983, as I'd just read.

I watched her crest the hill in my side mirror and I sat up to finish my fries and shake. Ten minutes later, boredom began to set in. This job sucked.

Luckily, Joe Beckwith was just as bored as I was. He left the shack, got back in his green minivan and turned toward me as Maggie had done. I ducked down in the seat as a loud drumbeat blasted through the night air. Green Day began singing "Do You Know Your Enemy" from the passenger seat of my car. The knuckles of my left hand tightened on the steering wheel as I scrambled to answer my cell phone, start my car and make a U-turn to follow Joe all at the same time.

"Hello?" I whispered for some inexplicable reason. The engine purred to life and I pulled away from the curb.

"Babe, I thought I'd wake up naked with a beautiful woman in my arms."

Makaio. My heartbeat revved like my car engine as I raced to catch up with my target.

"I have to work," I explained to both of us.

"Tonight?" He sounded disappointed.

Now I was devastated. "Yes, my job doesn't have set hours." A horn blared as I cut off a car to catch up with my mark.

"Where are you?" His voice no longer tried to undress me. It was, however, trying to butt in where it didn't belong.

"Makaio, I really can't talk, I'm busy."

"Tell me where you are and I'll help you with whatever job you're working on."

Yeah, like we'd work if he was sitting in my small car with me. I don't think so. "You'd cramp my style," I said, letting him know in no uncertain terms this was none of his business.

"Are you breaking the law?"

I glanced down at my speedometer. I was definitely breaking at least two laws at the moment, but I needed to find my target. I breathed a sigh of relief when I spotted the green minivan in front of me about five blocks.

"Define breaking the law," I asked casually as my pulse slowed.

"Driving like an idiot while talking on the phone and making people honk their horns at you." His voice had a hint of anger to it. Anger I didn't have time for.

"That's not very specific. I gotta go, Makaio, you're distracting me."

"I'd like to distract you in person, like I did earlier." Just like that, he made my libido flair.

Shit! The tire hit the edge of the pavement, the wheels pulled, and I dropped the phone as gravel flew. Thankfully, I was able to gain control of the vehicle. I glanced around for my phone. My face was burning from the adrenaline of almost killing myself, along with a little embarrassment. Okay, mostly embarrassment, knowing Makaio hadn't been asleep when my body responded to his magical fingers was like doing the walk of shame. Another reminder that I wasn't the *wham, bam thank you, Sam* type of gal.

"I gotta go," I said into the phone as I picked it up from the floorboard at my feet. I hung up before he had the opportunity to respond. At that particular moment, I really didn't need to think about his hands, what they could do, or what I had done.

As my target headed out Kaumuali'i Highway, I dropped back so all I could see were his taillights. He turned right on LeLe Road, and I slowed down to pull into a restaurant parking lot across the street, as he pulled into a local convenience store. Grabbing my new binoculars from the passenger seat, I zeroed in on Joe getting out of his car and entering the store.

He went straight to the coffee station where I could only see his head behind racks of bread. Standing in front of a large Kona Coffee display, it was obvious he was getting a fix of dark liquid caffeine. I could almost smell the island brew. I might have walked across the street myself to indulge, but the side effects of dealing with added energy and needing to use the restroom stopped me.

Joe's behavior was normal for anyone who worked dogwatch, but I was pretty sure he should have stopped to get the coffee on his way to work, not after he arrived. As he approached the counter, his entire body came into view. He reached into his rear pants pocket for his wallet.

Deeply engrossed in my first surveillance, I jumped when a giggle to my left caught me off-guard. I yanked the binoculars away from my face and dropped them in my lap. Pretending to fix my makeup in the rear view mirror, I watched a woman, accompanied by a much older man, walk toward the rear parking lot behind the restaurant. The way they groped each other on the way to their vehicle defined their relationship.

Once they were out of sight, I pulled my binoculars back to my face just in time to see my target smiling like an idiot at the clerk. His smile held almost as much meaning as the pawing hands of the couple who were undoubtedly making out in their vehicle right now. I adjusted the binoculars to scope out the object of his desire, who stood on a raised platform behind the counter.

And got an eyeful of boobs.

Boobs, that I could unfortunately identify. I knew them well, because they weren't just any boobs. They were Windy boobs.

I looked at her face anyway. She was sporting her practiced come-do-me-big-boy look that made men trip all over themselves to get to her. I returned my limited circular vision to my target's face and I could have sworn there was drool coming out of his mouth. He was giddy. He was laughing. And he was not looking at Windy's face. His eyes were glued to her chest.

Men.

He paid for his coffee and Windy did a little boob wiggle that sent him into a fit of giggles as he stumbled out the door like a drunk.

What the hell?

He staggered toward the minivan and bumped into a couple guys out on the town. I could hear the commotion even as traffic passed between us.

"Get off me, you stupid drunk."

Joe stumbled away laughing and practically falling over by the time he reached his car. Wow, I'd been following at a distance and he'd obviously been drinking the entire time. Not once had I noticed his level of intoxication. But there was no way I was going to let him drive. I started my car and quickly made my way across the street.

Joe stood at the side of his van, his key attempting to find the door lock when I pulled up next to him. Swaying back and forth, he giggled to himself as he leaned his head against the window for balance. It would have been funny, if he wasn't so pathetic. My gut clenched with anger. Anger at him and anger at myself for missing the obvious.

"Joe," I said through my open passenger window.

His head lifted and he stared into the window of his own van, like the person talking to him was inside.

"Joe," I repeated.

In slow motion he turned, keys in one hand, coffee in the other. His feet twisted awkwardly with alcohol-induced poor motor skills. It was like watching a tree fall in the woods. Would anyone hear it?

Timber...

He went down hard. A solid thud. No bounce. But it was followed by a splash of liquid and a bellow from another customer walking toward the store. I unbuckled and climbed across gearshift to the passenger side and looked out the window. Joe was on the ground looking confused, his eyes crossed, as the large man who got bathed in his coffee closed the gap between them, barking obscenities like a junkyard dog. The guy appeared rabid as he stopped and stared down at Joe.

"GRRRR..." he growled.

Afraid I'd see my second dead body, I interrupted from inside my car. "Ah...I'm really sorry, mister. My brother...is really upset. He's..." What the hell was he doing? "....He's going through a divorce."

Mad Dog was now looking at me as if he was going to eat me alive. I hopped out of my car anyway. His chest heaved, his jaw clenched and the tendons in his neck bulged. I swallowed, the dread of confrontation rising in my throat.

"Can I pay for your dry cleaning bill?" I noticed his clothing too late. They were covered with paint splatter. He wasn't really the dry cleaning type. "Or maybe I could buy you a six pack of Kona Big Wave?"

That got his attention. Beer always grabbed a man's attention. His breathing slowed as he wrung out the side of his t-shirt and looked me up and down.

"You going to drink it with me, sistah?" He leered.

"Ah...no, sorry." Looking for an excuse, I pointed at Joe. "I need to get my brother home."

The guy's leering started giving me the creeps. He stared at everything but my face.

"If there's no entertainment with the beer, you'll have to buy me two six packs."

Since when did women turn into entertainment for men? I was about ready to give him a piece of my mind when Joe suddenly saw humor in our situation. He pointed at the 'wet dog' and laughed hysterically.

Like an annoying parrot, he wouldn't shut up. His laughter became so unbearable, he had to stop pointing and hold his stomach. It had a nice effect on Mad Dog. His scowl was beyond rabid when he reached down and yanked Joe up by the front of his shirt.

My hands tingled. Adrenaline flowed through my system, begging to be used. Every muscle in my body screamed, *fight! fight! fight!* I'd never been in a real altercation, the whole day was turning into a bunch of firsts to be marked off my list of experiences. Sizing up my target, I wasn't sure who was drooling more, Mad Dog or Joe. Joe's face had the look of a goofy, happy, harmless drunk. Mad Dog, on the other hand, just looked uncontrollably violent. He was ready to swing at anything and everything and if I didn't stop him now…

Run!

That same strange male voice was back inside my head, warning me of the danger I faced. I gulped down my fear and ignored it, then tapped on Mad Dog's shoulder.

Luckily, I grew up in a house full of testosterone, because when Mad Dog whipped around with Joe still in his clutches, his body dangling like a wet noodle, I was ready for anything. I dodged Joe's flapping legs easily.

"Grrrrrr…" Mad Dog growled again.

"I'm really sorry, brah. He's drunk and doesn't have a clue what he's doing." I tried to reason with him while attempting to position myself.

Mad Dog looked at me, then at Joe, then back to me.

"You don't look like his sistah," he sneered.

"Yeah, we got different dads. I'd like to say he wasn't my brother, but my mom really wouldn't like that."

He understood the meaning of *Ohana*. No matter what, loyalty to family came first.

Just like that, he dropped Joe who crumpled to the ground in a fit of laughter. I winced at the sound of his elbow striking the pavement. He was going be seriously sore in the morning.

"Where's my Kona Big Wave, Sissy?"

I wasn't sure if he was referring to me being Joe's sister or the strength of my spine. It took a serious lip-bite to hold my tongue when all I wanted to do was grab the baton my dad had given me for my twenty-first birthday from my car and beat the ever-living shit out of the intensely narrow-minded, uncompromising dick-head in front of me.

The little rant in my head brought my anger back in check as I reached through my car window, past my baton, and grabbed my purse from the rear seat. I pulled out some bills and handed Mad Dog the money. He looked down at the cash in his hand and extended his palm out for more.

I wanted to slam the extra twenty I pulled out of my purse down his throat, but resisted the

KYM ROBERTS

temptation and placed it in his hand without touching him.

"Can you help me put him in my car?"

"He's not my *Ohana*, Sissy." He turned and headed for the store.

"Dick-head," escaped my lips as I bent down and grabbed Joe under the arms. I struggled to pull the guard I was supposed to be watching, to a sitting position and Joe decided to pick up on my bad language.

"Diiiii...eddd...Diiiii...eddd," Luckily for me, if you put it all together, it sounded more like a drawn out 'deeaad' than a 'dick-head'.

Mad Dog looked back at us, his expression one of a warring debate between coming back to kick our asses or going to get his beer. I shook my head and smiled, and Mad Dog resumed his quest for The Big Wave.

Thank goodness for small favors.

I tried to prop Joe against my car, his upper body sprawled against the side rear window. I quickly opened the passenger door while keeping my foot against his backside, prohibiting him from slinking down to the ground. Then I put his arm around my shoulder. Huffing and puffing, I grabbed his waist and dragged him to the passenger seat. Joe plopped down, grabbed hold of me, and pushed my butt to the floorboard as he fell backward across the front seats. His laughter bounced off the interior of my car as I struggled to get out of the cramped space.

Scrunched in the floorboard, with a drunk lying across my two front seats laughing like there

142

was no tomorrow, I pulled on the dash in an ineffectual attempt to dislodge myself. I looked up to see Pai smiling down at me.

"Baby Doll, I find you in the most interesting places."

CHAPTER FOURTEEN

I couldn't help but smile. He does that to me. He turns my predicaments into humorous stories to tell my kids, not the embarrassingly inadequate attempts of me trying to be an adult.

He reached down, grabbed my extended hand, dislodged me from the vise clamp squishing my body and pulled me up against his large frame. My breath caught, my smile disappeared. I stood looking up at the man with a twinkle in his eyes while his arms wrapped around my waist. I felt safe. He felt nice. Too nice.

I knew I was in trouble when his head started to descend. His lips hovering above mine, our breath mixing. There was a moment, right before our lips touched, that I needed to stop him, but I didn't. I welcomed his possessive claim on my body and soul and melted in his arms.

He was my fairytale, the one I'd dreamt about as a little girl. I saw us married with children running circles around us, laughing while the youngest sat on Pai's shoulders as his tongue swept through my mouth. It was the life my parents wanted for me.

I froze. Reality showered me like a hose spraying two dogs apart. I pushed Pai away with every ounce of strength I had.

Holy shit. I was not ready for kids.

"Baby Doll, it was only a kiss. Not a proposal."

"How do you do that?" I asked as I smoothed down the front of my clothes.

"What?" Pai wasn't looking at me anymore. He was looking past me.

"You always seem to know my thoughts."

"It's easy. You wear your feelings on the outside." He continued to avoid eye contact.

"No one else reads me like that," I insisted. Finally, his eyes returned to mine.

"No one else is looking at you the way I do." His voice sounded intimate.

My body tingled in response. He had a point. No one looked at me...or rather, *in* me the way he did. He wanted to know me. The good, the bad, and the disgustingly ugly parts of me. He didn't care.

It was strangely alluring, yet it scared the shit out of me.

"What? He gets the entertainment and I get the beer?" Mad Dog was back with his two six packs and some change in his pocket.

Pai turned in time to see Mad Dog look me up and down, and before I knew what he was doing, it was Mad Dog's turn to have his feet dangling in the air like a wet noodle. Part of me wanted to lean back against the car, cross my arms and say, 'Who's the sissy now, punk?'

But that unleashed anger of Pai's was barely contained as he got in Mad Dog's face and reduced him to a cowering puppy. I was witnessing a side of Pai I'd only imagined existed, and would never want directed at me. Even Makaio hadn't brought this out in him, and it again made me wonder if I really knew the man at all.

Mad Dog didn't deserve protection, but he also didn't deserve a pummeling.

I placed my hand on Pai's shoulder, praying the man I knew him to be, would come back. And something, from someplace I couldn't begin to identify, told me Pai would recognize my touch. My breasts rubbed against his flexed bicep as I pulled myself closer to him. He had to feel our bond.

Pai glanced back at me. The feral look — gone.

"Baby Doll, your timing is impeccable. I just wish your reasoning for that special wake-up call was a little different."

See, he knew me. He understood my motive for brushing up against him was to distract, not seduce. He knew me on the deepest level possible yet he still wanted me.

"I think you owe the woman an apology," Pai ground out as he returned his gaze to the man still dangling more than a foot off the ground. As big as Mad Dog was, I was totally impressed with the ease Pai held him. His arms were taut. His muscles bulged, but he stood holding the little-kid-of-a-man as if he would never tire.

"I'm sorry," whispered Mad Dog.

"I can't hear you, and I'm pretty sure the lady can't hear you either."

"I'm sorry," with a glance at Pai, Mad Dog finished, "Miss."

Pai set Mad Dog down and he slinked away with his beer still intact and his tail between his legs. Good riddance.

"Can you repeat that distraction move one more time?" Pai asked.

I laughed and got lost in his happy eyes. No one made my spirit soar the way he did. Unfortunately, Joe moaned behind me and reminded me of the job at hand.

"So what's his story?" Pai asked as he reached past me and sat up the drunk in my passenger seat.

"Apparently, he likes to drink when he gets to work. I didn't see anything out of the ordinary until he was paying for his coffee. Then it was obvious that he was drunk. He was staggering and giddy. It was weird."

"He hasn't been drinking." Pai replied in confident, matter of fact tone.

"What are you talking about? He's drunk as a skunk."

147

"Nope. Not alcohol. Maybe something else, but there's no alcohol in his system. Smell him." Pai stepped back and allowed me to get closer to Joe.

I leaned down and breathed in — waiting for my senses to be overwhelmed with alcohol. The only thing I could smell were remnants of the coffee he'd spilt. Pai was right. Joe hadn't been drinking, but he was definitely under the influence of something.

Like the mainland, Kaua'i had paid a huge price with the introduction of the meth. It ravaged our people and turned many into creatures of lore with no recognition of pride or *ohana*. They rejected everything and everyone they loved except for the ice they wanted to run through their veins. I wondered if that's why they called it ice. It turned its victims into cold-blooded animals without a care in the world for anything or anyone, but their next fix.

"His file says he's married. Do you want to call his wife and see if she wants to pick him up?"

Joe leaned over and nearly fell out of my car before Pai steadied him.

"Go ahead. I'll hold him while you call her. Ask her if we can search the car, and tell her I'm going to need Joe to take a drug test just to be sure."

I nodded and grabbed my cell phone. I dialed the number in my file and waited. It rang until voicemail picked up.

"There's no one there."

"Jade's werkhing…" Joe mumbled.

I looked down at the file, found his wife's cell phone number, and dialed it. When a female answered, I identified myself.

"Malia Fern?" She asked.

"Yes, I work for Lincoln Security—"

"Mal, it's Jade."

Jade. I looked down at the file in my hand. Joe Beckwith was married to Jade Beckwith.

"Jade?"

"Jade Tanaka Beckwith," she responded.

"From Kaua'i High?" I asked.

She laughed, "Go, Red Raiders. How did you get my number? Wait, you said Lincoln Security. Are you and Joe working together?"

"Uhhh..." This was the reason I didn't want this job in the first place. Delivering bad news was not my thing. Especially to the woman who was there for me when my friendship with Windy fell apart. I looked to Pai for help, but he had his hands full holding Joe in my car.

"Oh, my God. He's okay, isn't he?" Jade asked.

"He's fine, but he's...he's under the influence of something, and he can't work."

"Where is he?" She sounded more worried than angry. Which was a good sign, right?

"We're at LeLe's Quik Stop on LeLe Road, just down the street from his job." I paused before I delivered the blow that would turn her world upside down. "Is it okay for our boss to search his vehicle for the cause of his condition?"

"Of course he can. Joe doesn't drink or do drugs and he...he just left the house less than an hour ago. He was completely sober."

"Jade, it's not alcohol. I don't know what it is, but right now, he's passed out in the front seat of my car. Does he have any medical conditions?"

"None. He's totally healthy."

"You're sure it's okay to search the van?" I asked again, hoping she'd say no.

"Yes, I know my Joe. He wouldn't intentionally ingest anything bad. I'll call a cab and come drive him home."

"If you'd like, I can drive your van and our boss can drive Joe." Now the hard part. "I need to pick up a drug test at the pharmacy so we know what he's taking."

Jade cleared her throat, her voice gaining strength as she faced the situation head on. "That's fine. I'm a pharmacist at Menehune Pharmacy. Joe dropped me off before he went to work. I'll pick out the best test and meet you out front. And thank you, Malia."

"I'm sorry, Jade. I wish it wasn't like this." I meant it. I felt sick to my stomach with the pain I brought her. Deep down, I knew I wasn't responsible, Joe was, but it didn't make it any easier.

"Me too," she whispered.

I hung up and began searching the van. Joe still mumbled incoherently in my front seat, and Pai pitched in with the vehicle search while I filled him in on Joe and Jade.

I'd watched Joe walk from the van to the shack and back, so there was no way the dope was outside the car, and after a thorough search of the interior, we came up empty-handed. Not a cigarette, not a Tylenol, nor a syringe in sight. The van was spotless, including the car seat in the back.

Thinking of Jade married with a kid, made me feel like I was beyond immature. She was settled in a job, already a wife and mother. I can't even keep my car clean...and I don't have kids.

I gave Pai directions to Jade's house, and hoped he could find his way around the island as well as his tongue found its way around my mouth. I got into the van and headed for Lihue with him following me. Looking in the rearview mirror, I noticed how much room Pai occupied in my car, and wondered about the drive back to pick up his Jeep. My toes tingled for the umpteenth time in the last couple days.

How the hell did I end up with two incredibly sexy men in my life, when I'd gone so long without any?

CHAPTER FIFTEEN

I pulled into the Menehune Pharmacy parking lot and found Jade waiting in front of the store. Of Japanese descent, and a couple years older than me, Jade still didn't look old enough to buy a beer, let alone dispense prescriptions. Her white lab coat was rolled under her arm and her purse was slung over her shoulder. A white bag, no doubt containing the drug test I asked about, dangled down to her side. Her smile was delicate but warm, the kind people saved for their closest friends and relatives. She met me at the driver's door, and despite me being the deliverer of bad news, Jade gave me a big hug.

"*Aloha*, Mal." I really expected things to have changed in the last few minutes after she'd had time to think about what I was doing, but her greeting was genuine.

"Jade, I'm so sorry—"

"No, worries. This isn't the first time." Jade took over the driver's seat and I rounded the van to take the passenger side.

This wasn't the first time. *Hua.*

"Can you tell me if Joe was full of energy or sleepy?" Jade started the van and we drove north toward KaPa'a.

"Definitely sleepy, he passed out," I advised.

The look of shock on her face made me think we should have called an ambulance. Then she began to scrutinize me a little too closely and I began to get nervous. "Are you Menehune?" She asked.

At first, I thought she was joking, but her expression remained serious. "Excuse me?"

"Menehune. Are you from Menehune descent?"

Did everyone have little people on the brain? I hadn't even thought about the ancient race in years. Sure, I saw the name all over town on this and that, but no one actually talked about them as if they actually existed.

"Ah...no," I responded.

"The reason I ask is because Menehune men...well, they can become intoxicated when they are *subjected* to certain things."

I stared at her, totally speechless, but she chose not to enlighten me about the imaginary disease of the mythical men and got down to reality.

"I brought a test that identifies 12 different drugs. I think you should be looking for a drug from depressants or the opioids/morphine categories. I can't guarantee that, since so many people take cocktails of a variety of drugs, but those are the ones I would look for first, *if* I didn't know the cause."

I looked at the box and saw her logic eliminated amphetamines, methamphetamines, ecstasy, and cocaine, but the drugs left on the list didn't look any better. I didn't think we were looking for drugs smoked or injected, since we hadn't found a hypodermic needle, or any other paraphernalia, nor had we smelled anything in the van. However, that still left every drug in the depressant and opioid/morphine categories which could all be swallowed or snorted.

Ugh.

The potential destruction of Jade's family life was a depressing thought, and added to my resolve to avoid looking for 'happily ever after.' I really didn't want to see the pain in Jade's deep brown eyes when her husband tested positive. The pain of a lifetime of dreams washing out to sea. The pain of trust betrayed. Yet I knew, if I felt this bad, Jade felt infinitely worse.

My car was parked in front of Jade's small yellow house, when she pulled into the single car driveway. Pai came to the door with a sexy smile on his face as we approached the house. On anyone else, I would think it was inappropriate. On Pai, it was comforting.

Until he saw Jade. Then his face lost all emotion and Jade stopped in her tracks in front of the van. Something passed between them.

Something too familiar for a boss and his employee's wife.

I looked from one to the other, then Jade cleared her throat and said, "I've never met Joe's boss before."

If that wasn't the biggest lie, I don't know what was.

"Seriously?" I called her out on the obvious. Jade's eyes darted in my direction before she looked away. I knew that wasn't the truth. We may not have been close for the last five years, but some things never change.

Pai held the door open for us and Jade walked in ahead of me.

"You must be Joe's boss."

Pai's eyes searched Jade's, and then he shook her hand. "Alapai Lincoln. My friends call me Pai."

"I would have thought they'd call you...Al." Jade walked into the living room and approached her husband, who was sprawled out on a reclining loveseat.

Pai looked like he wanted to follow her. He turned instead, and leaned toward me as I passed through the door, effectively creating full contact down the lengths of our bodies. My stuttered step caused the corners of his mouth to quirk. Again, I would have thought this improper on anyone but Pai, especially after what had just transpired between him and Jade.

He reached out and steadied me off to his side. "He's starting to come around, but needs something for the nasty headache."

Pai closed the front door, and the comfortable living room suddenly seemed way too small for the four of us. Not for lack of space, but the extra baggage that seemed to be flying in the air around us.

Joe moaned and Jade kissed his forehead. His eyes opened and for the first time, they seemed to focus on something. Jade.

"Honey, I…"

"Shhhhh. I know." Jade kissed her husband and Pai and I turned away.

I was giving them as much privacy as possible. I think Pai was uncomfortable for a whole different set of reasons. Every fiber in my body wanted to walk out the door and never find out what was really going on. Unsure why I was still there, I turned to say goodbye, and saw Jade smiling weakly at me from the couch. Joe's head rested on her lap, and she gently combed her fingers through his hair.

Oh, shit. She believed it. She believed Joe hadn't done anything wrong.

"Can I have the test?" She asked.

"Uh—" I looked down at the bag in my hand. "Yeah, sure. Are you going to be okay?"

"Someone did this to Joe. He wouldn't do this to himself." Her voice was soft but strong, and I knew I couldn't leave. Not yet. She was going to need me when that test came back positive.

I started rewinding the night in my head. Joe walking into the store, getting coffee and…yes, he did take a drink, but there's no drug in the world that would act that quickly. I wanted to argue with her, but Pai stopped me with a gentle hand on my shoulder. I mumbled something about us talking about it after we knew what we were dealing with.

"Do you want some help?" Pai asked.

"Please. I don't think I can get him to the bathroom by myself."

I read the instructions in the box while Pai helped Joe to the bathroom and Jade followed. This test was pretty simple, pee in the cup, hold the sensor in the urine for ten seconds and five minutes later, we would know what drug or drugs he was using.

I handed the cup and the test strip to Jade, who excused Pai while she assisted her husband. Pai and I stood around awkwardly in the living room, feeling like we were intruding in this couple's private life.

Pai broke the silence. "You can watch the guards tomorrow. You don't need to go back tonight."

I knew with a short-term contract there wasn't a minute to waste if Pai was going to find out what was going on, and the last thing I wanted to do was to be alone with him, especially after what had transpired between he and Jade.

"I won't let you down. I'll get the job done tonight."

"Baby Doll, I feel your division of loyalties pulling you apart. Jade needs you here."

Jade walked out of the bathroom with a remarkably sober Joe. Sober, but judging by his squinting, the lights were too much to deal with while majorly hung over.

His betrayal brought out that juvenile side of me that wanted to bang their kitchen pots together and yell "Boo!" in his ear.

Jade supported her husband, who was actually taller than she was, with his arm slung over her shoulder while she held onto his waist. Joe pressed his lips to her ear in a tenderly appreciative kiss. If I didn't know any better, I would think he was sick, maybe just home from the hospital after having surgery.

"I'll get you some medicine for your headache." Jade smiled at her husband, and Pai stepped up to help Joe to the couch while Jade went into the kitchen.

If Joe was my husband, I'd pour a whole damn bottle of pain reliever down his throat, but this Jade was not the Jade I grew up with. Not the girl who dumped her spaghetti and meat sauce over her high school sweetheart's head when he winked at a cheerleader. Then again, if my instincts were on target, she'd cheated on her husband...with Pai. The old Jade would have never done that, either.

I was so confused by everything, the urge to run out the door nearly choked me. Jade was in denial and I really didn't deal well with women who made excuses for their man's behavior. She looked at me with conviction in her eyes, just daring me to voice my feelings and malign her husband's character.

I bit off what I really wanted to say, taking the easy way out instead. "If you don't need anything else, Pai and I are going to leave."

"No, I want you to stay for the test results." Her voice was gaining in conviction. How could she believe his shit? Yet, if she chose to believe someone drugged him instead of him taking it voluntarily, who was I to try and change her mind?

Pai and I stood around looking uncomfortable, while Jade went into the kitchen to make coffee. Joe just sat on the loveseat with his eyes closed. The five minutes passed faster than I expected and Jade went into the bathroom for the result. I waited for her departure from the makeshift lab, ringing my hands together until Pai grabbed one hand and squeezed it gently. Any minute now she was going to be making up some lame excuse for her husband's addiction.

Jade exited the bathroom, wearing the biggest smile you could possibly imagine. Her eyes went straight to Joe, who stood up and returned it with a goofy one of his own. The distance between them disappeared and Jade was off the ground, twirling around in Joe's arms in the middle of their living room.

Joe was completely sober. Not a noticeable trace left of being under the influence. No drooling. No stumbling. No squinting. Just happily in love. The two of them laughed, hugged, and kissed.

In between their love-fest, Jade exclaiming, "I knew," kiss, kiss, "you wouldn't do drugs," kiss, "or drink while driving."

"Thank you for having faith in me." Joe's eyes welled up with tears before they embraced in a very steamy kiss. That was all the excuse Pai needed. He grabbed my hand and we quietly headed for the door.

Jade interrupted our escape from the confines of Joe's embrace. "There were no drugs in Joe's system, the test was negative." She beamed at her husband.

Before I could argue that the test was a false negative, Joe turned toward us.

"Thank you for bringing me home. I'm lucky you came by."

I became acutely aware of Pai still holding my hand, I immediately pulled away, and decided to go along with the farce. "Can you tell us what happened tonight?"

"I don't know. I left the house and everything was fine. Jade and I were running late when we dropped the baby off at her mom's. After I took Jade to work, I went straight to the site, but I knew I wouldn't make it through the night without a lot of coffee, so I left. I'm sorry, Mr. Lincoln. I understand if you don't want me working for you anymore."

Jade turned toward Pai and a look passed between them. Something I couldn't identify and wasn't sure I wanted to.

"Mr. Lincoln, our baby has been sick, and Joe has been letting me sleep more than he should have. He's a good, *honest* man." Jade's emphasis on 'honest' made Pai squirm. Not visibly, but I felt it.

"What happened when you stopped for coffee?" I asked.

160

"I don't know. I ran in to get a cup and went to pay for it." His eyebrows clenched in concentration, and then he shook his head. "That's the last thing I remember until I was being helped out of a little car by Mr. Lincoln in front of my house."

If I believed Joe, then I was the only witness to what happened to him. I remembered the silly grin he got on his face as he looked at Windy. Something tickled at my brain. I missed something.

"Do you remember the cashier at the store?" I asked.

As Joe thought about it, his face went completely blank. Either he was a damn good liar, or something happened to him right before he paid for his coffee. There was no way any man would forget coming face-to-boob with Windy's chest.

The suspicion of missing something nudged at my memory and suddenly I believed him. Joe was telling the truth.

"I think you better make an appointment with your doctor and make sure there isn't a medical reason for what happened," I suggested.

"It's not necessary. There's nothing wrong with Joe." Jade looked directly at Pai.

"But—"

Pai interrupted me. "Make sure you're on time tomorrow, Joe."

"Yes, sir. Thank you, Mr. Lincoln." Joe shook Pai's hand with gratitude, and Pai and I walked out together.

The mystery wasn't solved, but I had another case to work. After I escaped my tiny little Pai-filled car.

Oh, boy.

CHAPTER SIXTEEN

Downtown Koloa is about three blocks long, anchored by the intersection of Maluhia Road and Koloa Road. There's one strip of shops facing Maluhia, and a few others located on the backside, with access through side roads and alleys. That's how I get to my apartment, and where we first caught sight of the Ducati Streetfighter racing away. My heart plummeted.

"That guy's going to kill himself."

I heard the concern in Pai's voice, and wondered if he'd still care if he knew it was Makaio taking the corner at Poipu Road twice as fast as the posted speed limit. At one moment, both vehicles had been stationary at the stop signs, and Makaio's hand actually raised to the visor on his helmet. Then it gripped the handlebar hard and his bike spat out gravel behind him. He was definitely pissed off about Pai driving my car.

Makaio thought I'd lied to him. He thought I was out on the town with Pai. I wasn't sure if I was relieved to have one of the sexy men out of my life, or not. I mean, now I didn't have to choose, right? Of course, not getting the *opportunity* to choose, kind of sucked.

We rode the rest of the way to the convenience store in silence, which would have been pleasant, had I not been thinking about how I'd hurt Makaio's feelings and what he probably thought of me. Then there was that twisted knot in my gut I refused to identify.

Pai pulled into the lot and turned off the ignition. I jumped out of the car before he could turn and kiss me. Not that I didn't like his kisses, I was just a little confused.

"I'll be right back. I need to get some stuff inside."

I nearly ran into the store but slowed down once inside in order to load my arms with energy sources for my late night stakeout. Lack of energy hadn't been a problem so far, but I knew that by three A.M. I'd be hurting. I grabbed a bottle of green tea and in my haste, hip-checked a boy grabbing an energy drink. He careened backward nearly taking out his mom in the process before she gained her balance and saved them both.

"Sorry, I—oh." I stopped mid-sentence.

The boy wasn't a boy, but a full-sized man standing just shy of five foot with facial hair.

"That's okay, I love to be woman-handled by the taller sex. That's why I married her." He grinned at the woman I thought was his mother, who was actually his very pretty wife.

"He most certainly does," his wife announced. Then she grabbed his face and kissed him hard in front of everyone.

A few customers 'whooped' before the couple broke apart.

"Well, I'm sorry. I didn't mean to knock you over."

"No, worries. I think I've been more than compensated." He winked at his wife who smacked him on the rear.

I returned to my mental list of treats and added a bottle of water, a green tea, a bag of chocolate treats and sunflower seeds to my cache. As I approached the cash register, I realized Windy was still working, and I suddenly wanted to dump my stuff and run out the door the same way I'd run in. Until she saw me standing two-deep in line. There wasn't a chance in hell I'd give her the satisfaction of seeing me cower.

"Well, if it isn't the little surfer girl who lost her top," she said in a sickeningly sweet voice loud enough to bounce off all the walls and have every man in the place turn to look for boobies.

Don't think I didn't catch the word 'little' in her description. I just chose to ignore it. Windy's announcement had the effect she craved, all the men looked in the direction of her half-exposed breasts. A smile of satisfaction curved her lips. She rewarded her audience with a little wiggle. She leaned over the counter, nearly spilling out of the low scooped neckline. I'm pretty sure at least one nipple peeked at its onlookers.

A drunk giggled behind me. I turned and a sense of déjà vu washed over me when the boy/man I'd plowed over in the drink aisle stumbled forward. His wife came running from the rear of the store, grabbed the items from his arms and threw them on a shelf before whisking him out the door without a word spoken between them.

An image of Joe stumbling out of the store flashed in my mind. Neither man had been on my radar as out-of-control drunk until they approached the counter. I looked around for a source. The ceiling, the shelves, the floor, I turned in three hundred and sixty degrees. Nothing stood out as a hazardous chemical or intoxicant that would cause the bizarre behavior of the two different men. I looked at the other patrons. No one appeared inebriated, or even the slightest bit intoxicated. Drooling over exposed skin, however, was a different story. They'd have to mop the floor in about ten minutes.

"*Aloha*, can I help you?"

The skinny guy with the nerdy glasses working alongside Windy looked at me expectantly. I walked past Windy still shaking her basketballs for the customer in front of me and approached her co-worker. A young guy in his twenties, who apparently got enough of Windy's boobs every day. He didn't give her wiggle-jiggle a second glance.

After paying for the over-priced stash of get-up-and-go junk food, I ignored Windy and headed out the door. Leaning against my car with his arms and ankles crossed, heat radiated off Pai like black top on a hot summer day. I tried not to notice the imposing sexual air clinging to him as he stepped away from my Mini and held the door open for me. I scooted past him and slid into the seat. He leaned over, and I couldn't avoid his eye contact, as he closed the door.

"Baby Doll, I will never pressure you to do something you do not want to do." He winked. "Unless you want me to."

He knew I didn't want to kiss him, yet I was dying to be entangled in his arms. He always knew my feelings before I understood them. "Thank you. I'll call you tomorrow, okay?"

Pai leaned over and kissed the top of my head.

"*Ā hui hou*, Baby Doll."

Until we meet again. I sighed with pleasure, relief and disappointment all mixed together in a jumbled mess. I started my car and tried to ignore his red Jeep as I passed it in the parking lot, but I couldn't resist that alluring smile. I smiled at Pai and waved goodbye.

It was going to be a long and lonely night at *The Garden of the Gods*.

CHAPTER SEVENTEEN

The streets were deserted. The skies were clear, and I'd counted almost two hundred stars in the sky by three o'clock. Pai had called another guard in to work Joe's shift...James Kamakau. Like a battery operated bunny — short, with really large ears — he ran around at full speed, checking everything from the lock on the secondary gate to parked cars on the street. He even ran off a couple who were making out in the back seat of a sports car near the entrance of the complex.

Luckily, I was a good block and a half away, near the emergency vet clinic, which rarely had middle-of-the-night business. Otherwise, he'd probably run me off, too. Although in all honesty, I kind of missed the happy-for-now couple. Between the screams of pleasure and the car rocking and rolling, it almost made me think they were on the rollercoaster ride of a lifetime.

Okay, not really. It was better to think of them at an amusement park, than to wish it was me in that back seat, getting busy with one of the cousins.

I watched the guard make his round of the complex through my low-light binoculars. They weren't as good as the night vision goggles I'd tried on at Pai's office, but they were easier to take away from my face in case an emergency patient arrived at the clinic. Plus I'm not sure how I'd explain the goofy space-age glasses that made me resemble a foreigner visiting Area 51.

I snuck out of my car for the third time that night and eased my way over the lava rock wall surrounding the site. It was the only spot I could easily scale thanks to a stone missing halfway up the wall.

The hour was approaching when a lot of people working midnights decide to take a nap. If he took a nap, I couldn't blame him. I needed a nap so badly I was ready to make a deal with him myself.

Unconsciously I got closer to the guard than I had on my two previous trips, and was amazed to see just how small in stature he really was. The man wasn't even five foot tall. He was muscular for his size, but that was probably over-compensation on his part.

A snap of the branch under my foot brought his flashlight swinging in my direction. I froze, bent over, barely hidden from his view behind a fern. If he'd been taller, he would have spotted me the second his light hit the area. I held my breath, afraid he'd walk through the wall of brush that stood between us. His cell phone rang.

"Lincoln Security," he whispered into the phone.

There was a pause, and then my target began moving around trying to scan the area as he held the phone to his ear.

"Sir, can I check the log for you after I finish my rounds?" He asked the person on the phone.

I could hear garbled yelling on the other end as his flashlight illuminated my head once more.

My pulse quickened with apprehension. How was I going to explain being in the bushes? Shit.

"No, sir, I'm not on a 'wild chicken chase.' Yes, sir, I'll get it for you right away," he whispered into the phone.

His flashlight swung away from me as he turned back toward the guard shack. As soon as he was on the path, I high-tailed it out of there, found my hole in the wall and returned to my car to watch his flashlight bob back and forth on his route to the guard shack.

Breathless, I decided that the next time he made rounds, I'd just follow his light through the property from the wall. If it disappeared for too long or stopped, I'd check on him. Otherwise, I wasn't going to risk getting caught again.

Over an hour later, my eyes were about ready to roll back in my head.

I'd been going back and forth between a chocolate-induced sugar high and a smacky cotton mouth from sucking on too many sunflower seeds. My water was gone, and I wished I'd bought two green teas for the caffeine. And now that I thought about it, my bladder was knocking on the restroom door.

A set of car lights approached. The first fifty cars that drove past had me on the edge of my seat, but I was well past the counting stage, so this one barely made my eyes focus. As it drew closer, though, it slowed down. And the slower it went, the more alert I became. The driver was obviously looking for something. But the only businesses open in the immediate area was Pearl's Hawaiian Pastries (did I tell you about the neon hula dancer sporting a cowboy hat and boots?) and the vet's office. You couldn't miss either sign.

I watched as the vehicle pulled into the parking lot of Sunny Snorkel Rental's west of *The Garden of the Gods*, and wondered if I was about to witness a burglary. The building was dark, the hand-painted sign unreadable in the dim light to anyone who didn't know the area. Hopefully, it was an over-zealous business owner coming to work early. Glancing at my watch, I mentally logged the arrival time of the vehicle at four-thirty.

Wide awake now, I zoomed in with my binoculars on the darkened car and caught sight of a blonde in the front seat of a Camaro SS. I couldn't see the color, but I was betting the car had black racing stripes and pink wheels. She pulled her shirt over her head and threw it in the back seat, followed by, what I thought was a bra.

I began to wonder at what point I would morph from being a private investigator (not a legal PI, just a surfer conducting a private investigation), to a voyeur. Most guys would be all over this, trying to get a closer look, but watching Windy primp for a hookup was not my idea of a good time.

The glow of her cell phone appeared as she brought it to her ear and a few moments later, she exited the car. Three inch heels appeared on the pavement, followed by a skirt so short, I would bet it didn't cover her ass in the back. She tossed her long hair over her shoulder in a practiced move of seduction. I couldn't see her facial features, but I didn't need to. My nemesis could be positively identified by...you guessed it, the boobs falling out of her tube top.

Makaio would make the right assumption if he was here. Windy was making money the old-fashioned way. Why else would she dress like that?

I had always wondered how she always managed to drive a flashy new car. I've seen her work as a hotel concierge, a tour guide, a waitress, and now a convenience store clerk, but none of those jobs could possibly pay for a new sports car every year. A second set of headlights appeared in my rear view mirror. I ducked down in my seat as it passed and headed straight for Windy. I couldn't get a look at the driver, but from the shadowed outline of his head, it was obviously a man. Windy leaned into the window of the red Mustang in classic hooker style.

The driver was no doubt getting an eye full, but after a few minutes, he drove away without even getting so much as a pinch. What was she up to? Windy returned and began walking in my direction. I put my hand on the ignition ready to beat it out of there if she recognized my car.

She didn't even give my Mini a second thought. She turned toward *The Garden of the Gods* condos and disappeared behind the hedge, right after she glanced up and down the road.

She appeared on the other end of the row of bushes and I couldn't help but notice her swagger had become much more animated. Chest bouncing, hips swaying, the cheeks of her ass were definitely visible. I could imagine her heels clip-clopped on the asphalt, like a horse in a parade. A parade of sexual seduction, in Windy's case.

The bouncy bunny guard exited through the rear of his small building and approached Windy with his flashlight illuminating her figure. It started at her face and traveled quickly down to her toes, but abruptly came back to her chest where it stopped. Almost like the delayed reaction, you have when you see a $100 bill lying on the sidewalk and you nearly fall flat on your face when you stop too quickly to pick it up. (Not that I've ever found a hundred dollar bill, my max is five.)

Windy's hand flew to her mouth with a coy giggle, a little boob jiggle, and I couldn't help rolling my eyes. She approached the guard, put her arm around his shoulder, and directed him to the gardens where I had hidden earlier.

This was it. This was the reason why Makaio and I hadn't seen anyone at the guard shack. The guard was off getting laid by a prostitute — Windy.

Pai was not going to be happy. I hopped out of my car and ran across the street, camera and cell phone in hand. As I entered the property, I heard a car engine near the entrance, followed by the low rumbling grind of the electronic gate being opened with a pass card.

Pai.

I debated on waiting for him, but changed my mind when I heard Windy's giggle in front of me. I couldn't make out the words of the guard, his deep voice too soft to travel the distance between us. Windy was leading him toward the narrow stretch on sand on beach.

I heard Pai's car turn toward the opposite end of the complex, engine noise getting farther and farther away.

Damn it. I debated calling him.

"Yurrr nooot sub p-post be eear." The guard objected. Sorta.

Windy chuckled.

They crashed through the underbrush, completely oblivious to the sacred grounds around them, but their route made it difficult to be quiet.

"Ooof."

"Dammit! You stupid idiot. You better make this worth my while." Windy's voice no longer held its sultry tone as she cursed him.

I stopped and listened to them struggling. Windy was definitely getting a work out by the sounds of her labored breathing. And it was another one of those moments when I wanted to be anywhere but there. Yet I had to get the pictures. Pictures of an act I really didn't want to see. I debated the whole reason why I was doing this in the first place.

Help me. His voice drifted over the brush.

Hua. Closing my eyes, I fortified my resolve to find out what was going at *The Garden of the Gods* and approached the sex-on-demand display, my stomach rolled in outrage and revulsion. I forced my body forward, when all I wanted to do was turn, gag, and lose all that junk food I'd consumed.

I reached the clearing, took a couple quiet, deep breaths and listened to the sexual grunts a few feet away. Pulling the branches of a fern back, I stuck the camera through the narrow opening. My index finger pressed against the smooth shutter release button and my flash lit up the area with quick bursts of light.

Damn, I forgot to turn off the flash.

I quickly snapped more pictures as Windy swung around, squinting for my camera lens.

Breasts exposed, tube top rolled around her waist, Windy held the guard to her bare chest. I snapped the picture, the flash highlighting her surprised expression.

My heart stopped. I froze in horror. Wendy wasn't making out with the guard, she was holding…the headless body of the guard in a standing position. Where was his head?

I couldn't help it. At that moment, I became a girly girl. My scream pierced the air as I stumbled backward and tripped on the root of a banyan tree.

Arms flailing, I grasped at anything to catch myself, but fell on my ass.

My childhood playmate had turned into a murdering, head-eating, sex monster. The scream continued to echo through the complex as I scrambled to my feet and ran for my car. I didn't care that I no longer had my camera or my cell phone. I just wanted the hell out of this garden of evil. Branches tore at my arms and legs, scraped my face as I ran to escape the demon. Panic completely consumed me.

On some level I was aware that I needed to gain control of myself if I was going to live, but I didn't seem capable of convincing my mouth it needed to shut up. Running through the garden, I hit the bamboo forest near the road and became lost in its density. I was making enough noise to wake up the dead, and yet I knew the guard wouldn't be waking up anytime soon.

My hair tangled in a low hanging branch and pulled me backward like the snap of a bungee cord. My left shoe flew off as I struggled to maintain my footing. I yanked my hair loose and it flung across my face, my sight temporarily obstructed. I stumbled and pushed myself forward several more steps as my blouse caught on another branch tearing across my chest. I turned to go the other direction and ran into a brick wall.

Hands grasped my arms and I realized it wasn't a wall. It was a man. A very large man.

Darkness masked the face of my captive. I struggled to get away, only to be held tighter. I kicked and screamed. Bit and clawed. I was a wild woman, hell bent on not losing my head.

CHAPTER EIGHTEEN

Trapped, and still too far from the road, I used the last weapon available to me. I bit down on his solid chest.

"Owwww! Shit, lady!"

My feet left the ground and all I could think of was being hurled across the ground right after he finished sneering in my face. (Technically he'd be sneering into a mass of hair, but I don't think either one of us saw it that way.) I gauged the distance to his body, reared my head back and slammed the top of my forehead into the bridge of his nose. We both toppled to the ground.

"I'm a police officer. Calm down," he said from somewhere in front of me.

Police officer? My vision was doubled, some features tripled, but I didn't see any uniform and there was no way I was falling for that trick, especially since he had a gun in his hand while he stood above me.

I waited for his move and prayed my vision would line up in single file. He shoved his gun in the back of his waistband and bent toward me, but his perfect ploy to ease my mind was destroyed as I kicked his ankles. Unfortunately, my assault sent him flopping on top of me with enough force to knock the wind out of a man the size of Pai.

Stunned, I gasped for air but continued to swing until he seized my arms, his fingers clamping down on my forearms.

"Calm down! Calm down! I'm here to help you," he insisted.

I froze under his weight, but struggled to breathe. Even if the lighting had been decent, I couldn't see his face, thanks to my hair acting like a mass of seaweed over my eyes.

"I'm going to get up," He warned. "I'll pull you to your feet so you can catch your breath. Don't attack me. I'm a police officer. I'm here to help you."

He released my arms slowly, as if he was waiting for me to attack. When I didn't, he quickly lifted his weight and jumped to his feet. I remained still, unsure if I should believe him or not. He reached down, grabbed my wrist, pulled me to my feet, and stepped back.

"Are you okay?"

That's when I finally recognized his voice. He'd asked me that same thing when I fallen flat on my face in the parking lot at my apartment.

"Makaio?" Disbelief and relief nearly buckled my knees.

He grabbed my arms to keep me from falling, but still kept his distance. Like maybe he was scared I'd knee him in the crotch. Any other guy and I probably would have.

"Malia?" He pushed the hair out of my face.

"Were you going to shoot me?" I asked.

"Not unless you pointed a weapon at me. Were you going to bite my nipple off?"

"If I had to. I'm sorry, but Windy..." I pulled on his arm, attempting to yank him back into the forest.

"Weren't you trying to get out of the forest?"

"Yes, but now that you're here with a gun, we can't let her get away." My breathing was still erratic, but I stopped.

"Wait a minute, who's Windy?"

"The chick who gave you my bathing suit top."

"Windy," he said it slowly, like he was conjuring up her image in his mind. "The one who gave me her phone number?"

A stab of jealousy went through me. I had no right to feel it, but it was there anyway. I nodded and tried to pull him into the woods.

He refused to move. "What'd she do to you?"

"She killed a man," I managed to say.

"She what?" Makaio released one of my arms. I had no doubt he was grabbing for his gun while he cautiously scanned the area.

"We can't let her get away. She killed that poor guard." My voice was gaining strength and conviction. Having a gun on your side makes you feel a lot stronger, but Makaio had another idea. He put his finger to my lips and pulled me into a squatting position where we listened to the silence surrounding us. Nothing.

"Let's go," he announced, starting to rise. "I'm taking you back to Pearl's." I started to argue, but a sudden movement in the brush silenced me.

We squatted again and waited for what seemed like forever, before Makaio decided to make his move. We ran through the woods, his hand tightly wrapped around mine, urging me to hurry. His route was so much better than the one I'd taken. Clear, and branch free.

Two minutes later, we were standing next to the wall, nowhere near my escape route, and Makaio lifted me over. He followed my retreat to the street, hauling himself over the ancient stone fence. I went into the crook of his arm and directed him to my car parked in the shadows up the street on the opposite side.

"Was Pai with you?" Dressed in BDU's and a tight t-shirt (did they make them any other size for men as large as Makaio?) his voice was stern, but I was pretty sure at least half of it was out of concern for his cousin's safety.

"No, I don't think so. I'm not sure."

He stopped and brought his face down to mine, searching me for answers I didn't have. "Malia, that doesn't make sense. Where's Pai?"

"I don't know!" I insisted. Thinking of Pai being in the woods without a gun was about ready to turn me inside out. "He wasn't with me. I heard a car come in, and I thought it was him, but that was before Windy killed the guard."

"Why did you think it was Pai?"

"The guard who was working tonight made sure the arm was down. No one could pull a car through without using a pass card, or busting down the arm."

"Why would Pai have a pass card to this place?"

"His company's providing security for the construction site. They were supposed to be here until the job was done, but the owner died."

"Who's the owner?" He knew the answer. He just wanted to hear it.

"The man I found on the beach. Peter Johnson. His partner paid Pai in cash to provide security to watch the site, but Pai's having problems with his guards. I told him the gate was open the morning I found Mr. Johnson's body, and he wanted to know where his security personnel were. So he hired me to watch them."

He began guiding me back to my car, strolling down the sidewalk as if we were a couple, arm-in-arm. "You're *working* for Pai?" He sounded relieved.

I nodded, and for a second I thought he might kiss me, but we still needed to find Pai, Windy, and the headless body of the guard. He pulled his phone out and dialed his cousin. Voicemail answered.

"How did you find me?"

"I was doing some work on the plumbing at Pearl's. So the next woman with an allergic reaction has a bathroom to use." His eyes tracked my arms where the bites were hidden by the night sky. "You said Windy killed a guard?" He put his phone back in his pocket.

"Yeah…she chopped off his head."

Makaio stopped. His eyes widened in disbelief. Beheading a person wasn't an easy task, I got it…and the crime scene would be beyond gruesome, but I know what I saw.

"Where did you see the body?" He asked.

"In the middle of the garden, closer to the beach."

"You stay here. I'll be right back." He pushed me against my car that I hadn't even realized we'd reached.

I clawed at his arm, pulling him back toward me when he turned toward the complex.

"If you go, I go." I lost my fear, determined not to lose him. If Windy had removed a man's head, she had a knife at minimum, but probably a weapon much larger. Like a machete. I wasn't about to let Windy come near Makaio with a weapon like that.

"Ain't happening. I'll go in and get her. You direct the dispatcher to where I'll be."

"Nope." My stubborn streak was wide awake now. "You either let me go in with you or you wait for backup."

"Malia." He had that exasperated look that guys get when it's time to do a macho thing and they need to shake the girl loose.

183

It kind of pissed me off. Sure, I'd acted all girly a moment ago, screaming and all, but a man got decapitated. That had to count for something in the excuse column.

I folded my arms across my chest.

"Okay, fine." He sighed. "Get in. We'll move closer to Pearl's. I had her call 911 when we heard you scream." He sighed and watched the wall around *The Garden of the Gods* like maybe it'd be his lucky day, and Windy would try to escape.

I wanted to point out that if the wall was too tall for me to scale, Windy wasn't going to be lifting her bowling balls over it anytime soon.

I dug in my pockets with hands shaking so badly my surfboard key chain fob clanked against the side of my car. Taking the keys from me, Makaio opened the passenger door and guided me into the seat before closing it. He scanned the area again, and for a moment I thought he'd take off for the woods, his need to catch a killer visible in his adrenaline charged muscles, but he didn't leave. True to his word, he walked around to the driver's side, got in and started the car. We quietly pulled down the street closer to the entrance, and Makaio dialed 911 from his cell phone.

"911," the sterile voice on the other end of the line answered.

"This is Officer Natua. I've been contacted by a citizen in regard to a…possible aggravated assault."

After talking to the dispatcher for a few minutes, Makaio hung up and called my brother, John.

John answered after a couple rings, his voice groggy with sleep. "Detective Kumu."

"John, this is Makaio Natua. I'm with Malia at *The Garden of the Gods* condo complex. She just witnessed a murder."

"Malia?" I could tell that made my brother wide awake. "Is she okay? What happened?"

"She's working for my cousin Pai, checking up on his security personnel." John cussed not-so-under-his-breath, and Makaio continued, "She says she saw one of the guards get beheaded."

"Do you have a body?"

"Not yet, I'm waiting for an on-duty officer for backup."

"Okay, give me the address and I'll be there shortly. And don't let her out of your sight. Is that understood?"

Makaio nodded. "Yes, sir."

He disconnected and I was surprised John didn't want to at least talk to me, hear my voice. Something. My eyes began to well with tears, but the sound of an engine dried up my emotions. The silhouette of the light bar on the top of a patrol car eased up behind us. Makaio pulled out his police ID and waited for the two officers to approach.

"Natua?" An officer asked as he came up to the driver's side of the vehicle and flashed a light in Makaio's face.

"Yeah." Makaio held out his ID. "It's Chun. Kāne's with me."

"Biagio?" I craned my neck to see the uniform behind me on the passenger side, and then rolled down my window.

"Mal, what's going on?" Kāne asked.

"Thank God, you're here." Now we could look for Pai and Windy with three guns.

"You okay?"

Makaio interrupted, opening his door and addressing Kāne over the roof of my car. "She's not doing very well right now, since she just witnessed a murder and the murderer is still on the loose. Are you ready to go make an arrest or do you want to sit here and chit chat?"

He sounded pissed off, and I wondered if that was his way of getting into combat mode. Kāne opened my door and I exited the car, ready to show them where the body was located.

Chun asked for the description of the suspect and what weapons they were facing. I told him it was Windy and I wasn't sure what she was armed with.

"Windy?" Kāne's voice was laced with disbelief.

I remembered he and Windy dated in high school, right before she dumped him for the quarterback.

"I know she eats up men and swallows them whole, but beheading? That doesn't sound like her," Kāne argued.

"Stay here. Keep the car running, the windows up and the doors locked," Makaio ordered. "We'll be back in a minute." He was ready to lead an army into battle if need be.

But I wasn't staying in my car. "Makaio—"

He grabbed my shoulders and guided me toward the driver's door. "No arguments. This is police business. You can use my phone and call Pai, find out where he's at. We'll be right back." He leaned in further, kissed my nose and pushed me in the driver's seat.

I watched Chun call something in on his walkie-talkie and a tone echoed from the two radios. With Makaio in the lead, the three of them disappeared over the wall, while I sat in the car and waited. Like a girl.

CHAPTER NINETEEN

I was wringing my hands like a sissy and the cowgirl hula dancer sign was really beginning to annoy me in front of Pearl's donut shop. It was just wrong, offensive even. Islanders don't wear cowboy hats or boots while dancing. Hula isn't a nightclub move, it's a celebration of life, spoken through the movements of every part of the body, not just the hips.

Sitting and waiting sucked. I wanted to be in there with the guys. I wanted to nail Windy's ass to the ground and prove I had a backbone. This whole case had me so jumpy I didn't understand myself. Makaio still wasn't back. Pai wasn't answering his phone. And the street was just as boring as it had been before Windy killed the guard.

Another car approached from behind. I could see the headlights shining through the windshield of the police car parked directly behind me.

Hua.

I slunk down in the front seat, grabbed my baton from the passenger side, and watched the vehicle approach from my side rearview mirrors. The lights extinguished before the vehicle pulled up in line and parked behind the police car. I prayed it was another officer and not Windy's accomplice. I put my hand on the key in the ignition, ready to make a run for it and decided next time I'd have more than my baton to protect myself.

Staring hard at the vehicle, I finally made out the shape of the car. A police car with no emergency light bar, which meant it was a detective.

My brother, thank God.

I jumped out of the car about the same time he exited his vehicle, which in hindsight might not have been the smartest move. Especially, since he was looking toward the condos. He spun around, pulling his gun from his holster and I nearly peed my pants.

News headlines flashed in my head. "Local Surfer Gunned Down by Police." Or "Local Surfer Dies by Her Brother's Hands in *The Garden of the Gods*." My favorite was, "Woman Shot by Police After She Peed Her Pants."

"Geez, Malia. Do you really think it's smart to jump out at a cop when you call him to the scene of a headless dead guy?"

"Sorry." I was so glad to see him, I didn't care that he was mad.

John re-holstered his .40 caliber pistol and met me halfway. This time, he hugged and comforted his little sister, who had seen too much. And as much as I hate to admit it, I let him.

We got in his car and John wasn't looking at my face, but my hair.

"Rough night?"

I couldn't tell if he was making fun of my appearance or if he was being sympathetic. It really had been a bad night. I ran a hand through my hair, coming up with several leaves, probably off the fern forest I'd been hiding in, and wondered if that's where my relatives got the last name Fern.

Maybe they were like me. Always running through the forests in a panicked state and ending up with leaves sticking out of their hair.

"It's been the worst kind of night, ever," I confessed.

"Tell me what happened while we wait for them to clear the area," John replied in a voice I knew he used on other victims and witnesses.

"Are they okay?" I bit my lip, afraid the night would get worse.

"I'm sure they are. It just takes some time to secure the scene." Again, his voice held the strong smooth resonance of a detective in charge.

I nodded. I knew it would take a while. It just seemed to be taking *forever*. I began with why I was there and how Pai had hired me. I told him I thought a car had entered the gate and I assumed it was Pai, but he wasn't answering his phone.

The furrows in John's face deepened. I told him how Windy had driven up during my shift and pointed to her car parked down the street. During my description, I struggled with the decapitation part, my hands twisting together, again. John gripped my hands and squeezed, his compassion getting me through the worst of it. I finished the story with my mad dash through the forest, losing my shoe and running into Makaio. John took notes during my tale and added touches of brotherly support throughout. It made me feel like maybe we'd crossed a line between childhood and adulthood.

Then a voice came over the radio. "332, clear the air. Can you start an ambulance for an unconscious male about thirty-five."

Dispatch responded there was an ambulance in route and I noticed John frowning again as he closed his notebook.

"Was that Kāne?"

John held up a 'hold that thought' finger, as he picked up his radio mic and called the officer. "1060 to 332."

"Go ahead, 1060."

"Do you have a crime scene for the Adult Crimes Unit to respond to?"

"Not unless you guys have taken on public intoxication." I could hear the laughter in Biagio's voice.

"10-4," John turned to me, really unhappy at this point. "Malia, is this some kind of joke? Cause if it is, I'm not laughing."

"What? John I didn't just go through hell to punk you. There's a man out there without a head. I heard Windy chop off his head."

"The man's just unconscious, Mal. Like I should be. At home. In my bed. But instead, I'm out here with you." The way he said *you* made me feel like the bothersome little sister again. He paused his chiding, ran his hand through his hair and turned toward me with a somber look. "Maybe dismembering that guy has messed with your head."

My breath caught. My indignation soared. I was beyond tired, yes, but I knew what I saw. "My head is not messed up! And I did not dismember anyone, Windy did!"

I couldn't fathom his lack of faith in me, let alone that he thought I was going crazy. He asked *me* for help. Yeah, I was determined to solve Peter Johnson's homicide, but I wasn't even sure it was a homicide any more. My gut said it was. Peter, or some imaginary voice in my head said it was. Everything else said it wasn't. I swallowed my pride for a moment and thought about the situation.

One burning question remained, "Where's Windy?"

"Are you sure it was Windy?"

Irritated, I pointed at her car parked down the street.

"Maybe she met someone for a boat ride from the dock." John suggested.

My response was interrupted by Kāne's voice on the radio ordering an ambulance for an unconscious man. John went back to his notebook, an uncomfortable silence easing its way into the car. But that didn't mean it was the guard I'd been watching. It could be the guy in the car. The one who drove inside the gate after I followed Windy and the guard into the garden. He was the only other one who was there.

"John, it has to be the guy who drove inside the gate." I began to fear what I had just said. "Oh, God. Is it Pai? Is Pai hurt?"

John was no longer looking at me. He was looking down the street. I gazed down the street wondering why something other than my concern for Pai caught his attention.

Then I spotted her. Windy wiggled and jiggled her way down the middle of the street, heels dangling from her fingertips. With her back to us, she rearranged her skirt to cover her ass.

The spawn from hell looked like she was just out for a leisurely stroll, if you believed hookers took innocent strolls at four am. It was exactly what I'd expect from the evil progeny of the devil. She was intermingling in the life of normal people, posing as innocent members of our society.

Windy hadn't been innocent since she was ten, and this was worse than just bullying and sexual promiscuity. This was murder.

"Get her! She murdered that guard!" I ordered.

John looked at me and sighed. He didn't know what to think. He reluctantly put down his notebook and got out of his car.

A few moments later, I was looking at Windy leaning over the front hood of the unmarked police car — where I sat uncomfortably in the passenger seat. The view of her cleavage was even more offensive with the knowledge that she cozied up to a dead guy. Her fingers wiggled on the hood, like she couldn't wait to get her maniacal claws in my flesh. I gulped and convinced myself that she was no threat with her hands spread across the hood. Her legs were extended even wider — much to John's irritation. He hadn't put her in that position, she had. Still, she glared at me through the windshield.

Her evil eye had never bothered me until tonight. Regrettably, I was out of strength to play her game of eye contact chicken. I lost miserably.

I told myself it was out of a bizarre fascination with how her tattooed boobs hung so low they touched the hood of the car. Her hair was wet and the front of her tube top clung to wet breasts. The garment was nothing but an ineffectual bustier. Her nipples stood out not just like headlights, but like those huge searchlights that dark city uses to call its super hero into action.

Did men really like all that?

John didn't seem too mesmerized after his initial, 'How the hell do I search those?' look. Now, he was telling her to turn around and lean against the car. He talked into his handheld radio for a moment, and then with a hand signal, which looked like one of those you give a dog to 'stay,' he told her not to move. An ambulance pulled up and John directed the paramedics to the construction site's front gate before he came back and got into the driver's seat.

"Makaio's fine. They haven't found a car or anyone else. Just the unconscious guard. Other than trespass, I don't have any reason to detain her, Mal." Windy's butt flared across the hood of his car like a hoagie bun full of spam.

"But she took off that man's head!" I couldn't believe he was going to let her go. If she were released, she'd come over to my place and chop my head off during my sleep. I had no doubt I would be missing an appendage I valued very much if she walked.

"There's no blood on the front of her."

"Duh. She's all wet. Obviously, she went for a swim after I saw her. Swab her hands, collect her clothes, and get the lab to look for DNA." I insisted.

John just looked at me. We stared at each other for several seconds. He didn't know what to do with me, and I was angry he wasn't going to arrest a cold-blooded killer.

This time, I won the battle of chicken. (I secretly think it was because he let me.)

He grabbed his radio mike and called Kāne. "1060 to 332. Do you have the identity of your victim?"

"Affirmative. James Kamakau. He's a guard with Lincoln Securities. The ambulance is leaving with him now. We'll be out in a minute."

"10-4."

Message received. Loud and clear. The guard I'd been watching...the man I'd seen dead without a head...was very much alive. John looked at me with sympathy and I pondered my mental health.

"Come on, I'll stop the ambulance, and you can tell me if it's the same guy."

I nodded in agreement and got out of the car in a state of shock. It was the second time that night my brain was so full, it was blank.

"Johnny, baby, can I go now?" Windy's sugary sweet voice caused my stomach to roll. She sickened me, and made me want to barf in her face, but I no longer felt like we were on an equal playing field. It was as if she suddenly had some secret powers that caused me to quake in my shoes. Or rather, shoe, since my left sandal was lost in the forest of tall bamboo across the street.

"Wait here a minute, Windy. We'll be right back."

"Okay, Johnny baby."

I could tell John wasn't happy with that nickname. I imagined a detective sergeant wouldn't want the other cops, or citizens hearing her use the term either. Then I wondered if he and Windy had a past together. The thought sent a shiver up my spine. I really didn't like the thought of my brother being with such a skank. A murdering skank at that.

I went around the rear of the car to avoid being too close to her and ignored her smirk. The ambulance pulled up to the front entrance. John motioned for the driver to stop and spoke to him for a minute before heading to the back door and opened it. He indicated for me to follow him.

My feet suddenly felt heavy. I was so tired and confused. Anxious to prove their patient wasn't the decapitated guard, but reluctant to see living proof that I'd officially lost my mind. I certainly didn't want the guy to be dead, but ... hua.

I took a deep breath and stepped into the back of the ambulance as John held my elbow to assist me up.

I looked at the guard in front of me, with the familiar uniform. He had the same shoes. The same pants...and shirt. The same muscular form. Same short stature. The same disproportionately large ears attached to ...the same small head. It was all connected to make a very much alive and intact guard. The one I'd watched all night. She hadn't chopped it off. Energizer Bunny guard, James Kamakau was lying in front of me completely intact. I watched him struggling to focus on the paramedic who had hooked him up to an IV. The paramedic brought out one of those lights doctors use to look in your eyes, ears, nose and mouth and as soon as the light hit James' eye, he shook his head. Blinking several times, and suddenly seemed more alert.

"What happened?" He sputtered.

"Just relax, you're in an ambulance. We're taking you to the hospital." The paramedic continued examining his other eye. As the beam hit James' second eye, a light bulb seemed to turn on in his brain. His very much alive and active brain.

"I remember. She came up and…"

I waited for him to finish, but got nothing. He stopped mid-thought.

"What?" I demanded. I can't stand unfinished sentences. They're torture. Movies that leave unsaid words on the tips of the lips of dying loved ones, drive me nuts.

Kamakau looked at me, trying to figure out who I was and why I was there. I didn't give him the chance.

"She came up and did what?" I asked, trying to soften my demand a little bit.

His eyes never left mine, almost as if he was too scared to look anywhere else.

"The curse of the Menehune," he whispered.

"The curse of the Menehune?" Oh, please. Not this crap again. Was he seriously going to waste my time? I wanted to scream, 'No! What did Windy do to you?' Instead I just looked at him, waiting for an explanation.

"She knows it. If she spreads the knowledge, we're all doomed. We'll have to leave."

"What are you talking about it?" I resisted the urge to shake him mercilessly and waited patiently. That is, if you consider tapping my foot with my arms folded across my chest and a scowl on my face as a picture of patience.

Kamakau looked away, his eyes leaving mine and focusing on absolutely nothing.

"Miss, you'll have to leave now." The paramedic was looking at me with a 'Hello lady, sick man here that needs to go to the hospital' expression on his face. I nodded and jumped out of the ambulance, where John waited for me.

"Is that the guard you were watching?"

I nodded but refused to establish eye contact.

"Did he say what happened to him?"

I responded with a silent shake of my head. I'd already made a big enough fool out of myself, I wasn't about to start talking about a stupid curse.

John closed the door, patted the side of the ambulance with an open palm and we watched it drive down the street. I couldn't look at him. I just stood there, holding my arms tightly across my chest. He placed his hand on my back and leaned in to whisper to me.

"I'll be right back, okay?"

I nodded and watched him approach Windy. Her body posture suddenly changed. She went from slouching against the police car with her arms crossed, to standing with her hands on her hips, chest thrust forward and one foot out as if she was pulling up her skirt to hitch a ride at the side of the road. No one really did that, did they?

Laughter broke out behind me, and I turned around just in time to see Makaio, Kāne and Chun walk up from around a bend in the drive. The three of them were having a pretty good laugh, probably at my expense, until they saw me. Their faces dropped in an attempt to look professional.

Makaio either had the most experience, or the most to lose. Only a twitch at the corner of his mouth gave him away. Kāne almost succeeded as he coughed through his laughter. Chun just plain sucked at it as his shoulders, hunched inward and shook convulsively. He covered his mouth with a hand that wasn't big enough to contain his laughter.

Hell would freeze over before I'd go out on a date with *that* guy.

If I couldn't sober their expression, the sight of Windy standing behind me did.

Kāne nodded at me and said, "We all make mistakes, Mal."

He walked past me and headed over to John and Windy. Chun, on the other hand, didn't give me a second thought as he beat his partner to Windy's side without even a glance in my direction. He only had eyes for boobs at that point.

I looked at Makaio, searching his face for any sign of interest in Windy. Any sign of interest in me, now that he knew I was crazy. He smiled, reached up to pull some plants out of my hair and I felt the need to defend my sanity, but couldn't. Maybe the body had affected me more than I realized.

"You need to learn how to use your camera."

"Excuse me?"

"If you'd known how to use your camera better, you would have known how to take pictures in low light settings without a flash, and you wouldn't have thought the man's head was cut off."

He was making excuses for me, which pissed me off for some inexplicable reason. I had no excuse for myself, yet hearing him make one for me ignited my fuse.

I turned away and stalked toward my car. I'm sure my lopsided mix of barefoot and sandal wasn't completely dignified, but I didn't give a damn. But passing Windy and her entourage of cops served to enhance my feelings of inadequacy. How was it possible for her to get that much attention? Not that I wanted their attention, but there were principles involved. My anger blended with frustration, self-doubt and self-loathing. I felt as stupid and incompetent as I'd ever felt in my life. And to make matters worse, tears threatened to spill uncontrollably onto my cheeks.

I needed to get out of there. The sanctity of my car beckoned. A drive with the top down, the cool wind drying my tears and blowing all the debris from my hair was all the therapy I needed. Then my pillow under my head for twelve hours straight. That would stop me from seeing dead people.

I reached my car and started to pull on the door when Makaio's hand reached past my shoulder and held the door closed. I hadn't even heard him behind me, which didn't help my damaged psyche.

"Malia."

Nothing in the world could make me turn toward him. Not only was my hair and clothing a mess, tears were streaming down my face. No doubt leaving tracks of mascara in the dirt and dust gathered on my face. I had no fight left in me.

There was no struggle when he pulled me into his arms and I cried like a baby. We stood there for what seemed like a lifetime. His arms wrapped around me, my hands clinging to the soft cotton material covering his expansive chest. His incredibly masculine scent soothed my fears as it awakened a deeper need in my soul. I didn't want to think about the outside world, just our bodies crushed together.

As the tears dissipated, I became aware of his need and looked up into eyes so deep and dark they seemed to draw me into their depths. It was like disappearing into a black hole and finding the meaning of the universe inside.

His arms released my body, suddenly replaced by his hands gently caressing my face. He wiped the tears away with his thumbs and then his callused palms held my face inches from his. His head turned slightly as his lips slowly descended toward my own. My breath hitched with anticipation of his kiss as my eyes traveled to his mouth. As our lips were about to meet in what I knew would be an exquisite kiss, his head snapped up.

An instant later, he was grabbing my arms and shoving me backward across the street. My feet moving faster than I thought possible, we flew across the pavement and tumbled into the ditch. Makaio landed on top of me in belly flop fashion. Again. The air exploded from my lungs like a bullet exiting the barrel of a gun, the force burning my lungs and throat. My vision flashed white as his chin made contact with my forehead. I attempted to suck air into my lungs with no success. The distant sound of screeching tires perforated the haze. Crunching metal followed as Makaio shifted his weight to enclose me under his body.

I struggled for air, wondering if I would ever take a breath again. I attempted little breaths with minor results, success making me greedy for more. Finally, Makaio lifted his weight, and I gulped at the air like a fish out of water.

"Sorry. Are you okay?" For the second time in less than an hour, he looked down at me with concern written all over his face. I nodded, taking in another drink of air, still struggling to get oxygen into my dehydrated lungs.

"Yeah," I gasped, then looked closer and saw blood all over his bottom lip. "You're bleeding!"

"I'm okay, but…" He nearly went cross-eyed as he looked at the point of impact for his chin. "…you've got a nice goose egg forming in the middle of your forehead."

My fingers searched for the growth and located the source of my pain. Blood began throbbing under the skin. "What happened?"

"There was…an accident." He was looking at me as if he was waiting for me to lose my mind completely.

Maybe I had because for the life of me I had no idea what he was talking about. "What?"

"Someone hit your car." His voice held more sympathy.

My body was numb, incapable of movement. No. Not my car. Not my cute little convertible MINI Cooper. Not the one bit of therapy that would get me through this night. It couldn't be. He was mistaken.

Makaio rolled to my side, and I sat up to see how much damage my car had sustained, but it was gone. Someone had stolen my car, not hit it. I scanned the street where it had been, but all I could see was a big white monster truck with a bizarre hood ornament — long horns jutting out from the front hood.

What the hell was that?

If the monstrosity wasn't bad enough, I caught a splash of red, barely visible under its tires.

No. No. No. That could not be my car. My car wasn't that small. It wouldn't fit under that obnoxiously huge truck. Okay, maybe it would if the truck was airlifted and placed down gently over the top of it, but not without the help of a helicopter. I looked up. No lights shined down from a helicopter.

It had to be red skis under the truck.

"Can you get up?"

Unable to talk, I nodded in response and Makaio gently pulled me to my feet. John stood at the door of the truck talking to the driver. He appeared dwarfed by the mere size of the tires and height of the vehicle. The driver's side and front end of the truck appeared intact, including the long horns on the hood. I hoped the passenger side was mangled beyond repair as I stared at the small scrap of red metal underneath it.

My car.

"Darlin,' I appreciate you helpin' me out. I don't know what happened. One minute I was drivin' down the road mindin' my own business, the next I was sittin' on top of a lil' foreign piece of crap."

Pearl. That no good, two bit…pastry cook.

I lunged for her. My anger erupted like *Pu`u `O`o* on Mount Kilauea. I was totally out of control in pursuit of revenge, my anger building like the molten lava ready to spew. Pearl jumped behind John as he helped her from the vehicle, but it wasn't John that saved her. Makaio grabbed me first, denying my emotions, along with a probable murder rap.

"She did that on purpose!" I raged. My feet and arms extended toward her while Makaio held me off the ground with one arm around my waist.

I could hear blood rushing through my body to my ears, deafening me. Just as I thought I might break free from Makaio's grip, another vehicle pulled in between Pearl and me. I could no longer see the woman who took my baby away from me. The happy face of Pai sitting in his Jeep replaced it. He blocked out everything else with his bright smile.

"Brah, I'm guessing Malia doesn't want you holding her in your arms."

My arms and feet drooped like my hair around my face.

"You can leave, Pai." Makaio said, gritting out the response with some pent up emotions of his own.

Sobbing from the other side of the jeep drowned out any response Pai could give.

"Makaio! What have I done?" Pearl wailed like the doorbell on her pastry store.

In unison, we all looked toward John, who had backed away from the truck while trying to extricate himself from a sobbing Pearl in his arms. He gave Makaio a dirty look and curtly swung his head. Clearly my brother wanted Makaio on the other side of the jeep dealing with Pearl, not holding me like a lover.

Makaio looked down at me. His expression asked permission to leave, but his eyes asked if he could stay.

All the fight was out of me. I gave up. "Go ahead."

Makaio released me and Pai jumped out of the Jeep with a smile of victory for his cousin. Makaio sneered in return. His expression softened when he turned and kissed my cheek before heading for Pearl.

"Baby Doll, you looked a lot better when I left you. Where's your shoe?"

"I lost it somewhere over there in the middle of the bamboo. I should be able to find it. It's not too far from the wall."

"Just sit and relax in my Jeep. I'll find it."

Pai lifted me up into the driver's seat and leaned over me to grab a flashlight out of the glove box. I pointed to the spot where Makaio and

I came out of the trees and he took off in search of my sandal.

I watched as Windy blew kisses over her shoulder at Kāne and his partner. They may as well have drooled all over themselves as they watched her sashay to her car, hips swaying enough to compete with the best hula dancer around.

Come on. Women don't *really* walk like that.

Once she was in her car, they finally turned and approached John, who was calling in a tow truck. Fluids were leaking out of the pickup onto what was left of my car. Ol' Pearl had succeeded in damaging the undercarriage of her truck, which was the bright spot of my night. At least there was some justice in the world.

I looked at Makaio's face, bearing a miserable expression what with the weeping Pearl going on and on about her stupid truck. John advanced toward me with an unreadable expression on his face. I couldn't tell if he was angry at me, Pearl, or at the whole world. As he got closer, I realized his anger wasn't directed toward me at all. It went beyond me. I turned to see Pai approaching with my sandal in his hand and that ever-present grin on his face.

"I've been trying to get in contact with you, Mr. Lincoln." John meant business, and I hoped Pai didn't become flippant.

"Sorry, I've been busy. You must be Malia's brother." Pai reached out to shake John's hand, despite the fact that John looked as if he was ready to slap cuffs on him.

"I need you to come down and give me a statement."

"Yes, why don't we plan on meeting tomorrow? Right now, I want to get Malia home. She's had very little sleep lately." Pai glared at Makaio who returned the look with an added dose of resentment attached.

Ready to give up on all of them, I attempted to get out of the jeep, only to have Pai stop me. "Let me help you." He squatted down, put the sandal on my bare foot and gently struggled to buckle the strap around my, once again, swollen cankle. If the rest of me looked like that, I didn't want to know.

Kāne decided to add his two cents. "Hey, Mal, if you wanted to be treated like Cinderella, there are easier ways of doing it."

Pai let each vertebrae in his back unroll slowly as he stood up to his full height and turned toward Kāne, who looked like he was going to pee his pants. Pai approached him from one side, while Makaio descended upon him from the other, both men looking like they were ready to engage in physical warfare. I envisioned tribal tattoos on their faces, ancient weapons in their hands as they went into battle.

Kāne drew his taser and John jumped in front of him before the situation escalated.

"It's been a long night, guys, let's not make it worse by over reacting to a juvenile comment."

"Sorry, Mal, I was just teasing," Kāne added. His apology wasn't necessary, in my opinion, but it mattered to Pai and Makaio, who backed down in unison.

"I'm sorry for bringing everyone out on a wild goose chase." And I was. It had been a humiliating night.

"Anyone would have made the same mistake if they saw the picture you took." Kāne turned back to the accident scene that involved the death of my car.

"Where is my camera?"

"Makaio's got it along with your phone. Didn't he show you?"

"No…"

Pearl had somehow reattached herself to Makaio like a cougar starfish hanging onto a rock, making it impossible for him move around Pai's jeep. Instead, he scooted to the passenger side and stopped.

"Malia, I tried to tell you but you walked away and when I caught up to you, you were upset and then…" He skipped over the part where he was about to kiss me when Pearl annihilated my car. "There just hasn't been any time to tell you."

It was true. There had been no time to talk about anything. I had no reason to be mad, despite the clinging Pearl. I nodded my understanding and Makaio pulled my camera and phone out of the side pocket of his camo shorts.

I was surprised to find they'd survived being tossed to the wind and our little episode in the ditch. Then again, I probably had a bruise somewhere on my body in the shape of a phone or camera from cushioning their impact. Taking a deep cleansing breath, I turned on the camera and hit the review button. My last picture, the one that had scared the ever-living crap out of me, showed Windy just as I remembered her. Bare boobed, her eyes wide, mouth open even wider with the shock of being caught in the act written all over her face. She held on to…

Dear God…the headless body of the guard.

My body shuddered at the graphic image. The pure animalistic violence was beyond my comprehension causing me to block out the image by squeezing my eyes closed. How could that be? I opened my eyes staring at John in disillusionment.

Pai and John moved in closer to look at the graphic photo like bypassers attracted to the gore of an accident scene. Makaio spoke first.

"Look again, Malia. The fern is blocking the view of his neck and her bo….his head is covered by her…chest."

Unable to view the senseless violence a third time, I peeked with one eye closed. Pai and John moved closer to the screen that I now held at arm's length. Even Pearl gave up her rock to lean across the passenger seat and view the picture. John chuckled. A low rumble that built upon itself before he turned away in a full blown explosion of his amusement. I looked from John to Pai, who struggled not to reveal that gorgeous smile. But no, there it was in its finest (and whitest) before his head fell back in laughter.

Pearl jerked her head back and then began to laugh in what I would describe as a cackle before I yanked my camera toward my chest.

Obviously, I was missing the big picture. Again, I took a deep breath, pulled the camera away from my body and looked at it with both eyes open. I looked past the 'eye-catching boobs' glowing in the middle of the screen, delicate tattoos circling from below, and saw that in fact, James Kamakau's head *was* attached to his neck, but it was hidden underneath Windy's boobs in the most bizarre sexual act ever photographed. (Probably not, but I'm not exactly a connoisseur of porn.)

I was the very definition of an eye-witness gone bad. I'd reacted with emotion and bias. My own bias against Windy. Imagining she was a wicked seed of the devil himself. (She still might fit that description, but she didn't commit murder.)

Pai gave me one of those big happy smiles with a low hearty chuckle. Even John completely forgave his little sister for pulling him out of bed. I did, after all, give him ammunition to use against me for years to come. Pearl continued with her wicked witch laugh and I leaned back in the front seat of the Jeep like a limp rag. The revelation of what I had *really* seen began to release the tension and horror of the fictional images trapped in my mind.

Makaio pulled Pearl back and leaned across the passenger seat of the Jeep to whisper in my ear. "I don't want to be smothered by silicone implants. I like the real thing."

I looked up and saw the heat in his eyes as they traveled the length of my body.

Damn, that man could make me sweat.

Pai cleared his throat and leaned in with one arm resting on the driver's seat, his other arm effectively trapping me in, as it extended to the dash.

"Baby Doll, are you ready to leave? I think you've earned a personal massage for the next two hours...at least." He winked and I felt the flush spread across my face.

At least Makaio's declaration had been private. Pai's claim was made and staked in front of way too many people. My brother sized him up in a way I hadn't seen him do since my senior prom, while Makaio looked ready to meet his cousin toe-to-toe again. His earlier concern for Pai's welfare was completely forgotten.

Pearl managed to keep her claws on Makaio, leaving scratches all over his pumped up bicep while pulling him away from me. Suddenly envisioning what wild sex with an older woman might be like, the term 'cougar' now made sense.

"Darlin,' are you goin' to finish fixin' my plumbin'?"

The torment in Makaio's eyes was evident. Be with me, finish helping the old broad (I was probably the only one to see her that way), or kick his cousin's butt.

"Brah, you can't leave the woman high and dry, or in this case...wet. Pearl needs you to fix her plumbing. Isn't that what you do best?" Pai sent his cousin a happy grin.

Makaio glared at Pai, who truly was enjoying his cousin's predicament. The tension in the air was palpable.

I don't rattle easily, at least I didn't before I pulled off Peter's arm. Since then, life had been a living hell...mixed with every emotion possible, including balls to the wall explosive passion and I was beginning to understand the real meaning of bipolar, but enough was enough. I turned toward Pai and started in on him first.

"Pai, leave Makaio alone. He was there when I needed him. You weren't." I watched Pai's face become one of humility before turning on Makaio, whose expression had turned smug. At least until he realized he'd been caught.

"Makaio, stop acting like a pit bull ready to attack, and go finish Cougar lady's restroom so she doesn't let any more women down when they trust her to watch the door to the men's room." Pearl was about to object, but I pointed a tired finger and stopped her cold turkey. "You better have insurance on that monstrosity you crunched my car with, or so help me, I will put those horns where the sun doesn't shine."

Pearl's face scrunched up in outrage at my threat, Makaio held her arms and John once again stepped in. This time, he sighed before giving his

I'm-in-charge speech. (Not the first time he acted that way around me.)

"Ladies, the officers will fill out a report and give you both an accident form with all the information you need to give to your insurance companies. Pearl, they'll need to know where you want your truck towed. Malia, is there anything you want to get out of your car?"

Craning my neck to look past all the people blocking my view of my crumpled car, tears began to well. Just like that, the pent up emotions of the past couple days, spilled over and I could no longer speak.

Pai came to my rescue this time. "I'm going to take Malia home. Makaio, go through her car and get any personal effects for her. You can drop them off tomorrow."

Makaio nodded in agreement and turned Pearl away before the woman could open her mouth. I swore if she said one word, I was going to kill her. The hell with the witnesses. Temporary insanity was just one word away from taking over my body.

"Mr. Lincoln, I need to speak with you." John wasn't about to let Pai take control.

The tears were rolling freely down my face now as Pai picked me up and carried me around to the passenger side of the Jeep.

"Can it wait until morning? I'd like to take Malia home."

My brother took one look at my face and ran his fingers through his hair. "Fine. But first thing in the morning, I want you downtown."

"You got it, boss."

I looked at the sun starting to rise to the east. There was no way Pai would make it to John's office, and my brother wasn't fooled. The day a man like Pai looked to John for instructions was the day the gods wiped Hawai'i off the map.

CHAPTER TWENTY

I let the scents of the island do their magic. The cool morning breeze blew my matted hair out of my face, replacing the odors of car fluids and burnt rubber with salt air, hibiscus flowers and fresh rain. Pai was helping me escape my car's tragic death scene. It was probably melodramatic of me to think of it that way, but she was my baby.

The new song by Bag of Toys playing on the radio should have energized me for a journey to the beach. Instead, I found myself sinking further into the leather seats, ready to sleep for the next twenty-four hours just as soon as we reached my apartment. The jeep turned to the right and the tires hit the uneven surface of a gravel drive. Expecting to see the parking lot of my apartment, I opened my eyes to see lush trees pass by on each side of the vehicle. It wasn't my parking lot. It was the road to Lani's condo.

Hua.

All the relaxing sensations I'd just experienced were gone. Pai hadn't taken me home. He'd taken me to his place.

"I thought a nice Jacuzzi would relax you before you went to bed..." He was smiling at me now, with that sultry, sexy smile of his which was just too damn alluring for me to handle. Especially now.

"...I'll be on my couch. Relax, Malia. After we get you cleaned up and relaxed, I need to go to the hospital to see my guard. I need to hear his side."

"But I don't have a bathing suit."

Pai groaned. A sexy, animalistic noise that made my toes tingle. I'm sure he was picturing us in the Jacuzzi with no clothes on.

I know I was.

"Baby Doll, you are a tease without even trying to be."

He should talk. He and his cousin were driving me insane. It just wasn't fair that I'd met two incredible men within twenty-four hours of each other, both of whom made me think about sex day and night.

"Yeah, it seems you aren't the only woman to feel that way."

Hua. He did it again. "How do you know what I'm thinking?" There was no logical explanation for it.

"I told you. You wear your feelings on your sleeve." Pai wasn't looking at me. I got the impression he was hiding some deep dark secret.

"If that's true, why can't anyone else read my thoughts? Makaio doesn't have a clue."

"That's because my cousin only hears what his body tells him. Not what other people's bodies have to say."

"Why don't you get along?" In so many ways, the two men were alike. I could see them playing football together, going to college together, going to the bars and picking up women together. Women. It was over a woman.

"See, even you can read what others are thinking when you try." Pai's smile appeared strained.

"Who was she?"

He sighed heavily. His chest expanding nearly distracted me, but I refused to look.

"My girlfriend. She decided to try some handcuffs in the bedroom, but she gave Makaio the honor of locking her up."

My heart sank into a bottomless pit. I felt betrayed. Used. Stupid. Yet Pai was the one who'd been hurt. His cousin had dealt him a serious blow that I still couldn't fathom him doing. "Makaio slept with your girlfriend?"

Pai shrugged, acting like it was no big deal, but obviously, it was.

"I was consumed with expanding the Lincoln Security Firm. I think she sought out Makaio as revenge for my neglect."

"Ahhh." What could I say to that? Pai was a nice guy. The woman he loved had betrayed him, but what made it worse was the disloyalty of his cousin. A man I'd been intimate with. (Sorta.) If I

217

was going to let Pai kiss me, I should probably tell him I'd done more than just kiss Makaio.

"I know what you did with Makaio."

My embarrassment and shame clenched my gut. Hands clamped in my lap, I didn't know what to say...or do. Had Makaio gotten on the phone as soon as I'd left my apartment and rubbed it in Pai's face? I couldn't look at Pai as he punched in the code to the gate and headed down the drive.

He parked the car and we sat there, staring at the front of the darkened bungalow with silence filling the space between us. His hand caressed my cheek, then he turned my face, forcing me to look him in the eye. "You're different, Baby Doll. I don't know why, but you're worth fighting for."

His eyes traveled to my lips as his head slowly descended. Strong masculine lips paused a fraction from my own. His scent was glorious. Where Makaio was a wild ocean current, Pai was all cool sea breezes, slowly seducing me with his exotic comfort. Two completely different men pulled me just as strongly. My desperado was gone; my knight had taken his place.

Pai's lips captured mine in a slow exploratory waltz filled with heat. His hand traveled from my cheek to my neck where it caressed my increasing pulse before descending to my collarbone. As it slipped to the front of my neck, our kiss intensified, his tongue dancing with my own and then he was gone.

He pulled away. (Before I did.) A fact I found extremely disturbing since I'd just been in a very passionate embrace with Makaio not even an hour earlier. Shouldn't I be the one stopping all these kisses? His fingers played with the ticklish spot in the hollow of my neck.

"Baby Doll, I'm a patient man. I'll wait for you to decide."

He smiled, pecked my lips (still burning from his kiss) and got out of the Jeep. I watched him walk around the vehicle, and visualized him carrying me through the front door.

I quickly unbuckled my seatbelt and jumped from the vehicle. Pai smiled down at me as I landed on my feet. I refused to be steered toward Pai's bed. The pain in my cankle, however, had returned full force causing me to hobble forward. Unaffected by my behavior, Pai casually put his arm around my waist, and took some of the pressure off my foot as we walked up the sidewalk together.

I looked toward the conspicuously dark main house. "Where's Lani?"

"She had an early flight to Oahu. She took her son over to her brother's house."

"Oh." We were alone. That did not bode well for my resolve.

"I'm not going to get into the Jacuzzi with you. We'll save that for when you're ready."

I'm pretty sure my body was ready. Luckily, my brain was smart enough to keep my mouth shut.

"I won't look if you want to get undressed and get into the Jacuzzi."

Of course, I wanted to. Every inch of me hurt in more ways than one. I nodded as we reached the door and Pai released me to unlock the door. We replayed the brushing of our bodies as I entered his temporary home. He smiled. I groaned, pretending it was from pain, not the desire coursing through my body.

"Can you really read all of my thoughts?" A woman needs secrets.

"Unfortunately for some women, not a thought goes by that I don't hear." Pai winked and I'm pretty sure my face turned the shade of a Flamingo Lily, the bright red variety.

"Every thought?" I looked up through my lashes.

"I would say the color of your cheeks resembles the pink variety of the Flamingo Lily."

Hua.

Pai coughed, a strangled sound escaping his mouth. "You're thinking about my balls?"

"No!" At least I hadn't been. Maybe.

He cleared his throat. "Then why did you say testicles?"

"I didn't." I denied.

"*Hua* translates to testicles." He insisted.

Damn. He really could hear everything inside my head. "I know what it means, but my brother taught it to me when I was a kid. He caught me cussing at the beach with my friends. He said if I was going to cuss, I needed to say it in our native tongue so not everyone understood what I was saying. By the time I slipped in front of my mom, I'd been saying it for years. Old habits die hard."

Pai's eyes crinkled. "How many guys heard you say '*hua*' before you knew what it meant?"

"Too many," I confessed.

He grinned.

I grinned. Then his balls really did slip into my mind. I ran/limped for the bathroom and slammed the door.

I looked in the mirror and cussed again. *Hua.* No wonder Pai could resist me. I was surprised anyone was able to tolerate me.

I don't even want to tell you how filthy I was, or what my hair looked like. My makeup was far from supermodel material, and the goose egg in the middle of my forehead looked like a third eye. I stripped down, brushed out my hair, cleaned off all the dirt and dried mud from my body. Wrapped in nothing but a towel, I went out on the patio where Pai sat in a deck chair near the bubbling Jacuzzi with his laptop open.

He looked up and his eyes darkened with pent up desire. Damn my libido with its off the charts activity. His eyes traveled down my body and back up to my chest. Then he looked back down at his computer.

"You better get in the water before I forget how patient I am."

I scampered across the patio and tripped into the Jacuzzi with a splash, the towel going with me. I caught a glimpse of his smile as I settled down in the warm pulsing jets. Just what my sore tattered body needed.

"I'm sorry I didn't answer your calls this evening. I met with Misty Johnson, Peter's widow, while you were watching the construction site. She was pretty upset at the time and I didn't want to leave her.

"Misty said her husband had been clean for almost eight months. Last week, she called Daven when she hadn't been able to reach him. Daven told her he was worried that he may have hooked up with the wrong people, but he would be home the next day and let her know what was going on. That's why he reported Peter was missing when he got home. Apparently, Peter had been drinking heavily every night and one night, he caught him doing meth with some women outside the hotel bar. Daven didn't want to tell her, so he ignored Peter's behavior and went to Oahu to another construction site. When Daven returned to Kaua'i, he found Misty's messages on the phone in the condo he was sharing with Peter. Peter was gone and Daven knew he had to come clean about Peter's behavior. He also told the police that Peter had been squandering their investment money with his drug habit."

"Wow, that poor woman." While I was relieved Pai hadn't abandoned me for no good reason, I felt guilty for accusing him of doing just that. Misty Johnson had lost everything. Her husband and the dream of a happily ever after. It was depressing. And Pai had made sure she wasn't alone.

My body reluctantly began to succumb to the water's massaging sensations, the bubbles working their magic on my sore, exhausted muscles. I leaned back, rested my head on the padded pillow, and watched Pai through half-closed eyes.

"Yeah, but she doesn't believe it. She said her husband got addicted to the OxyContin when he had back surgery. He never spent a lot of money on his drug addiction. He just used too much medication and convinced different doctors to prescribe him more. He recognized the problem himself before it got too far out of control. She said he never 'hit rock bottom' like you'd expect from most addicts before they acknowledge their problem. He was ashamed of his addiction and put himself into rehab."

"Maybe he was stealing from the company instead of using personal funds so she wouldn't know about it. He wouldn't be the first spouse to hide his problem." I was done looking for something that wasn't there. I had barked up the wrong tree with this investigation just as I had with Windy and the guard. No more wild ghost chases for me.

Help me.

My body spasmed and splashed with an electrical charge strong enough to shove me under water. I came up sputtering water from my nose and mouth.

Pai was on his feet charging across the patio. "What the hell was that?"

"Stop!"

He froze in his tracks.

"I'm not dressed." I pulled my chest against the side and motioned him to sit back down. I didn't need him scrutinizing me. I looked like hell before I got in the Jacuzzi, and now I was freaked out of my frickin' mind.

Scared he was only reacting to me going under water and that I really was losing it, I whispered, "Did you hear him?" It may have been the first and only time I prayed someone could read my mind.

"The man in your head saying, 'Help me'? How could I miss it? Whose voice was that?" Pai slowly backed away, watching me for any more sudden attacks on my brain.

I slumped forward and rested my head on my arms over the edge. "Thank God. I thought I was going crazy." I lifted my head and rested my chin on my arms to confess. "The first time I heard it…was when I rolled over Peter Johnson's body. I heard him again last night at the convenience store with Joe. He told me to run from that nutjob you stopped from attacking me, but for the most part, I've kind of been ignoring him."

Pai returned to his chair and remained silent, as if he was debating how he should respond. I visualized myself in a strait jacket and began to regret my confession. Dead people can't communicate with the living.

"Who says they can't?" he asked.

"So you believe dead people can talk?" Waiting for him to make fun of me, sarcasm dripped off my words.

"Do you believe I can hear your thoughts?" He had me on that one. He could hear my thoughts and he heard Peter's voice in my head. Weird shit was happening that I didn't particularly care for.

"That's why I want you to work for me full-time."

Even though I was listening, my eyes had closed and I wasn't sure if I had heard him correctly. "What?" I asked, distracted by my freaky life.

"I want to hire you full-time."

"Why?" I asked.

"I think you can help me get to the truth. I think Peter may be guiding you and if I get you in front of the right people, Peter just may reveal the key to his murder." Pai's fingers tapped away on his laptop.

Curiosity got the better of me. I opened my eyes and sat up to get a better view of the man who thought a surf instructor who dropped out of college her senior year could help him at anything. "Why would you think that?"

"Let's just say it was a feeling I got from Daven Raines. Peter told me Daven was a very calm and controlled guy. Misty said the same thing. Daven came to her aid when her husband had the car accident. He stood by his partner's side when money was tight from medical expenses, and when he went into rehab. By everyone's account, Daven has been the model business partner."

"So what's the problem?" This case was sounding more and more like I'd be barking up another tree without a leg to stand on.

"Everything seems to occur when Daven's not around."

"That tends to point toward his innocence, not guilt." The more I heard, the less I wanted to get involved. How many times could I look like an idiot in a week?

"That's my point. Innocent people get drawn into the middle of crap. Daven Raines makes sure he's never in the middle, but always there in the end to pick up the pieces."

"Pai…"

"Baby Doll, I hired you because my pride won't stop me from getting to the truth. Don't let yours stop you from taking on this case."

Ouch.

I leaned back and let his admonishment sink in. Pai waited in silence, until I finally asked, "This doesn't have anything to do with the fact that my dad recommended you to Peter Johnson, does it?"

"No."

"Or that my dad is trying to get me a full-time job other than teaching tourists how to surf?"

Pai smiled. "I won't deny that it came up…"

"Ha!"

Pai raised his hand to shut me up. "But that's not the reason why I want you working for me, and I think you know it."

I capitulated. "Okay, fine, but, I still don't completely understand. The only job I've done for you, I totally screwed up and I have zero experience in any kind of security work."

"That's a matter of opinion. Did you rescue Joe and find out why James was missing on the job?"

"I don't think 'rescue' is the right word to define what I did, and I don't know what really happened to either one of them. I thought James had been decapitated."

"The man fell for the oldest trick in the book. A female decoy showing a little cleavage. Well, more than a little, but he left his post to get some action. Chances are he did it more than once. You said Windy was walking as if she knew where she was going and who she was meeting. Right?"

I replayed the scene in my mind. Windy changing clothes in her car, then approaching a potential john in the street. When that didn't pan out, she headed straight for the guard shack. It was as if she'd been-there-done-that.

However, the guard didn't act that way. He had checked her out with his flashlight, sure, but he wasn't grinning from ear to ear. His actions were typical of a guard approaching a trespasser. When she arrived, his behavior was by the book.

"Who was the guy in the car?" Pai asked without missing a step on his laptop.

"I don't know, just some john that decided not to buy."

"Or he was the one directing Windy to set the trap."

Pai was right. Windy's sole purpose had been to get the guard away from the shack. She'd known exactly what was going to happen when she shook her boobs for the guard. He didn't.

"The guard wasn't expecting Windy. He approached her as he would anyone else who walked up to the condo at that time of night. Until he saw her boobs. That's when his behavior changed." Just like Windy planned. She had set a trap and the guard had been snared. The knowledge resonated deep within the marrow of my bones. Windy was guilty. I just didn't know what she was guilty of.

"And that's exactly my point with Daven Raines. He's guilty. I just don't know what or how much he's responsible for, but sometimes, you have to listen to what your body is telling you."

I no longer found Pai's ability to read my thoughts scary or embarrassing. It actually helped our level of communication tremendously. (At least while we thought about the case.)

"Why would she try to lure the guard away?" I asked while my mind focused on her method.

"I don't know."

Looking at Pai, I expected him to smile, at the direction of my thoughts. Instead, he sat there working on his computer like a distracted husband in front of the TV. He'd missed my mental comment to him, which made the situation even funnier.

I started giggling. My giggle turned into a burst of suppressed laughter. Pai looked up at me quizzically with the corners of his mouth twitching with the infection of my laughter.

"What's so funny?"

"Windy's…" I tried to tell him, I really did, but I couldn't. The laughter took over my body, shaking my shoulders, tightening my stomach muscles, tears forming in my eyes. Pai was looking at me, laughing from the pure contagiousness of my uncontrolled amusement.

He knew about Windy's boobs, and he knew about her burying the guard's head in her chest, but he didn't know Windy's last name.

In between my fits of laughing and my attempts to control the spasms of hilarity, I filled him in on the joke.

"Windy's...last name... is Trapp. She set a...*booby trap*." I choked on the punch line.

I heard Pai's laughter roar as my body cramped from my own. His happy eyes were spilling tears faster than my own. Noise was no longer coming out of my mouth. I snorted trying to catch my breath, possibly the most unfeminine noise you've ever heard. Pai leaned back in his chair, losing control completely. I gasped for air, and he toppled over backwards.

Streams of tears running down my face, I jumped out of the Jacuzzi and ran to him. Lying flat on his back, laptop on his chest, and his legs still straddling the sides of the chair, Pai was still laughing and crying when I got there to ask him if he was okay between my own giggles.

Suddenly, he was more than okay. His laughter subsided and his smile disappeared. His eyes turned dark and he set the computer aside. He hopped to his feet with the ease of a child, not a man over six and a half feet tall. He was standing so close to me I couldn't breathe, again. His eyes devoured me. Every naked inch of me.

Oh, God. I should run. Grab a cushion. Something. I didn't.

"Malia…" His voice was husky. I liked it when he said my name that way. Especially when he rubbed my wet arms from the shoulder down to my elbows. "You're cold."

I saw his telltale lingering glance at my chest. Yeah, I knew how my body was reacting to our proximity and why he thought I was cold, but I was about as far from cold as a woman gets. Pai groaned that deep animal noise he'd made earlier and released me long enough to pull his shirt off and slip it over my head. Then he turned toward the house.

"You're killing me, Baby Doll. Go to bed, it's late."

More like it was early — the sun just about to capture the entire sky. I looked over my shoulder to see if he was going to join me.

"You have an appointment in a couple hours and I need to go check on James."

"When are you going to sleep?" I knew it sounded like an invitation, but I didn't care. His blue eyes were as dark as the night sky.

"Neither one of us will get any sleep if I stay here. I think it's safer for you, if I go to the hospital. Our time will come."

He said it with such certainty, he amazed me. I swayed from one man to the other depending on whom I was with. I didn't have a clue which one was right for me. So far, each one had been exactly what I needed at the moment in time I needed them most. At what point would that change? When would I be able to decide which cousin was the man for me? Or was I doomed with indecisiveness until they both told me to take a hike?

He prodded me toward the house, but the pressure of his hand on my ass was completely unexpected.

I actually yipped with surprise. Shocked that he would step over the line of knighthood, I glanced back to see him smiling from ear to ear with that sexy, lopsided grin.

"I needed that. Now run away and sleep, my Hawaiian Princess."

"You lied to me, Pai."

He looked at me, trying to figure out what I was talking about.

I smiled, pleased that somehow I'd hidden something from the man who'd seen every last inch of me. "You said you wouldn't look."

As I ran upstairs like an inexperienced teenager, unsure of my own desires, I heard his soft laughter. "*A hui ho*, Baby Doll."

Until we meet again.

CHAPTER TWENTY-ONE

Music blared somewhere, ruining the deep, mindless sleep encompassing me. I didn't want to wake up. Soft, smooth cotton sheets caressed my skin, while the mattress hugged my body like a feather pillow. It was heaven and my enemy was ruining it.

I stumbled out of bed to grab my cell phone, surprisingly more refreshed than I would have expected after five hours of sleep and, finally realized the heaven I'd experienced wasn't my own bed. I was in Pai's room. In his shirt, and nothing else. I followed the sound of Green Day and located my phone near the door on the floor with my dirty clothes. I should have recognized it wasn't my bed sooner. My own sofa bed was about as far from heaven as hell.

"Hello?" I answered with what I like to think of as my sexy, deep throat morning voice.

"Good morning, Baby Doll."

"Pai?" My voice croaked, ruining any arousing image he might have of me lying in his bed, which I wasn't.

"Does anyone else call you Baby Doll?"

"No. Do you call other women Baby Doll?"

"No. You're the only one."

"Why do you call me that?" I could almost hear him thinking about it as I rubbed the sleep from my eyes.

"When I first saw you running along the road, I had this urge to hold you tight and never let go. Kind of like a little girl with that one favorite doll, she cherishes. It just came out of my mouth without me even thinking about it."

"Oh." Clearly, the man knew how to make a woman feel special. I'd had a favorite doll as a child. I'd even moved her to my apartment, without my brothers' knowing it. (I left her in the box in my closet, but she was there just the same.)

"I've made an appointment for this evening with Misty Johnson."

"But you've already talked to her."

"I didn't know Peter was inside your head at the time. I think there's something we can learn by putting the two of them back together."

I didn't tell Pai that I really didn't *want* Peter to come back in my head. "What time is it now?"

"Eleven o'clock."

"Have you slept yet?"

"Not yet."

I could also somehow tell he was so tired that he was driving on autopilot, and I began to worry about him. At the same time, I felt guilty for my hours of slumber.

"I'm fine, Baby Doll."

"Yes, you are definitely *Fine* with a capital F, but you need to go to bed." And as soon as I said it, I knew what *he* was thinking. "Alone."

He chuckled as I read the dirty thoughts coming through the airwaves of the phone.

"See, you're beginning to listen."

"I think anyone would have read that thought." Then I got to the hard question. The one I needed to ask but didn't want to ask.

"No, I don't have any women's clothing for you to wear, but I called Lani and asked if you could borrow some of hers."

"You called Lani!"

"Would you rather I call your brother?" Pai sounded amused.

I was mortified.

"I told her about your car and the guard. She understood immediately."

Hua. I'd never be able to face her.

Pai made a strangled noise. "It's going to be difficult listening to you thinking about balls all the time."

"I wasn't thinking about balls." I insisted, half-heartedly.

"Un-huh." He wasn't convinced.

Neither was I.

"There's an extra set of keys in the kitchen drawer near the phone to Lani's place."

I opened the drawer and pulled out the keys. "Got 'em."

"I'll be home in about a half hour," Pai stated.

Be careful and *mahalo*, Pai."

I hung up and ran to take a two-minute shower. Once again, I couldn't risk being caught by a hunky man.

Some women would kill for my problems.

As I stepped out of the shower stall, a male voice echoed through the room. At first, I froze in excited fear. (Pai can do that to me.) Then I realized it was my brother's voice on the answering machine. In not so polite words, John told Lani he knew that she'd worked with Pai in the past, and if she knew where he was, he needed to get his butt down to HQ for his statement. Now.

I chose to ignore the message. The phone line was the same for the main house and the in-laws quarters and the call wasn't for me. Pai would listen when he got home and make the necessary arrangements. I made the bed, grabbed my belongings, and then took the keys to Lani's place out of the kitchen drawer. Wrapped only in a towel, I locked Pai's door and ran for the main house. Once inside, I called my brother Kionni from my cell phone.

"*Aloha*, Malia. What do you need now?"

"What do you mean, 'What do I need'?" It irritated me he knew I needed his help, just like it pissed me off that he always had his shit together.

"You always need something. That's the only reason you call."

"Actually, I called to ask how... you and your girlfriend were doing." I struggled to remember her name while I pulled on a pair of capris, jumping around in circles as my foot got tangled in the pant leg. I fell against the doorjamb with a grunt.

"I don't have a girlfriend. I haven't had a girlfriend in several months. Are you fighting with your clothes again?"

Pai wasn't the only man in my life that could read me like an open book. "Funny." I decided to stop playing games and go for it. "Can I trouble you for a ride?"

"What happened to your car?"

It pained me even to talk about it. "A drunk driver hit it last night and totaled it."

"You okay?" His obvious concern softened our sibling rivalry.

"Yeah, I wasn't in it." I pulled on a bright green halter-top with pink lace around the neckline that didn't require a bra and looked at myself in the mirror. Not bad considering Lani is built like Linda Hamilton in *Terminator 2*, and I'm more like stick-woman with muscles.

"I've got an appointment at a site at eleven-thirty. I can pick you up after that."

I stopped looking at how Lani's pants fit my ass. If he didn't pick me up now, I'd be here when Pai came home. Not an option.

"I really need to get to work. I've got lessons starting at noon. Can you pick me up and then I'll drop you off at the site and head for home."

"You're funny, sis. You're not driving my truck the day after you wreck your car."

"I didn't wreck it. It was parked." I was starting to remember why the little twerp got on my nerves.

"You still got your motorcycle license?" he asked.

"Yeah, but it's at Mom and Dad's, and I sold my bike when I bought my car."

I really liked my bike but on the Garden Isle, where we get more rainfall than any other place on earth, it's nice to have a roof over your head when you need it. My helmet saved my hair, but not my clothes. Since I couldn't afford to have a bike and a car, I did the next best thing and bought a convertible.

"I just got a new bike. I'll let you ride it."

His generosity caught me off guard and made me suspicious. "You're going to let me ride your new bike, but you won't let me drive your truck?"

"The bike didn't cost as much as the truck and it's a small one that fits in the bed. I'm at Mom and Dad's now. I'll grab your license and be at your apartment in about twenty minutes with it."

He started to hang up without saying good-bye, which is another one of my pet peeves he indulges in. "Wait! Kionni!" I heard him laughing, he knew his behavior irritated me and he loved to push my buttons.

"Yeah, sis."

"I need a helmet and I'm at Lani's place."

"Okay, I'll be there in fifteen minutes. Open the gate for me."

I ran my fingers through my hair and looked in the mirror. My complexion is dark enough I can go without makeup and my hair is straight enough not to worry about the style, but with the green top and tan capris, I could seriously blend into the island backdrop. I grabbed a ponytail holder, pulled my hair back off my face and then took a washcloth to my teeth. My goose egg had improved — it was now the size of a robin's egg, in color and diameter. I couldn't ask for more than that.

Fifteen minutes on the dot, Kionni honked his horn at the gate I hadn't opened yet. I looked out the bedroom window and saw his ruby red truck sparkling like a gemstone. He treated that truck like a baby, and it glowed on the other side of the iron bars.

I ran down the steps, pressed the remote entry at the front door, and went out on the porch. Kionni pulled up in front of the house and I got a glimpse of his 'bike' in the bed of his truck. It was orange, and that was just the beginning.

The driver's side door slammed shut shortly after the engine turned off and Kionni walked around toward the backside of the truck. Today he was wearing a pair of tan slacks and a white button down shirt. His smart-ass face wore a giant shit-eating grin, one that made the sibling in me want to tell him where he could stick that 'bike,' but I needed the ride.

"What the hell is that?" I asked.

"You don't like my bike?" Kionni feigned innocence.

"That's not a bike."

"It's street legal," he responded and opened the tailgate.

Kionni unstrapped the orange monster in the bed. Okay, it was a mini monster, but it was definitely a monster.

"You expect me to believe you bought that?"

"I didn't say that. I said, 'I just *got* a new bike.' I won it." Kionni unloaded a bright orange scooter from the back of his truck with very little effort.

"That's not a bike. That's a scooter."

"Yeah, but it's transportation and you need it."

"You could give me a ride." I looked at him, trying to hide my anger and plead for a ride in his truck at the same time.

"We don't have time to go by your apartment before I go to the site. What are you up to?"

"I'm working a case."

He laughed. "You're not a PI. Is Lani crazy?"

I kept my mouth shut. He didn't need to know the case didn't involve Lani. The less he knew the better.

"Maybe you'll earn enough money to pay your bills." Finally, Kionni turned to open the passenger door of the truck, and I stuck my tongue out at his back. But quickly pulled it back in my mouth when he turned around. At first, I thought he had a basketball in his hands, which made me take a closer look.

This had to be some kind of cruel joke. It was actually a motorcycle helmet that looked like an orange.

"You have got to be kidding."

His smile belonged in a toothpaste commercial. I looked back at the scooter. The logo of an orange soda product stood out obnoxiously in bright blue letters on the side panel. I couldn't help it, I groaned.

"Hey, look at it this way, it's better than a hotdog. Can you imagine wearing a wiener on your head? Now, guys will just ask to see the melons to go with the orange."

I glared at him, not trusting my mouth to behave if I opened it.

"And, better you than me," he said as he put the helmet on my head, still grinning that obnoxiously white smile that made me want to smack off his face. Instead, I took my frustration out on his hand as he tried to snap the chinstrap in place. I swatted it like a nun whacking a student's hand with a ruler. Not that I'd ever been whacked by a nun, but the visual was nice.

Kionni laughed, handed me my motorcycle license and turned toward his truck.

"As soon as I get a rental car, you can have it back." I told his retreating back.

"Nah, that's okay. You've just become a tax deduction for me. You're welcome, sis."

I knew I had to thank him, but it was pretty damn hard to say something nice when he was laughing at me and making me look like an idiot. He probably tweeted about this before he got here so all our friends would get pictures of me riding it in various places across the island. Normally I love technology, but right now, I had a feeling that social media would make me a laughing stock.

"Thank you, Kionni," I mumbled.

"What? I'm sorry I didn't hear you." I knew he had; he just wanted to make sure I knew that he knew he had saved my butt once more.

"I said THANK YOU."

"Anytime, sis. By the way, under the seat is the charging cord. It will only go for two to three hours before it needs charged again. You've got a full charge now. *A hoi hou.*"

"*A hoi hou aku.*" Goodbye and good riddance is what I wanted to say.

My brother pulled out of the gate as Pai was coming in. I saw Kionni nod in Pai's direction and take a second look at the incredibly hot man driving toward me. He blatantly spied in his rear view mirror and I waved him on, not wanting my little brother to see my interaction with Pai. Or for him to hear Pai call me Baby Doll. Word would get back to my parents, and within moments, they'd be calling a wedding planner.

As far as I was concerned, my family and friends would find out about my wedding after it happened, and not before.

Once Kionni was gone, I straddled the scooter and started it up. Pai pulled up next to me and gave me that lopsided grin of his.

"Baby Doll, can I see the melons that go with that orange?"

"I used to think you were funny, Pai." I

said in utter amazement over his telepathic gift.

He laughed at my attempt to be mad, which was impossible, and I grinned back at him. One day, I might look back and think the vision of me on this mini-monster was funny. Like when I was a hundred years old.

"My orchard princess. Baby Doll, I will dream of all the delectable fruits you can offer me."

"Good night, Pai, get some sleep."

"*A hoi hou, Ki`i pēpē.*"

I winked at his Hawaiian version of Baby Doll, unsure which one I liked best. I headed down the drive on my new orange burst of power, feeling as stupid as I looked.

Normally when I drive, I have a tendency to people watch. I've always loved checking out the tourists and their goofy outfits. Now, I looked like one of them. I drove straight to my apartment with blinders on.

As I pulled into the lot, I saw my brother John waiting for me, a blank expression on his face. At first, I didn't think he recognized me. Then I figured he must have pity for my plight that kept him from laughing. I took the helmet off, waiting for a burst of laughter or a choked back gurgle, but his face remained blank. If he wasn't going to bring it up, neither was I.

"Knock, knock."

"What?" What the hell was he talking about?

"Knock, knock," he repeated as the light bulb went on in my head.

"Very funny, Johnny baby." I thought Windy's nickname might distract him, but was disappointed when he continued with his poor attempt at humor.

"Knock, knock," he repeated with the deadpan expression of a hardened cop. I glared but gave in since he wasn't going to stop until I played along.

"Who's there?"

"Banana."

I rolled my eyes. "Banana who?"

"Knock, knock."

"Enough already, John." He continued to look at me, his eyebrows raised, waiting for me to respond. "Alright! Who's there?"

"Banana."

"Banana who?" I walked toward my apartment, forcing him to follow me if he wanted to continue his juvenile antics.

"Knock, knock."

I reached for the key above the door and unlocked it before asking, "Who's there?"

"Orange."

"Orange who?" Finally, he reached the punchline I knew was coming.

"Orange you glad you aren't a banana? A banana helmet would drive all the monkeys crazy." He laughed at his poor attempt at being a comedian.

"That's pathetic. You need some sleep if you think that's funny."

John plopped down on my sofa bed as if he owned the place, and missed my snarl. I went to the fridge, poured the two of us a glass of iced tea, and then plopped down on the couch next to him. I guess I owed him a little kindness after getting him out of bed for nothing last night. Especially since he looked like he hadn't been home yet.

"What's with the board?" John nodded toward my dry erase board.

Crap, I forgot about that. "Nothing." I took a drink of tea.

"Malia, this isn't a game. It's time to let me do my job, and you go back to your surfing lessons."

I bit my lip. He was tired. And he was definitely NOT telling me I was just a dumb surfer.

John's humor ran out right after mine. "Where's Mr. Lincoln?"

"Uh…who?" I asked a little taken back.

"Alapai Lincoln. I've been to his office, I've called his cell and office number. I even called Lani's after Dad told me they knew each other. He doesn't seem to have a home address except for on the Big Island, and I have no idea where he's at."

"Oh, well, why would you think I knew where he was?"

"Because, this morning, you left the scene of a wild goose chase with the man who was supposed to bring you home." His voice tightened with displeasure.

Evading his question, I asked my own. "Why are you looking for Pai? You've acted like this case was an accident from the beginning, so what's the point of taking his statement?"

"Because Peter Johnson *was* murdered. Someone bashed in his skull and then dumped him in the ocean. The toxicology report came back clean and the ME ruled he was dead before he hit the water."

"But what about his partner, Daven Raines? He was there, too." I insisted.

John's brow lowered. He wasn't pleased I knew as much as I did about his case. Too bad. I stared back at him. He shouldn't have asked me to get involved.

He closed his eyes. I'm pretty sure he was seeking the support of a Tiki god. When he opened them he gave me more information than I thought possible. "Daven Raines had a date the night Mr. Johnson disappeared. She picked him up at the *Garden of the Gods* and left Mr. Lincoln with the victim."

"That's impossible." I argued. "Have you talked to her? Did she identify Pai?"

John nodded, forgetting all the competition between us. "I took her statement this morning."

Unease spread through my gut. I wasn't ready to believe what John was trying to tell me. "But—"

"Windy identified him, Malia."

"Windy?" I jumped off my couch, walked the distance of the room to the door, and turned around to face off with my brother. If we were any closer I might strangle him. "Windy! You believe that skank?"

John stood up and closed the distance between us, his face washed with sympathy. "I'm

245

sorry. I know you like this guy, but I have two witnesses who have given statements to the fact that Alapai Lincoln was the last person to see Peter Johnson alive."

He put a tender hand on my shoulder, but I shrugged it off and opened my door.

"Where can I find him, Mal?" John asked.

I thought of Pai lying in bed, sound asleep, and I did the unspeakable. "I have no idea," I lied.

CHAPTER TWENTY-TWO

I left Pai about twenty messages before I went to work. The guy must sleep like the dead, but I knew I couldn't go back to Lani's to warn him. Especially when I saw John's car sitting down the street from my apartment. So I went to work and watched my brother drive past the parking lot when we arrived. I wanted to flip him off, but he's *ohana* and he was just trying to do his job.

It was a perfect day for surfing — if you were a five year old, or a *haole* who'd never seen the ocean until yesterday — the swells were about twenty-four inches. The fronds of tall palms swayed in the breeze, and I spotted a lone Hawaiian monk seal playing along the lava rocks on the sandbar. At seventy-five degrees, the skies were clear with a few puffy white clouds, and Poipu Beach wasn't, for a change, jammed to the brim with tourists.

Just surf instructors training to be sharks by stealing my customers. I literally watched two students saunter off with the competition as I walked up to the metal shed with the sun-bleached sign, *Aaron's Surf Zone painted on the front*. The move was classic – offer the same price, throw in a free t-shirt, and my big fish was hooked. Grumbling I unlocked the shed and pulled out several old boards and stacked them against the wall.

When I was seventeen, we were 'the' company to go to. Today our owner, Rob Aaron, didn't care that we were being destroyed by fancy tents with loudspeakers and rockin' boards. Not to mention good-looking instructors who didn't mind being island fantasies. Rob didn't care; he was living the dream in a tent on the beach. He also swore he had a big deal in the works to get us a new stand at a great spot. (Did I tell you Rob's head was in the clouds?)

Most of our instructors had moved on to greener pastures, like the stand selling "I Survived the Big Waves at Poipu Beach" t-shirts. In return for my loyalty to my first job ever, I was stuck teaching with Rob. We worked together mostly, though his brother had come in from Oahu to help out for the last six weeks, and taught on our days off. I'd never met him, but Dave and Rob were twins, so it wasn't like I was missing anything.

This was the price of monogamy — a partner in his fifties going on thirty, a beer gut with a distorted lizard crawling across it and long stringy hair — on his back. His head was shaved bald. I'd hinted (more like told him flat out) that he should let his hair grow out and shave his back.

He thought I was funny.

It was the only serious conversation we ever had. (I tried to sneak it in every week.)

"I don't need lame land instructions, I dominate mountains. Let's hit the waves, Hot Cheeks." Our star pupil interrupted Rob's instruction about the importance of a properly performed belly flop.

This was the part of the job I hated. The 'professionals' who knew everything about nothing. Before I could put the know-it-all-snow-boarder from Utah in his place, Rob piped in.

"No problem, brah. Malia will take you out."

I looked at Rob. He winked.

I smiled. He hadn't let me teach a *real* lesson in years. I almost felt sorry for the tanned-face dude with the ghostly white body.

"Yeah, Malia," he fist bumped his buddy, "I'm ready for some *private* lessons."

Nope. I felt no remorse whatsoever. I let my eyes travel the length of him. He had fairly large feet for a guy under six feet, which could help or hinder him, depending on his balance. His droopy board shorts had seen better days, but at least they covered his pasty knees. His chest must have been waxed a month ago, as stubble covered every inch. The *ewww* factor was off the charts with this dude;

his chest somehow managed to glow *through* the stubble as well. He had extra full lips that might be acceptable on a woman, but on a guy it was just plain creepy. His eyes were lost behind aviator sunglasses and shaggy blond hair.

"You should leave you sunglasses here," I advised.

"Nah, I never go without them."

I shrugged. He would in five minutes. "Grab your board and carry it on top of your head." I showed him how to balance the board.

"That's for girls." He put his board under his arm.

I shrugged again, and headed for the beach.

"Hey! Watch it, buddy."

Obviously, my pro didn't carry his own snow skis either. I didn't look back; I knew what happened. Mr. Pro had smacked someone with his board. I smiled. This was going to be the highlight of my day.

Two hours later, my shift was over. Normally, I hated to see it end, but today I counted my blessings. Mr. Pro smartass snowboarder ended up dry-heaving salt water on the beach without his sunglasses, (we did manage to find them — broken), while his buddy managed to hook up with a cute college chick on spring break during the 'lame land instructions.' Both of them got up several times, riding their waves into the beach to follow them up with flirtatious high fives. Mr. Pro wiped the coral reef with his shoulder and had large raw bloody patch to prove it. (He also didn't get the phone number he'd been vying for.)

Belly flops are so important, but you learn all about those while you listen to the instructor, on land.

A forty-ish woman came out to scratch something off her bucket list, and turned out to be one hell of a surfer. (Remember, we were on baby waves.) A family of five tried it and had a great time laughing, falling, and catching maybe half their waves. They enjoyed the whole experience — together. That's what it's all about.

I tried Pai's number again, but got voicemail. Frustrated, I stomped my way down the path to the Mauna Koa Resort, a high end hotel at the western edge of Poipu, covering 7,000 acres. The hotel had rented Rob a spot on their land since the late eighties. The luxury resort had two hundred units spanning across the property, four pools and a two-acre lazy river, and three restaurants. Not to mention numerous bars that I've visited a few times. With Rob's rental space, we were allowed to change in the restrooms off the luxurious open air lobby. We were also allowed to pitch our classes twice a week to their clientele, who lounged and chatted in the plush seating area. Lately, however, I got the impression that Rob's relationship with the hotel was sliding downhill, he'd canceled three of our last six sales pitch sessions — and they were our major source of customers.

I changed into Lani's borrowed clothes and hit the road with my backpack and orange helmet. Even the tourist staring at me on the mini-monster didn't faze me as I rode past Spouting Horn, remembering the times my brother had threatened to throw me into *Puhi's* dangerous lava tube. The rock formation brought in droves of tourists, who loved watching the water spray fifty feet in the air. For the locals, it was wrapped in tales of danger and human triumph over a giant lizard threatening anyone who dared swim or fish in the area. (And brotherly threats to scare the crap out of their younger siblings.)

What did bother me was the marked patrol unit that followed me from the lot at Mauna Koa through the old town streets of Koloa, right up until the very moment I turned toward my apartment. Then it continued on toward KaPa'a and I pulled into my spot, not knowing how I was going to get to Pai without leading my brother straight to him.

The surprise waiting for me in the parking lot brought back all the confused emotions I'd been able to forget about for a few short hours. Despite knowing he was a player of the worst kind, my heart fluttered when I saw Makaio standing with his back to me at my front door. His short, cropped hair displayed an attractive head. I know, right? How can the back of a man's head be attractive? (I work for a bald, middle-aged man. Heads can be sexy — or not.) Makaio's shoulders bunched with muscle under his grey t-shirt and stood the breadth of my doorway. His back V'd into a tight waist with a rounded ass my hands were dying to latch onto.

He heard my approach, turned and grinned. Not the full-blown smile his cousin would have given me; rather, the sexy, smart smirk I'd already come to adore. I waved and parked the scooter in my spot while he took the steps down two at a time to stand next to me as I dismounted. When I turned around, he was in my space, making it hard to breathe. Or think.

His eyes traveled from my chest, draped in a green halter with pink lace that hugged my curves and gaped in all the right places, to my wrinkled capris. Then he took my helmet off for me and my hair fell to my shoulders.

"Do you have any melons to go with that orange?"

The dumb look on my face along with the slight amount of drool dried up instantaneously. I glared at him, lips pursed, hand on hip. I was pretty sure he'd mistake the twinkle in my eyes and the increased rise and fall of my chest for anger. I didn't need him to know it was from his proximity.

"I could kill Kionni," I confessed.

He frowned. "Who's Kionni?"

"My brother. He gave me this stupid scooter and this ridiculous helmet. Then he proceeded to tell me all the guys would ask that same, stupid question. And so far, you're the second man to ask. Why did you ask me that stupid question?"

"You have a green top with pink lace that clings rather nicely to your...your body."

I looked down at my chest from a new perspective.

"You had another piece of fruit on your head." Makaio held up the orange helmet.

I needed to change. Driving around like an orange was one thing, combining it with a watermelon top was just asking for trouble, or stupid comments.

"So tell me, who's the other guy asking about your melons?"

I rolled my eyes and walked around him toward my apartment. I was not going to get in the middle of Makaio and Pai anymore than I already was.

"I brought your stuff from your car, but before you get your hopes up, you need to know Pearl's truck leaked oil all over everything."

I stopped and looked at the bag he held out for my inspection. My anger returned hotter than ever. I was pretty sure he could see smoke coming out of my ears. It had to go somewhere. If it stayed inside, my head would have already exploded. I clenched my teeth and snatched the bag out of his hand.

I should have thanked him. My mind, however, was preoccupied with hate for my car's murderer.

"That bitch is going to pay for this," I ground out and stomped up the stairs.

Makaio's phone rang behind me.

"Natua," he answered.

I looked back and found him staring at my ass.

"Yeah, what do you need, John?"

I listened with unabashed interest to his conversation with my brother, anger dripping off me in chunks.

"The cause of death was blunt force trauma?" He listened to my brother for a moment, his eyes still admiring my backside even though I'd turned halfway around. "Okay, so why are you calling me?" Makaio's eyes left my body and traveled across the parking lot to the back entrance of the ice cream shop across the street.

Part of me hated losing all that attention, the practical part understood that cause of death and sexual heat didn't mix. But still...

Makaio's teeth clenched together. "Pai."

Oh, crap. I bit my lip and waited for the hammer to fall. His gaze turned back to me, accusingly.

"Great. My cousin was the last person to see him alive. What do you want me to do about it?"

He was watching me, waiting for my reaction. Unfortunately, I didn't catch on quick enough. My lack of reaction told him I knew Pai was the last one to see Peter Johnson alive.

Makaio's eyes narrowed. A vein on his forehead pulsated.

Hua. I turned and opened my apartment.

"I'll see what I can do." He hung up his phone and followed me inside.

I put the bag of my oily belongings on the counter and grabbed a bottle of dishwashing soap and rubber gloves from under the sink, hoping to salvage what I could — credit cards, driver's license, a pair of earrings.

Makaio took a deep breath behind me. "What are you doing with this stuff on your board?"

I glanced backward and saw him staring at my dry-erase board that hadn't been updated. "Nothing." Technically, it wasn't a lie.

Makaio studied it without saying a word.

"What did John want?" Even though I wasn't afraid of Makaio, the silence filled with sounds of him breathing directly behind me, put my nerves on edge.

"Peter Johnson was murdered after all. It looks like Pai was the last person to see him alive and John wants him in his office...now."

"Pai was awake all night. His phone is turned off, because he needs some rest. He'll talk to John this evening when I wake him up for our appointment." I turned on the water and looked in the bag containing my sludgy purse, the files, the binoculars and my purse. *Ewww*.

"What appointment?"

"We're supposed to meet with...a witness." I filled the sink with soapy water.

Makaio grabbed my arm and turned me around. "This is a murder investigation, Malia. It doesn't wait for other people's schedules. Time is important and I need to get Pai to your brother. Now. He can sleep later."

"But—"

"Did John ask you if you knew where Pai was?" It sounded like an accusation.

I averted my eyes, looked at the sink filling with water. "Pai's innocent. You know it and I know it. You have to help him. You owe him that much."

"I *owe* him? He's this close," his fingers appeared in front of my face with less than an inch of distance between his thumb and index finger, "to being arrested for murder." Makaio no longer had the patience for twenty questions, he demanded. "Where is he?"

I bit my lip, which was turning into hamburger. "You're not going to hurt him, are you?"

Makaio shook his head, but I couldn't tell what he was thinking. His expression was beyond my ability to understand. Which didn't say much for our relationship or my ability to hear his thoughts. I paused and stared at him, trying to read his thoughts before I gave him the address. He had that same stoic gaze my father and brother mastered. They must teach Deadpan 101 at the police academy.

"Promise me, you won't hurt him."

"Malia…" Makaio sighed and rubbed his hand against his scalp, his short hair looked untouched.

I knew I was back in the middle where I didn't belong, but I refused to let violence break out between the two of them. "Promise me."

He grunted the words, "I promise."

I buckled and gave the address.

Makaio typed the address in his phone. "Is there a gate?" He looked like he hoped I didn't know.

I gave him the code. "13-6-22-25. He probably won't answer the door, he hasn't been sleeping very long."

KYM ROBERTS

His interrogation didn't stop. "Do you have a key?"

I shook my head.

He figured out what to ask next. "Is there a key somewhere?"

I gave in. "On the back patio under a rock with the inscription 'Pelé Rocks' engraved on it." I really needed to study up on the whole investigative technique thing. I always seemed to be giving more answers than I receive.

I turned off the water. "Do you want me to come with you?" I asked.

"No." Makaio turned and headed toward the door. "If Pai can't make your appointment, I'll go with you."

"Pai's innocent. It won't take long for John to recognize that. Tell Pai to call me when he's done and I'll let...our witness know we've been delayed."

Makaio walked out the door without another word. I immediately picked up my phone and called his cousin. My loyalty...divided.

CHAPTER
TWENTY-THREE

Waiting around for John to figure out Pai was innocent didn't really sit well with me. I needed to do something, and it was time to conduct an interview — all by myself — with Mutt. I hadn't forgotten about him witnessing the payment between Pai and Daven Raines. He thought it was a drug deal at *The Garden of the Gods*, which was understandable considering the time and location. But I also knew Pai was holding something back. Something he thought was important.

It was time to find out what that was, before it was too late. I also needed to find out how Mutt knew Peter Johnson's identity before anyone else.

I spent the better part of the afternoon calling everyone I knew in an attempt to locate Mutt.

Nothing. It was just as I suspected, no one knew his real name.

I even tried Lena, an ex-girlfriend of Kionni's who worked in the records department at KPD. Luckily for me, her broken heart didn't last long since she met her current boyfriend the same day of the breakup. That relationship was now on its second year of monogamous bliss, and Lena was actually grateful to Kionni. Go figure.

Too bad her computer checks of the moniker 'Mutt' went nowhere. She got absolutely zilch. Without a name, I couldn't even google him. The only place I'd be able to find Mutt was at the Lawa'i Bay, the beach where I lost my top.

Hua.

I glanced at my wall clock and realized I didn't have enough time to get to Poipu before our interview with Misty Johnson. And I hadn't heard from Pai, which meant my brother still had him in police custody. I would have to conduct the interview of Peter Johnson's widow by myself. Solo.

Desperate to look, and act more like an investigator and less like a beach bum, I ransacked my closet for something professional. As a surf instructor, my required dress-for-success attire was a wet suit. I had two of those but not much else. I emptied at least half of my clothes on my sofa bed, and finally came up with a black strappy jumpsuit. To make it look less club-ish and more I'm-a-grown-up-with-a-career, I added a sweater with multiple shades of blue. (My mom and dad had given it to me for Christmas. At the time I smiled and thanked them, internally swearing that I'd never be caught dead wearing it — hopefully, that was true.) The outfit was completed with a pair of silver earrings and some sensible flats that looked more businesslike than the five-inch hooker stilettos I normally wore with the jumpsuit. I grabbed a clip for my hair and took one last look in the mirror.

I looked exactly like what I was — a twenty-year-old trying to look forty, who hadn't slept or eaten properly in a week. Ugh.

I quickly snarfed down my dinner — a spam sandwich and a taro turnover — then grabbed my purse, cringed when I picked up the bright orange helmet and headed out the door.

The night sky was clear. Diamond shaped stars sparkled in a deep black backdrop — it was heavenly. Purse strapped over my shoulder, I rode the scooter to Ms. Johnson's condo at Kukuiula Bay along the southern shore, where high-end condos stretched along the beach. It was also half an island away from where her husband had stayed with Daven Raines.

I parked the scooter and realized I actually found the ride on my little orange monster fairly enjoyable. Go figure. I scoped out the property; each unit appeared to have a variety of condos of different sizes. Pulling my hair into the clip I'd stashed in my purse, I walked to where I thought number 702 would be located. My first guess was wrong; 802 was marked on the side of the building.

Danger! Peter yelled in my head.

My heartbeat kicked up about a thousand notches. Yes, it was his voice in my head, again. I turned to check out the opposite site of the complex, thinking I'd spot 702, and I could have sworn I saw a figure move away from the condo across the grass. I stepped into the shadows, scanned the area for further movement and found nothing. The only noise was the beat of island rap music slipping out into the night from the condo on the opposite end. And strangely, the blood in my ears pounded along with the beat of the music.

Convinced I was just freaking myself out, I made my way across the grass to 702 and rang the bell, glancing over my shoulder the entire time. I heard movement on the other side of the door, and a few seconds passed while someone obviously peered through the eyehole. Finally, a timid, "Who is it?"

"*Aloha*, I'm Malia Fern with Lincoln Security. Mrs. Johnson, could I speak with you for a moment?" Knowing I'd made the appropriate introduction, I still jumped a little when the door opened. A tall, willowy blonde, she wore a shabby chic dress of peach floral and off white lace. Her feet were bare, and her hair was tied back with a long scarf that extended down her back. Her shoulder bones jutted out with the angular look of a Hollywood starlet with an eating disorder. She had a frail beauty, marred only by the tight lines of stress and grief on her otherwise perfect features. She was at least a decade younger than her husband was. In fact, I was pretty sure she was my age.

She shook my hand timidly, giving me a small smile of welcome as she introduced herself and asked me to come in.

"Please, have a seat."

I sat down on a bamboo-framed sofa with fern print cushions. Ms. Johnson then sat in the matching chair off to my right, sheer curtains billowing from the open patio door. I could hear tinkly music playing in one of the bedrooms down the hall and imagined a baby sound asleep, oblivious to the vicious reality of his father's death. (I dearly hoped that child never learned how his father's body had been desecrated when someone (me) pulled off his arm.) Guiltily, I gazed at Ms. Johnson, waiting for some sort of sign that would give away her knowledge of my crime.

The only thing I saw was unbearable grief.

"Is Mr. Lincoln coming?"

"Ahhh… Mr. Lincoln is actually working the case with the police as we speak." (Technically, that wasn't a lie.)

Ms. Johnson nodded.

I pulled a pad and pen out of my purse and pushed forward into the interview. "Can you tell me when you last saw your husband?"

"He came to Hawai'i on the thirteenth, right after our new foreman for the construction site at *The Garden of the Gods* showed up unexpectedly at our house in New Mexico." She paused and looked at me. "Are you related to Kionni Fern?"

"Yes, he's my younger brother."

"I see." A hint of wariness crossed her face.

"I can assure you if Kionni or I had done anything wrong, our older brother, Detective Sergeant John Kumu wouldn't hesitate to put us in jail."

"Oh, I wasn't aware of the relationships between the three of you."

I didn't know what to say. I sat there smiling sympathetically (hopefully). I suppose from the outside looking in, our relationships might taint your impression of our impartiality. To a certain extent, I would protect my brothers, and they would protect me, but I'm pretty sure none of us wanted to do jail time for the other. And it wasn't like we wanted to work together. We didn't.

Ms. Johnson closed her eyes, took a deep breath and exhaled slowly. "My husband and I started this business venture about two years ago. It was my dream to return to Hawai'i. My dad was stationed here when I was a kid, but like most military families, we moved around a bunch. It was my husband's dream to build and sell condos, and then live in our own condo at the complex he built. We met Daven in Albuquerque, and they hit it off immediately. They formed a company and bought the property where *The Garden of the Gods* is located. Everything was going fine, until my husband broke his back in a hit-and-run car accident and had to have surgery. He was in so much pain all the time, but he never showed it to me. He always tried to maintain high spirits and a positive outlook toward our future here."

She smiled in remembrance of her dead husband. From the dreamy expression on her face, it sounded and looked like they had a marriage made in heaven.

Love. Peter interjected.

A lump formed in my throat. Pai was right. Peter was here with us, and he was dying to communicate with his wife.

"He became addicted to the pain medicine and it changed him. He started to lose his positive outlook and became paranoid. He began to hint about his lack of trust in Daven. I knew something was wrong, but I didn't know what." She grimaced in self-admonition. "Or maybe I just didn't want to see my husband as anything but the indestructible force I imagined him to be.

"Daven had been so supportive during Peter's surgery, his recovery and then through the rehab. He'd done everything with the business and he'd been there for me, as well. He took the baby to daycare for me and stayed with Peter while I worked. He actually did some repairs on our house. We couldn't ask for a better friend in our time of need. Then Peter started getting jealous and saying weird things like Daven was trying to take over his life. He even blamed his car accident on Daven...and said Daven was trying to get him out of the way so he could marry me.

Traitor. Peter's feeling of betrayal tore at my gut. I couldn't tell if it was from when he believed his partner was hitting on his wife, or now.

Misty continued. "The self-confident man I adored was suddenly a complete stranger. By then, I was desperate to save my marriage. I didn't think Daven was the problem, but Peter did, so I sent

Daven back here to handle the business. Things got a little better, but something was still drastically wrong with my husband."

A tear rolled down her face as she stared off in the distance, reliving the moment when her world changed.

"I'd never seen him weak. He'd always been my rock. I was the emotional one, but Peter's mood swings became unbearable. I tried to explain it away because of the pain, but our relationship was changing into something ugly." Her lip curled up as if she could still taste the sourness of their rotting relationship.

"He became unrelenting in his demands for perfection. I think his need for excellence finally defined the problem for him. Before his accident, he was an easy going man who encouraged and nurtured." She took another deep breath to calm herself and I waited for her to continue. Her grief so incredibly raw, I could almost see her heart bleeding.

I felt Peter's heart. It poured with sorrow and the need to beg for forgiveness. I wiped the tear that spilled from my eye as Misty continued.

"Then Peter told me he was addicted to his pain medicine. He said he needed help. He couldn't do it on his own. When we walked him into the rehab center the next day, I have to say, I've never seen such strength of character as Peter displayed at that moment. I was so proud of him."

Tears rolled freely down her cheeks as she described a man I hadn't known but wished I had. This family had lost more than a husband and a father. They had lost hope for the future. With the death of this one man, their world was now a shadow of what it had been. She sniffed and refocused her story.

"Peter came out of rehab stronger than ever. We still had bumps to get over and wounds to heal, but I totally believed in my husband again. I began to wonder if what Peter suspected about Daven was true."

Fresh tears brimmed her eyes. Misty paused and grabbed a tissue from the table next to her. She turned away, a new grief reaching her core. I stared at the wood grained floor, wanting to sink into its depths. (Was this the way all interviews went?)

"Excuse me a moment. I'm going to make some tea, would you like some?" Misty asked.

"That would be great." (A Long Island tea would be too much to hope for.)

Misty left the room and all I wanted to do was run. I hated dealing with other people's grief. I tend to internalize it and feel it, which is totally unprofessional, just ask my brother John.

The clink of ice in a glass announced Ms. Johnson's return with our tea. She'd washed her face clean of any sign of her tears, the slight puffiness around her eyes the only hint of her sorrow. Gone with the tears was her desire to talk about her loss. She moved onto the reason for our business as she handed me a blue tumbler filled with unsweetened tea.

"My husband came here to ensure the *Heiau* was protected, and because the funds for the condos were disappearing faster than the condos were being built. Daven appeared oblivious to the problem but said he'd look into it. Then the site became plagued with thieves and vandals. When Peter asked Daven for receipts, he always promised to send them, but never followed through. Peter explained he needed the paper work to make insurance claims, but by then, Daven couldn't find the receipts. He said he was having problems with the bookkeeping. Then Daven admitted he hadn't made police reports either. So without the receipts and the police reports, we couldn't recoup the thousands of dollars in losses we'd incurred.

"Daven wasn't the business manager we believed him to be, and my husband and I decided he should be here. Peter stayed with Daven at the condo rented by the company. They seemed to be getting along fine, and Peter was happy with the way they were working together to make things right since the construction had not progressed as planned. It was supposed to start nine months ago, but was delayed for six months."

I continued writing as Ms. Johnson took a drink of her tea.

"I understand your husband didn't want to hire more guards from Lincoln Security Associates. Can you tell me why?"

Ms. Johnson fiddled with her coaster on the table. "Peter wasn't against hiring more guards. He just wanted to wait until after they met with an accountant to have the books reviewed. Daven paid Mr. Lincoln with the last of the petty cash fund."

'Do you believe Mr. Raines was stealing funds from the business?"

"I honestly don't know. It could be he was just a lousy manager, but I have my doubts."

"Were the books ever audited?"

"No. My husband was supposed to meet with the auditor the day he disappeared. Daven was in Honolulu again, and the auditor called me."

"Why would Mr. Raines suggest that Peter may have been using again?" I asked.

"Daven is bitter. His mother had been in and out of rehab so many times that Daven finally washed his hands of her. He believes that once an addict, always an addict, just waiting for the right trigger to fall off the wagon."

"Is there anyone else that may have wanted to hurt your husband?"

Misty shook her head. It sounded like Mr. Raines had the perfect motive for killing Peter. Money.

"Did your husband accuse Mr. Raines of stealing from the business?"

"No. He never believed Daven would go that far. He didn't trust him, he believed Daven was hiding something. I was the one who pushed him to come here." Misty's eyes filled again.

Not wanting to dwell on her pain, I pushed forward for the information I needed. "What did Mr. Raines tell you?"

"Daven said Peter admitted his problem hadn't gone away. He and Daven agreed for Peter to sell our portion of the company. Daven was going to have the papers drawn up, but in the meantime, he had a meeting in Oahu he had to attend." Misty covered her mouth with the wadded tissue in her hand, the pain of her next words contorting her face. "While Peter's body floated in the ocean, I believed he had done the unspeakable and not only fallen off the wagon, but cheated on me as well. I would still believe it, if it wasn't for your brother Kionni."

"My brother?" What could he possibly add to this?

Misty blew her nose. "Daven told me your brother was the one who introduced Peter to a drug supplier on the island. When I couldn't find Peter, I called Kionni and accused him of the worst things." Her voice caught with emotion as she tried to continue. "Kionni insisted Daven was lying. He said the only other man he'd ever known to be as honorable as Peter was his dad.

"Peter was a good man who faced a horrible disease he didn't choose to start. I'm the one who failed him, not the other way around." Misty's shoulders slumped in defeat, and her eyes slipped to the floor.

Somewhere deep inside me, Peter tried to hide his pain. The sorrow that he wasn't there to hold her, protect her and tell her everything was going to be okay. He was hurting more than I thought possible after death. His broken heart tore at my chest.

I reached over and put my hand on Misty's knee. "I think you did everything you could to find your husband, which needed to include looking at the possibilities no one wants to think about. I don't think your husband would think badly of you for that."

Misty wrapped her arms around her middle, squeezing her body tightly. "Thank you, I hope you're right."

"I know I'm right." I changed the direction one last time. "How much money was taken from the company?"

"I don't know. At this point, I may never know."

"Why?"

"I've decided to walk away and let Daven handle everything."

"But wasn't this your dream?"

"I just don't think I can do it without Peter," she sobbed.

Again I struggled to keep the interview on track and myself from becoming too emotional. "When was the last time you talked to your husband?"

"Peter called me after meeting with Daven and Mr. Lincoln at the site. He wasn't happy, but it wasn't anything he was stressing over. The last thing he said to me was, 'No worries, honey. I've got you and our boy.'" Her voice hitched but she continued, "That's all that matters. I love you.'" Misty pinched the bridge of her nose. "My husband was a very strong man. He recognized his problem with painkillers and sought help. He didn't fall off the wagon as Daven suggested to the police. His toxicology report proved that."

Will always love you.

It was the longest thing Peter had ever said to me, and I knew it was important for me to pass it on. I reached for her hands and clasped them tightly in mine, knowing that Peter would somehow be able to touch her heart through my hands.

"From what my brother told me, your husband was the most honorable man he'd ever met. Peter loved you and your son beyond the barriers of this world or time." I hoped that did Peter justice, especially since I could feel his tears spilling inside me. All semblance of professionalism lost, I openly cried as I looked into Misty's grief-filled eyes and something passed between our hands. I'm not sure what it was, but I felt it pass through our finger tips and saw it on her face. The love she felt for him, and he felt for her. It wasn't like a beam of light from heaven or anything like that. It was more subtle, a glimmer in her eyes, a softening of her expression, she changed somehow and became more peaceful.

It took all three of us a few moments, and a bunch of tissues for Misty and me, to get back on track. Peter calmed, and the turmoil in my chest eased momentarily.

But the one thing I couldn't ignore, was how convenient it would be for Daven if Misty signed away the Johnson's hopes for tomorrow and their dreams died with Peter.

CHAPTER TWENTY-FOUR

Before leaving, Misty and I talked about her son. It was a topic she and Peter needed to be reminded of, one of joy and hope for the future. I actually held the baby in my arms as he slept and let Peter communicate all the love and knowledge every father wants to give his child. I don't know how it worked, I just know that their son smiled in my arms and Peter smiled in my heart. Their son brought them together with his birth and bound them for eternity.

After making Misty lock up all of her doors and windows, I left the Johnson's condo with mixed emotions. Determined to help a widow who desperately needed closure, not certain I could give it to her, and a little creeped out by the feelings of a dead man in my body.

Peter had talked to me more than ever. I sensed his spirit reaching through my own to touch his wife and son. Even now, he was there, but he was agitated and angry. Which put me more in tune with the night noises beyond the rhythmic hum of the surf breaking on the rocks. Beyond the calls of young Shearwater seabirds crying out to other fledglings on their virginal flights to the ocean. To the tiny sounds that didn't belong.

Normally, the environmentally conscious yellow lights illuminating the narrow path to the parking lot would make me feel good. It showed ecological awareness for our native birds on their initial voyage to the sea from their nests. Tonight, I found myself wishing for bright white floodlights to reduce the silent shadows threatening to engulf me in the midst of *Ti* plants. Muscles tense, I made it to the parking lot where my heart skipped a beat.

A large, imposing figure leaned against the vehicle parked next to my scooter. My helmet dangled in his hands. Part of me wanted to run. Run back to the Johnson condo. The other part wanted to kick his hulking ass for messing with my property.

My indecision held me stationary. My intuition reached out to him. Waited. Wondered. Watched. And he looked up. Giving me a glimpse of the smile spreading across his face.

"I doubt you could kick my 'hulking ass' and there's no reason to run back to Ms. Johnson. She's been through enough."

"Pai!" My heart skipped another beat for a completely different reason. I couldn't help but run to him. Glad he wasn't behind bars. Ecstatic he wasn't wearing a bright orange jumpsuit.

My arms wrapped around him, and my face smushed against his ample chest. God, he felt good. Smelled good. I held on, my fingers digging into the corded muscles of his back, and relief formed a lump the size of a turtle egg in my throat. There was the slightest change in his posture as he returned my embrace. Then he slowly pushed me away and held me at arm's length. His smile seemed a bit sad. His eyes questioned me with a veil of secrecy. I wanted to question him, but his look told me he wouldn't answer. Not yet.

"I came to help, but I didn't get here in time to go in with you."

"I could have used you. I'm not sure I asked all the right questions."

"You did great. The most important thing is that you gave them their good-bye. Without you, it wouldn't have been possible."

I smiled, a little self-confidence returning. "You can't possibly know that. We should go back in together."

"Malia, you did great. She's given all she can give. Peter has exhausted himself. I didn't stay because you needed me. I stayed…"

If Pai continued talking, I didn't hear his voice. I heard *need* racing through my mind, sexual attraction kicking into my gut. I shook my head to focus on what Pai was saying.

"What?"

"I stayed because I need you."

Thoughts of his tongue doing incredibly nasty, yet deliciously yummy things to my body invaded every space of thought I could spare. I rubbed my ear, trying to allow our conversation in.

"Pai, I told you I would help, and I meant what I said."

I couldn't seem to focus on the here and now. His tongue was replaced by something bigger. Better. I looked away, unable to look at him with the fantasy rushing to be fulfilled.

God, I'm so hard it hurts.

"What?" I screeched.

"Are you okay?" Pai touched my arm, the heat nearly burned my skin.

I jumped away. "What did you say?"

"I said I know you'll keep your word." Pai looked at me warily.

"No. No, that's not what you said." I knew what I heard. "You...you said, 'God, I'm so hard—'"

I blushed. Yeah, it was dark, but there was no way he'd miss the heat infusing my face. I could hide the heat surging through my unsated body, but my face was another story.

Pai's expression became masked and stoic — not giving away a sliver of emotion.

She can't possibly hear me.

"Of course, I can hear you, you're in my head!"

His nostrils flared. I could see them and feel his shock in the night air. He shook his head slowly. "No, I'm not."

"That's impossible, I *hear* you," I insisted.

"You hear me, Baby Doll, because you're in my head."

And everything you heard is true.

I looked down, below the waistband of his dress slacks. In the pitch dark, I'd be able to see that. He was — I took a breath and took another step backward. Holy shit.

"What the hell is happening to me?" I asked.

"It seems you are growing stronger."

I made a noise that wasn't quite a laugh, but not anywhere near a sob. It was jammed pack with disbelief.

Pai reached out and pulled me to him. The sexual tension was there, but the need to just *be* took over. Standing with our bodies touching at every level, he caressed my temple and told me about his day. His desire, however, remained obvious.

"Thank you for all your phone messages. I didn't see them until after Makaio arrived, but I appreciate the heads up. I spent most of my day with your brother. He thinks I had something to do with Peter Johnson's death. Apparently, my irresponsible avoidance played right into the hands of Daven Raines. He told the detective I was the last one to see Mr. Johnson alive, which Raines and I know is a lie. Unfortunately, we seem to be the only ones who know the truth. So…" The sigh that escaped his mouth expressed more weariness than exasperation. "I'm a person of interest to the case."

Guilt washed over me. I shouldn't have lied to John. I should have taken him to see Pai immediately, but I just couldn't believe my brother would take Windy's word over mine. Pai was innocent. (Okay, innocent wasn't quite the right word to describe Pai.)

His chest rumbled with laughter against my ear.

"This isn't your fault, Malia, and you're right, innocence is a thing of my childhood."

His lips pressed against the top of my head. I squeezed him harder.

"I would have avoided your brother out of my own competitiveness with Makaio. Peter Johnson was my client. I was hired to protect his property, but obviously the property wasn't the real target. If I'd done my homework I would have known that before Peter got killed."

I'd seen Pai angry on a couple occasions. Angry with Makaio. Angry with Mad Dog. This, however, was different. His anger was tearing him up inside. The feeling was so palatable that I felt the need to use mouthwash. So intense, it became my own.

"I left that night without even realizing Peter was in danger. My blindness cost Peter his life. Somewhere, I missed the signs of danger."

My blood heated with his fury. My fists clenched with unused exasperation as I absorbed his irritation.

His teeth ground together. "I should have known something was wrong."

Part of me wanted to yell at him. Pummel him. With fists so tight, I could feel the flesh of my palm give under the bite of my nails, but those weren't my feelings. I wasn't angry with Pai and I didn't want to hurt him. He was being too hard on himself. I knuckled down to express my true feelings and not the ones bombarding my mind.

"You may have been able to save him that day, but you couldn't protect him indefinitely without knowing all the facts. We still don't know exactly how or where Peter was killed."

I forced my thoughts away from the anger. Away from the foreign mixture of my feelings (and thoughts) all jumbled with Pai's, not to mention Peter's pain thrown into the mix somewhere. I thought of…Mutt. He was the key. He could clear Pai and point John in the direction of the real killer. There was no doubt in my mind Daven Raines belonged behind bars, and Mutt was going to help me put him there.

"I know the guy who originally saw you with Peter and Daven Raines, but there's no way he will voluntarily talk to the police. We're going to have to find him and somehow trick him into meeting John."

"And how do you propose we do that?"

"Your size should help." My eyes unwittingly traveled the length of his body. My mind took the tour as well.

"I like the way you think."

My gaze went back to his face. His smile didn't hold sadness. It held heat. Raw. Blistering. Heat. I stumbled backward, falling into my scooter. The sudden change in my body temperature flowed through my body and burned every nerve with overwhelming desire.

"Malia?" Pai reached for me.

I backed away.

"Is it that bad?" Pai looked apprehensive.

I think I panted. "No. It's just a little too…" I waved my hands in the air trying to encompass exactly how much raw sexual need coursed through my veins. "It's too much."

"It seems our link has progressed to another level. I'm sorry I subjected you to how a man's mind works." The expression on his face didn't really convince me of his regret.

I held onto my scooter for strength. Every inch of my being wanted to reach out and rip the business clothes from his body. My hands shook as I grasped the seat behind me, and my knees threatened to buckle. My breathing became labored as if I'd run a couple miles. Or just had sex. Or was in the middle of sex. God, I needed a cold shower. I was so hot I didn't think I could stand it. The only way to relieve it was to strip off every bit of my clothing and run for the cool ocean water.

"Are you telling me…?" I couldn't finish it. Couldn't fathom being able to read someone's thoughts so clearly. Couldn't comprehend my ability to experience his emotions. The axis of the earth seemed tilted. Tilted in a different direction than it had two minutes ago. I struggled for stability on legs that just didn't want to hold me any longer. My vision hazed at the corners. My body threatened to hyperventilate.

"It'll be okay."

Pai's voice continued to soothe. It crooned me toward relaxation. He murmured words I didn't understand. He reached every one of those burning nerve endings as he spoke. I listened without comprehension. I wondered if he spoke aloud or if I was still reading his thoughts. Another jolt. Flames of heat rocketed back through my body.

This time, Pai pulled me close, held me tight, despite the high temperature radiating off his body. He seemed to cool my overheated shell, like the chilly effect of an air conditioner's breeze blowing over my body. My breathing leveled. My thoughts calmed.

"Is this the way you feel every time you read my thoughts?"

I waited for his response, afraid to search for it in my mind.

"At first, it hits you like a Mack truck filled with Ecstasy. After a while, you learn to tone it down."

A Mack truck didn't plow into me. It bulldozed me into road pizza. Pai had just told me more than he'd meant to. I wasn't the first person he'd experienced this with. I pulled away with such force, I lurched backward and Pai fell against his Jeep.

Oh, shit.

Pai confirmed his guilt. He knew I knew without the explanation ever coming from his lips.

KYM ROBERTS

"Oh shit...oh shit...oh shit!" My feet were doing the tap dance of a firewalker as I turned around and around and around. "Fuck!" I shook my hands out, trying to rid myself of the pulsing blaze going down my arms into my fingertips.

Fuck is what we need to do.

I couldn't help but realize a man's thoughts really did turn to sex this often. He had to stop. "Stop it! Turn it off right now, Pai! I can't take it!"

Pai grabbed me from behind and held me in a bear hug. His arms wrapped around my body while his breath caressed my ear. He whispered more words, words beyond my comprehension that flowed through my body. At first, I thought he was going to follow through with his thoughts — bend me over and fuck me right there in the parking lot. And, well, a part of me welcomed it.

No, to be brutally honest, I desperately craved it. To the point, I felt like...an addict. I needed it. Every description of the drug Ecstasy I'd ever heard, mentioned the desire to be touched as a need. A prerequisite. A necessity of life. A need you had to control, or become lost to the drug.

Again, the imaginary air conditioner cooled my body and dampened the fire. But my heart still pounded against his arm, surprising me as I became aware of its matching musical drum beat in Pai's broad chest blanketing my back.

"Breathe," he said in my ear. That time, I knew he spoke out loud.

I filled my lungs with air and then exhaled slowly. Pai groaned and unwrapped me. I didn't want to think or feel what that meant. I stood on my own two feet while he created distance between us. The silence stretched. We each paced off the excess energy threatening to implode our minds. He was purposely blanking his mind of any thoughts. I *knew* it, without knowing it. Yet I was afraid he wouldn't be able to continue to keep me out of his head.

"How many women have you…?" What was I going to say? Fucked because of addiction? He stopped in mid-stride, turned with both eyebrows lifted, waiting for me to complete my sentence. My thoughts. "…felt this with?"

His hand rose to the back of his neck, like the muscles were suddenly so tight he could no longer move before he massaged out the kinks.

"I've had glimpses of it my entire life. The part about hearing someone else's thoughts. I didn't feel their emotions or any… any of the other stuff until about a year and a half ago. The first woman I felt this with…I was blown away. I thought she was my soul mate. How else could I have such a powerful connection?"

I knew what he meant. I thought of the image I'd had of us having kids. His rueful smile tore at my heart. He knew what I was thinking. I knew he was watching the vision slide down the drain. Suddenly, I didn't know if it was my disappointment or his I was feeling. Maybe it was both.

He cleared his throat. The smile was gone. "She was my fiancée." He paused before dropping the bomb, "The woman Maiko slept with."

It was my turn to react, *"Oh, shit."*

"Yeah." He crossed his arms across his chest, restraining himself from touching me. "We didn't separate because of my business. I left her because the feelings became so intense, I couldn't breathe. I was drowning in her emotions and desires. Coupled with my own, it was overwhelming. I was so desperate I couldn't function. Finally, I sought help. I turned to the only person I knew who could help me. My grandmother."

I waited for him to explain, hopeful there was a cure, but there wasn't.

"She sees things you wouldn't believe. Things that would scare the ever-living shit out of you. It did me. Her power is beyond the human realm. Luckily for me, she was able to teach me how to control the influx of emotions and the thoughts I got... from women like you."

Did he honestly say 'women like me'? I wasn't alone. I was in a category of women. A group of freaky, fucked-up women.

"You're not a freak, Malia, nor are you fucked up. You're a very special woman in a group of women I can communicate with telepathically. You're a Guardian of the Menehune."

I stopped breathing. "Wait...what?"

"We've been chosen to protect the Menehune—"

I held up my hand, stopping him from going a direction I wasn't even ready to consider. "How many women?" I wasn't sure I wanted to know how many women he had mind sex with either, but it was somehow the lesser of two ridiculous scenarios. And I purposely blocked out any of his thoughts. I didn't want the truth. If he chose to lie, I'd accept it whole heartily.

He didn't lie.

"I don't know. I've been trying to remember all the girls throughout my childhood, throughout school. I just don't know. At the time, it was random thoughts. You're the second since my ex-fiancée and like her, it's no longer random thoughts I hear and feel. It's more. Much more."

I didn't really want the answer to the next question, but I had to ask. "How much do you experience...with these women?"

"Thoughts. Emotions. ...sexual desires."

Panic welled up inside me. "With all of them?"

Every one of them.

Whoa, no way. He did not just tell me I was part of a fucking harem.

Once again, I felt my stomach grasp his emotions and hold on tight. This time it laughed, uncontrollably. He was amused.

I was not. I cleared my mind. At least I think I did. He was not going to translate my next thought. I sensed Pai pulling in the reins, toning down his own response, because of me. For me. He didn't laugh out loud. The dimple I found so incredibly sexy, hid.

My hands went to my hips. "How exactly does you having mind sex with a bunch of women relate to protecting the Menehune?"

His eyes twinkled with humor, but he kept the topic serious. "I don't know how it all works. The Menehune have not needed protection for over a century, but for some reason our Guardian powers are awakening inside of us."

"How come I don't feel anything with Peter? Isn't it the same thing?"

His head cocked to the side. "I would suspect it's because he's communicating through worlds, or because he's in love with his wife. I don't really know."

"So it's only sexual if you're not in love with someone else?" It made sense to me. Like an unwritten rule of monogamy governed by the gods.

"I hadn't really thought about it that way, but if you're wondering if I've been with all of them, I haven't. After my *kapuna wahine* taught me about the endowment, I have refrained from the indulgence. Until you."

I disregarded the flare of his nostrils, the scent of his arousal, the pulsing of his blood in his nether region. (Did I really smell his arousal and just think 'nether regions'?)

"What about guys? Did you ever experience this with a man?"

"I don't swing that way." He was laughing at me, again. His face didn't show it. His soul did. Over the obvious signs of his sexual prowess. I was starting to experience all of his feelings, and I didn't find it the least bit funny. More like…exhaustingly stimulating.

All of a sudden, it was gone. All of it. He turned it all off. I don't know how, but it was gone, like it never existed. Never awakened in me. Leaving behind fatigue. Exhilaration. Swaying on my feet with clarity of vision. Drained of every last ounce of energy, I was ecstatic. I felt alone. Free. A dichotomy of sensations flowed through my body.

"We should go. This isn't really a conversation to have here. Let me put your scooter in the back of the jeep and we'll go back to your place."

"NO!" Okay, that was probably a bit of overkill. I wasn't sure if my reaction was from him wanting to put my scooter in the back of his jeep, or from his earlier intentions of running his tongue down my body. I needed to ride. I needed to feel the wind in my hair. I needed freedom.

He didn't stop me.

I turned and straddled the scooter without meeting his gaze. He may have turned off his thoughts for me, but I was sure he was still reading my body. He handed me my helmet without saying a word, and I didn't want one. I put it on, started my bike and rode off. No more two-way communication between us. It was the road...and me.

With Pai in my side mirror. Watching me drive away.

CHAPTER TWENTY-FIVE

I rode the orange beast until my arms and legs were numb from the vibration of the tires bouncing on the road. My thoughts frozen. My heart deadened. I returned home not wanting to see anyone, or think about mind sex, or the implications of being a Guardian or anything else. The pillow on my bed was my only goal. I tripped as I pulled my leg over the side of the scooter and tweaked my cankle once more. Too tired to care, I righted myself and dragged my battered body up the wooden stairs to my apartment. I unlocked the door to my apartment already half asleep.

"Malia! Wait!"

I turned to find the man I'd been looking for had somehow found me. Mutt scampered up the steps radiating the stench of his namesake despite the oversized, long sleeve button-down covering his t-shirt. As much as I wanted to talk to him, I didn't want it to happen in my home. Given no choice, I stepped inside and allowed him entry.

"How did you find where I lived?" I asked with more than a little bit of suspicion in my voice.

"I didn't. I heard you were looking for me and I came by Private Kaua'EYES', but it was closed. I started to leave, and then I saw you getting off your scooter. What happened to your car?" Mutt made his way inside and plopped down on my sofa bed.

(*Ewww*, I'd probably have to fumigate it.)

Apparently, he hadn't been trained to wait for an invitation to sit on someone's furniture.

"It's a long story. How'd you get here?" There hadn't been any cars in front of the business, nor were there any in the rear parking lot.

"I'm parked down the street at *Joe Brah's*. I figured if you weren't here I'd go in and get a beer. You got any beer?"

I left the door to my apartment unlocked, making sure Mutt knew he wasn't staying too long, and plopped my purse on the counter.

"What's that on your board?" Mutt asked.

I glanced at the board. That sinking feeling of a secret disclosed to the very person I didn't want to know, hollowed my gut, and allowed fear to creep in where I didn't want it to be. In my best act of casual cleaning, I swiped the board twice with the dry eraser, praying I was still one step ahead.

KYM ROBERTS

"Oh, that's just our family tree, we were trying to work out the other day." It sounded lame to my own ears and the only way I could think to cover it was to push through and pretend fear wasn't filling every inch of my body. I did what every safety class tells you not to do, I turned my back on him, opened the fridge to get a couple beers, and hoped my act of complete comfort would disguise his checkmate. Then prayed for some magical, mystical Guardian super-power to get me the hell out of this situation.

My body tensed. My failure imminent, Peter yelled in my head, *"Look out!"*

But I was too slow. Pain radiated through my core from the base of my skull down to my toes. I wobbled with two beer bottles in my hands. One crashed to the floor as I staggered sideways, trying to catch myself.

Darkness hazed the edges of my vision and confusion latched onto my mind. An arm raised high above my head, and then began to descend upon me. With the reflexes of a turtle, I attempted to block the blow unsuccessfully, and dropped to my knees, the second bottle crashed to the floor and echoed far away in my brain. This time, the pain took away my vision, but cleared my uncertainty.

A sneaky, dirty junkyard dog was attacking me. My only chance of survival was to play possum. I slumped to the floor, my chest and stomach pressing against the broken beer bottles I'd been about to offer my attacker. I knew I was bleeding, but I forced myself to lie still, waiting for the mangy mutt to make his next move. I was ready, a shard of glass tucked in one hand, the other ready to grab whatever weapon he had.

My pulse pounded at the two wounds on my head. Warm blood trickled into my hair. Instinct made me want to raise my hand to the injuries, but I refocused on my attack.

My hair became his handle as my head snapped back. Pain shot through my scalp and I caught a glimpse of a blade coming toward my neck. Fear dumped strength and adrenaline behind my defense.

I slashed out at his wrist with the broken glass. The knife fell from his hand and blood splattered the front of me, but that didn't stop my onslaught. I followed through with my right elbow in a backward motion towards his face. (I hoped.) Through the fog in my head, I heard Mutt howl as I made contact with his mouth. Teeth sliced at my elbow and he staggered backward, tripping over my coffee table. Mutt crashed to the floor, and I scrambled for his knife.

Trying to get up while holding his hand over the wound on his wrist, Mutt rolled to his side for leverage. Like a cat ready to take on a vicious mongrel, I attached myself to his back and shoved him, face first into the floor. Returning the favor, I grabbed a fistful of his matted hair, raised his head and smashed his face into the wooden floor planks. I didn't feel his nose break. Didn't feel the pop of the cartilage and bone. Didn't feel remorse when blood pooled on the floor below him.

I pushed up off of his back, my blood and his mixing all over the place and left him there, moaning. Stepping away, I held the blade of his large k-bar knife in his direction, the point ready to stab the ever-living shit out of him if he even tried to attack me again. My breathing labored, I leaned against the wall for support and noticed some of my hair sticking out of the handle of his knife. If he had chosen to stab me first, instead of hitting, I'd be dead. As it was, my head pounded so hard it felt like it might fall off with each quake.

Mutt finally rolled over, holding his mangled wrist, blood seeping through his fingers. He sat up with his eyes closed and leaned back on my sofa bed. Blood flowed from his nose and mouth. It covered my floor, my smashed coffee table, the glass glistening in the red sticky substance. I needed a new place to sleep.

"I nee...an...ambooance," Mutt said weakly.

"You tried to kill me, you son of a bitch! You don't need anything!" I couldn't let go of my anger. If it was gone, I might collapse from exhaustion and pain. My hands, already shaking with fatigue, begged to drop to my sides. My legs would be next.

"Pwease..." his voice was weak but I still wasn't buying it. It could be a trick. I staggered back to the kitchen, and grabbed two towels from the drawer, one for my head and one for his wrist. Throwing the towel in his direction, it hit him in the face. Mutt winced with the contact, but took the towel and wrapped it around his wrist.

"If you want to live, you might want to wrap that tightly. Why were you trying to kill me?" I demanded more than asked.

Mutt started to pull himself up on my sofa, then saw the slow, deadly shake of my head. No way was he getting comfortable in my house. My couch was ruined, but I didn't care. He'd die before he got cozy.

Mutt's response would have been unintelligible to the average person. For someone who'd been communicating with the dead, it was somewhat understandable and I couldn't help the involuntary lift of my upper lip. The taste of scum never went over well with me. I was pretty sure he'd just told me his boss told him to kill me.

"Who's your boss?" It wasn't a question. A question was posed when you didn't know the answer. I knew the answer. I just needed him to confirm it.

"Raineth."

There it was. The slimeball I'd never met had sent Mutt to kill me, but how did he know about me?

The shadow in the garden outside Misty's condo flashed through my mind. It hadn't been my imagination.

It had been Mutt. He had been watching the Johnsons. He'd seen me approach. Knew I did errands for Private Kaua'EYES' and had reported me to a killer.

"What were you doing outside Misty Johnson's apartment?" I accused.

"Nuthin," he lied.

"Did you kill Peter Johnson?"

For the first time, Mutt looked shocked, innocent. His head snapped up at attention. His denial spurted from his lips, "No, I thidn't thew it!" Juicy and garbled, his voice was laced with a nasal hum it suddenly adopted when I broke his nose and blood flowed down his throat. "I thwear I thithn't keel anyone! M-thee keeled 'im."

He didn't have to swear, I knew he didn't. I understood his denial, but I didn't understand who he said killed Peter Johnson.

"Who?"

"M-thee. M-thee keeled 'im."

"Who's M-thee?"

My patience with his inability to communicate was wearing thin. I didn't care that I was the source of his dysfunctional voice. All I cared about was getting answers. Knowing he wouldn't be able to say the name any better a fourth time, Mutt made a hand gesture for a pen. I grabbed a pad of paper and pen from my counter and tossed it in his lap.

Mutt took pen to paper, and with the skill of a three year old, wrote on the pad with his left hand. Turning the pad on his lap, he held it up for me to read.

In between drops of blood, "MD" was written on the page.

"A doctor killed him?"

He shook his head, almost as emphatically as he had when I asked if he killed Mr. Johnson.

"No. That'th what Winthy thalled im."

The hair on the back of my neck prickled. Mutt's speech was becoming more and more difficult to understand, but I knew he was telling me the name of the woman behind the man. I understood her name. Very well, in fact. Windy.

What role did she play in all of this? That was something I'd have to figure out later. For now, I needed to call the police.

Without saying a word to Mutt, I crossed over to my purse and pulled out my phone. Makaio answered on the third ring.

"*Aloha*, I was afraid I'd never hear from you again." His deep sexy voice unwound my tightly controlled emotions.

Ignoring the pull, I blurted out, "I've been assaulted and the suspect is in my apartment."

"What?! Malia, hang up and call 911."

At the same time, Makaio was instructing me to call the police, Mutt was begging me not to.

"Pleath thon't call the Poleeth."

I ignored both their pleas with a roll of my eyes, relieved to be in the driver's seat again.

"The suspect is Mutt, and he witnessed Peter Johnson's murder."

Makaio's voice turned away from the phone. "Pearl, call 911. Tell the police to go to Private Kaua'EYE's Investigations in Koloa Town. There's a burglar in…"

"Don't tell her where I live!" It was too late.

"…Malia's apartment above the office."

"Dammit Makaio! That woman is more of a threat to me than Mutt is any day."

"I think I rethenth thath."

"I don't care what you resent, Mutt. Sit there and shut up." I guess I sounded like I was in control. I didn't feel like I was in control, but Makaio and Mutt both shut up, so I guess I was.

"Makaio, Mutt and I will wait patiently for you to get here."

Mutt glanced at the door and muttered something about not messing with me or I'd break Makaio's nose as well.

"You're damn right I'll break his nose, and I'll break your nose a second time if you don't keep your mouth shut." I ran my hand through my gooey hair in frustration and winced.

Damn that hurt.

"I'll be there in ten minutes. Grab your baseball bat just in case."

The line went dead. How did he know about my baseball bat? Then I remembered the rather unforgettable orgasm I'd had while lying on top of Makaio's chest. On my uncomfortable sofa bed, where my baseball bat protruded into the room from underneath.

If he'd been here I might have been embarrassed. As it was, Mutt didn't know about it. My casual trip to the sofa bed with the knife held close to my body in a white knuckled grip was met with wary eyes.

"Scoot over," I ordered.

Mutt moved like a dog dragging its butt on the carpet.

I pulled out my bat and looked at my captive. Mutt's lower lip pouted, but something else caught my attention. His right eye twitched.

Twitch. Twitch. Twitch.

His un-bandaged-but-not-so-scratch-free hand went up to rub the involuntary contraction. His hand shook. Mutt was in need of a fix.

Well, shit. My control probably had about a ten minute window before all hell broke loose.

CHAPTER
TWENTY-SIX

While waiting for the cavalry to arrive, I finally got most of the story out of Mutt. Apparently, he had an addiction to special K, or ketamine. It's a controlled substance frequently used with marijuana or Ecstasy. In powder form, it can be used to lace another drug or a drink. In liquid form, it can be injected. Ketamine isn't one of those drugs you mess around with. Besides being addictive, it causes mental illness and can cause fatal respiratory problems, but apparently the lure of the k-hole, a distorted vacuum that alters the user's perceptions, was too much of a temptation for Mutt to resist.

MD supplied the drugs that Mutt needed to survive, while they killed him slowly from the inside out. MD scheduled jobs at night, stealing copper and anything he could find from different construction sites on the island to pay for his drugs. MD got Mutt his job at *The Garden of the Gods*. MD... killed Peter Johnson with a hammer. Daven Raines didn't actually do the job, he just ordered it done.

And MD instructed Mutt to kill me.

As I held out a bag of ice for Mutt to apply to his nose, a part of me felt bad for him. Not a huge part, but a teeny tiny part way back in the recesses of my mind that could identify with the draw of the drug. I'd experienced a similar draw. The downright unstoppable, undeniable, all-consuming pull to get a fix, but my drug of choice had been Pai.

Was that what Mutt was feeling? If I'd had sex with Pai, would I be as miserable a human being as the one in front of me? Looking at Mutt was enough to make me abstain from sex for the rest of my life.

Maybe I should join a religious order. A convent. I'd seen reruns of *The Flying Nun* on TV. She was pretty cool, in an ultraconservative way. Could a nun wear a bikini and go surfing?

Right before my encounter with Mutt I'd experienced the exquisite high, then the horrible low of withdrawal. If I hadn't been subjected to the intensity and appeal of an addiction, I probably wouldn't have shown him any compassion. After all, his injuries were a hazard of the job he'd accepted as a would-be murderer.

When I'd felt the lure of the drug, I'd asked for help from Pai. When Pai became consumed by his ex-fiancée's thoughts, emotions and drives mixed with his own he turned to his *kapuna wahine*. Peter Johnson had gone into rehab of his own accord because he'd recognized he was out of control.

Mutt sought out more drugs and turned to a life of crime. Strength of character was at play.

Makaio made it to my apartment in about five minutes. I heard the engine of his motorcycle splitting the peace of the night air. A rain of rocks struck more rocks and pinged off my scooter. His feet barely made any noise on his ascent to my apartment. I crossed the room and opened the door just in time to save it from his shoulder.

He stumbled in, gun at the ready, startled and breathing heavily. His chest rising and falling in a muscle shirt designed for his physique.

Damn, he was hot.

The muscles on his arms were sculpted, blood pumping their bulging contours up a notch. (What I wouldn't give to watch him work out.) Makaio caught my sigh, his chest puffing out further. He strutted his masculinity for Mutt and his sexuality for me. I mentally smacked myself and hurt the cuts on the top of my head.

"Are you okay?" His eyes raked across my face before they reluctantly returned to Mutt.

"I am now. Thanks for coming." The need for control no longer a necessity, I thankfully plopped down on the small bench next to my door before my legs shot out from underneath me. "Mutt was just telling me about how he was supposed to come here to kill me." I was feeling powerful. I'd defeated my murderer.

"Have you checked him for weapons?" Even though he asked the question, I knew my answer didn't matter. He was going to check him no matter what, and as much as I wanted to deny my stupidity, I had to warn Makaio. Another mental head slap. Ouch.

"No, but I will." My willingness to help went on deaf ears.

"Lay flat on your stomach with your hands on the back of your head."

Mutt's eyebrows drew together as he pleaded for leniency. "Buth my nothe ith bro'en and my wristh ith cuth."

Makaio's gun raised a hair. His hands tightened around the grip. His jaw flexed. His voice deepened.

"Get on your stomach. Now."

I prayed Mutt wouldn't mess with him. If he did, he was going to lose. Real quick.

He didn't. Slowly, he inched out flat and lay on his stomach. His bloody fingers intertwined on the back of his head.

My heart stopped. I couldn't breathe. Couldn't move. Mutt's shirt had risen with his arms extended to his head, and the black handle of a second knife stuck out of the rear of his waistband. I would have asked, 'Who carries two knives?' but my voice was gone. My body, aware of my deadly mistake, sent all my blood to my center mass. My fingers and toes disappeared in a sea of jellyfish stings. My inability to hold myself up had me leaning back against the wall. Weak. Mentally and physically. If I'd been standing, I would have fallen in a crumpled heap.

In contrast, Makaio's voice was hard as steel.

"If you move, you are one dead mother-fucker."

"I wathn't 'oing tho use ith. I wath done."

All I could see was the knife. My mistake. My huge mistake. No. It wasn't huge. It was beyond huge, but my mind couldn't grasp any other words. Just…Huge.

Makaio placed the knife on the kitchen counter, then cuffed Mutt's left wrist to his belt loop at the small of his back. I'm not sure who was shaking more. Mutt in need of a fix or me scared half to death. In the beginning, I had beat Mutt physically. In the middle, I got sloppy. In the end, Makaio had probably saved my life. What would Mutt have done if I'd let my guard down?

Mutt answered my question for me. His alter ego wiped away the man I'd been talking to. Gone was the whining, wimp of a man I'd given a towel and a bag of ice. He was replaced by a man with horrifying hostility and hatred.

"You thupid bitth. You juth had tho call the polith. I thould have cuth you to pietheth."

Still holding my bat, I lost that piece of sanity I'd been clinging to. He thought he should have cut *me* to pieces? Anger consumed me. Anger at my stupidity. Anger at Daven Raines. Anger at Mutt. I didn't hear the blood pounding in my ears. I didn't feel my fingers grasp the bat in a home run grip. I didn't feel anything but pure, unquenchable fury.

"You son of a bitch!"

I charged him. Scoring, my only goal. Makaio was faster. He was between Mutt and me in a blink. His hand splayed wide across my chest. Nothing sexual. Just stopping my forward progress. His face tight. His eyes dark and dilated. He said one word.

"Don't."

That was it. That was all it took for him to bring me down. I guess that's the difference between a crazy person and someone who just went crazy for an instant. I lowered my bat and turned away, not wanting Makaio or Mutt to see my shame. Shame over my stupidity and loss of control. The ravenous ache to tear Mutt to pieces still gripping my insides with no way to extinguish it.

A thud, followed by a wheezing scream sent me on the defensive. Instinctively I lifted the bat and swung back around. Makaio held Mutt by his bloody shirt against the wall, his feet dangling off the ground. His face reddened as his airway constricted. Mutt's eyes were round with fright. I shouldn't admit this, but it soothed me to see his fear. Lifted my shame and that need for violence clawing at my gut.

"What were you supposed to do here?"

"Thill 'er." He said it so easily, as if I was just a cockroach to crunch on the floor.

"Who killed Peter Johnson?"

"M thee."

303

"Who?"

I interpreted, knowing Makaio would never get the name with Mutt handcuffed. "MD, like doctor, but he's not. That's just what everyone calls him."

Makaio nodded in my direction without taking his eyes off Mutt. "Where's MD?"

Silence filled the air. Mutt didn't answer and I held my breath, waiting for the hammer to strike. Makaio slammed Mutt against the wall with a thud. Despite watching the whole thing, I jumped. It startled me and forced me to intake oxygen, like coming up for air after being under water too long.

Makaio's thoughts flooded my senses. *MD might be on his way here to finish the job.* His body erupted with testosterone and aggression. My bat cocked in awareness and anger, ready for the potential threat to come through my door.

"Where's MD?" Makaio's jaw barely moved. His teeth clenched through his words, his voice deadly serious.

"Thaines wath goin' tho thend M-thee tho thill the dead thuyth wife."

Makaio's face drew back with a lack of understanding. Mine fell with comprehension. I felt my skin sag almost as much as the heart in my chest.

"Oh, God. MD is going after Misty, Peter Johnson's wife."

Makaio captured my gaze with his own. "Misty and her son?" He looked back at Mutt for confirmation. Mutt nodded.

My door slammed open, jump-starting my heart. I swung around with that home run swing I'd been dying to use. My Louisville Slugger going for the high and outside pitch. My favorite.

A head bobbed in a matrix type move. Slow motion. Inhuman. I missed the curveball. Strike one.

"Shit, Malia! My head's not a baseball. I'm here to help."

Pai. How had I missed his arrival? We were connected. Right?

Yeah, Baby Doll, we're connected.

My lips dried. My body went from adrenaline dump to extreme sexual awareness in a matter of seconds. Milliseconds. Heat raced through my body. I wanted to push him away. I took a step toward him instead. *Oh, God, not in front of Makaio. Turn it off, Pai!*

He turned it off. Everything. Just like that it was gone, but when he spoke, his voice held a trace of sexual awareness laced with fear.

"What's going on? Is that your blood?" Pai's eyes nearly popped as he took in my battered apartment and my disheveled appearance.

I looked down to see my shirt a disgusting smear of blood in different stages of drying. *Blek.* Most of it wasn't mine. "No, it's not mine. I'm fine, but Misty and her son are in danger."

Makaio dropped Mutt on the floor. In turn, Mutt began sputtering like the obnoxious handcuffed loser he was. I didn't even bother trying to translate through his new lisp. It was all worthless dribble.

Help her!

I shook my head.

"That wasn't me," Pai stated the obvious.

"I know."

"Was it Peter?" He asked.

"I think so."

Help her! Peter sounded desperate.

"What's going on?" Makaio asked.

"Misty Johnson's in trouble. She needs help, now." I pulled my phone out.

"Where is she?" Makaio was all business. Deadly business.

"You won't know how to get there. I'll call for a marked unit." I didn't want Makaio chasing after this MD. It was a bad idea. I felt it in my chest. The loss Misty experienced flashed through my mind. An endless ache that would never stop. The pain would lessen over time, but the hole would remain empty. Forever.

Help Misty and my son!

So in touch with that feeling, I didn't expect a blindside. Not from Pai.

"I'll take you. Let's go."

Makaio looked back at Mutt lying on his side, unable to get up and no longer a threat. I didn't want to tell him it was okay to go, but I did anyway.

"Don't worry about him. I got him. I already called 911, so they should be here any minute. I'll call them back and tell them to meet you at Misty's apartment."

Makaio turned and looked at me as if he was memorizing my face. Like he would never see me again. I'd heard his thoughts when fear for my safety had raced through his mind. Yet now I couldn't hear anything. Nor did I feel that strong sexual need I'd felt with Pai. There was still a hell of a lot of attraction between us, but it was blanketed with uncertainty. Pain traveled through my side and arm, telling me something I didn't want to know. Like one of us might not...

Frozen, I refused to acknowledge the meaning, lest it came true. Yet I knew I couldn't tell him to stay. It would kill him not to go.

And he left, without another word. Pai hot on his trail and all I had to look at was Mutt's ugly mug.

Numb. Wishing I'd stopped him from leaving. Wishing Pai didn't know the way. Wishing everything was different and that I couldn't hear Pai's Jeep tear out of my apartment's parking lot.

I pulled my cell phone from my pocket and dialed 911. Makaio and Pai needed backup. Now.

I gave the dispatcher the address. Told her Officer Natua was on his way in plain clothes with his cousin, and I described them both to a tee. I did not want them dying by friendly fire. I pushed the end button and stared at Mutt.

He seemed to be my focal point. My point of concentration. Not that I was in labor, but it felt like I'd been through labor. I was supposed to be connected to Pai, but every fiber of my being screamed for Makaio.

CHAPTER TWENTY-SEVEN

Forty-five minutes is a hell of a long time to wait when someone you care about has been shot. My worst fears had come true and I'd let it happen. Guilt left a hole in my chest a mile wide. Makaio had been shot when he raced to Misty's rescue. MD was already at the scene, breaking into the screen door that I'd insisted Misty lock. (I was pretty sure it was Peter's idea coming out through my voice.)

The confrontation left Makaio with two bullet holes in his body and MD missing a chunk of his brain. (The fact that I knew Makaio would be injured before it even happened was not comforting – I'd let him go.)

I paced in a small circle, waiting for more news about Makaio's condition. My side and arm radiated with pain deeper than the strikes I took on my head. The whole thing didn't make sense — my arm and side weren't injured, Makaio's was and I was quite literally feeling *his* pain…or I was certifiable. Either way, if I told my brother, he'd have me in a padded cell within the hour.

John insisted Makaio was stable, and since I'd already refused to go to the hospital for my own bloody scalp (there were tears in the flesh but nothing that would require stitches according to the paramedics)my brother thought it best I stay with him at my apartment. After all, I didn't need medical attention; the bleeding had stopped even before my head was bandaged up in mummy gear.

He called my bluff when I threatened to call Dad and dared me to do it. Because we both knew Dad wouldn't let me go anywhere, under the circumstances, even if he did want me to be with Pai. (I was pretty sure John would nix any chance of either cousin receiving a nod of approval after tonight. His protective big brother streak was in full-gear.) Besides, if Dad found out it was Makaio Natua I wanted to check on, he'd drive me straight to my parents' house and lock all the doors. So I didn't argue with my older, pain-in-the-butt brother. I stayed at the crime scene, blood covering the whole frickin' place, and made John call every fifteen minutes for a status update. Two could play this game.

John stopped my hundredth circle. "We need your clothes."

"For what?" I demanded. Not the least bit happy.

"For evidence that the whole thing happened the way you said it did." John looked down at his notes.

"You don't believe me?"

John's shoulders drooped before he closed his notebook and lifted his head. "I believe every word you said, Mal. I just have to be able to prove it eight months from now when this case goes to trail."

"Fine." I stomped to my closet, yanked a t-shirt off a hanger and grabbed a pair of shorts and undergarments from the shelf, before turning and making the same pouting march to bathroom. I know I was acting like a two year old. Having permission to change was music to my ears. Being forced to wait for John to tell me I could move in my own apartment, however, was like being in prison.

John stood at the bathroom door holding a brown paper bag. I snatched it from his hand and slammed the door behind me. I gave up my clothes as evidence, ditched the mummy hat, and took a quick shower while John supervised the crime scene tech photographing my bloody sofa bed, my bloody trash, the bloody floor. Blood everywhere. Like every speck told the story. I guess they did to a cop.

An attempt to towel dry my hair only resulted in shots of pain slicing through my side. My arm, and just below my right ribcage, burned from the inside out. I'd looked for injuries several times, but there wasn't a mark on my skin. So the pain wasn't real, or was it? My body kept telling me it was, while my mind insisted it was the shock of the whole night.

I'd been brain dead when I'd left Pai at Misty's, with no idea I was a target on Daven Raines' Murder-To-Do-List. It was hard to grasp that one of my surf buddies tried to kill me just to get a fix. The kinship we had within the small group of surfers I met on a daily basis was similar to *ohana*. We tested our skills against nature. Together. Not against each other. I never expected one of them to try and kill me, especially not someone like Mutt. You expect a dog to be loyal.

Deep down, I really believe he would have chickened out. Otherwise, he would have pulled that second knife and stabbed me in the gut when I gave him the ice, not left it stuffed down the back of his waistband. Right?

My phone rang, "Do You Know Your Enemy" breaking the unnatural silence. I yanked open my bathroom door and was met by John holding out my phone, still restricting where I could go in my tiny apartment.

The song of my ringtone hit a little too close to home. I saw John's chin lower, his head shaking from side to side. I wasn't the only one questioning my musical choice.

'Alapai Lincoln' flashed on my screen. My heart lurched into my throat. I blurted out, "Is he okay?" before Pai could say anything.

"He's fine. He lost some blood, has a broken thumb that's going to need a cast and he's going to have a few scars to show off to the women, but he's going to be fine."

I slumped down on the bench near my door, too relieved to care much about John's displeasure over my location. My next question was a formality. A part of me was curious, the rest of me didn't care past, 'He's going to be fine.'

"Where was he shot?"

"Once on his right side and once on his forearm."

"Okay." All my nervous energy vanished in the blink of an eye. I rubbed my side, it was so sore, but I knew I deserved every bit of it. "Does he need someone to take care of him?"

I wasn't prepared for Pai's answer. "Our *kapuna wahine* is going to take care of him. He lives with her."

Makaio lived with his grandmother. Their *kapuna wahine* was going to take him home once he was released from the hospital. I expected Makaio to have a bachelor pad. If not by himself, then one he shared with some other guy. Not live with his *kapuna wahine*.

"Malia. I'd like to see you, if that's okay? We really need to talk."

I didn't want to talk. I didn't want to do anything but sleep. It was all just too exhausting. Finding Peter Johnson's body. The lack of sleep. The tension with Makaio. The lack of sleep. The triangle turned square with Joe, Jade, Pai and me. The lack of sleep. Windy and Pearl — MY CAR. Lack of sleep. Reading Pai's thoughts and being drawn into the powerfully addictive feeling mixed with deep sexual arousal. Sleep. Fighting Mutt and then trusting him not to hurt me when the traitor may have been waiting for the moment to bury his knife in my body. THE LACK. OF. SLEEP. Knowing Makaio was heading for a deadly situation and letting him go anyway, despite feelings for him that I didn't understand. And the lack of sleep compounded by pain radiating through my body.

All I wanted to do was sleep. Just sleep it all away. Get back to normal. Whatever that was.

No, that wasn't true. I wanted to see Makaio. I'd nearly fainted when John told me he'd been shot. The pain had come on suddenly before that, doubling me over and making John run to my side. I'd denied everything, telling my brother and myself that I was okay. But I wasn't. I'd felt the cold hand of death when Makaio left, and I let him go anyway. That wasn't an easy thing to live with. Pai's phone call had released the tension coiled up in my body. Allowed me to relax. But I couldn't see Makaio. His grandmother was there. He needed family. Not me.

"Pai, can we talk in the morning?" A glance at my watch told me it was approaching dawn a little too quickly.

"Malia…"

I interrupted him, irritated he was pushing me where I didn't want to go. I didn't want to hear anymore.

"Please, Pai." My petition for a break went on deaf ears in the peanut gallery. John's voice, the voice of reason, delivered my sentence.

I hate that voice.

KYM ROBERTS

"Malia, you can't sleep here. Your front door won't lock and there's still a man out there that hired someone to kill you. It's not safe."

I turned toward John. "I can go to Mom and Dad's house."

"Then I need to tell them everything in case Raines shows up there." John pulled his cell phone from the inside of his suit jacket pocket.

He was right. By going to my parent's house, I put them at risk and despite my dad being completely capable of protecting himself, would he be able to protect my whole family against Raines?

John's argument gave Pai all the encouragement he needed. "I'll pick you up in twenty minutes. I'll take you to Lani's and you can sleep in her bed. Alone."

John looked down at me, shook his head and raised his eyebrows. "You can stay at my place."

The invitation about killed John. He liked his freedom from family obligations as much as I did, but he didn't want me with Pai. I turned away.

"Fine, I'll stay at Lani's." I knew when to give up the fight. Right now, my life was so unpredictable I couldn't get a grasp on reality and the last thing I needed to do was give my brother permission to stick his nose in where it didn't belong.

Thinking about whether or not I'd actually seen into Makaio's future was something else I didn't want to think about. Along with the question of whether or not I'm some kind of freak who can talk to someone with my mind. I am simply not crazy enough to believe in things as outrageous and ridiculous as that.

In the twenty minutes it took Pai to get there, John and his crew finished processing my apartment. He'd taken my statement with his mini recorder so I was done for the night. Crime scene technicians were at Misty's condo processing it, and Pai had already talked to a detective at the hospital with Makaio. I found some nails for Pai to secure my door and waited in his Jeep.

Next stop for John? Talk to Mutt. Next stop for Makaio? Spend the night at the hospital with his grandma by his side. Next stop for Pai and me? Bed. Alone. At Lani's place. Sometimes life can be rough. Other times, when you're looking forward to a bed… it can be almost wonderful.

Pai smiled. One of *those* full smiles. The one I liked so much with the dimple on his cheek. I couldn't help but smile back. That dimple told me so much. Pai was reading my thoughts, controlling his reaction, and blocking me from reading his. How he did it, I had no idea.

We rode the rest of the way in silence. Pai, content with his blissful inner self. Me, wondering if I really had a 'purpose' in life.

Living in my world had taken on a whole new set of ups and downs and questions about the future. And this whole new pile of crap about being a guardian of a race who is tasked with safekeeping the balance of everything good and evil in our society? It was pretty hard to swallow.

I mean, hell-ooooo? I just solved a murder case. Wasn't that enough?

We arrived at Lani's and true to his word, Pai let me go to bed without even a handshake or goodnight kiss. He did offer me a couple ibuprofen for my splitting headache.

I should've felt relieved but wasn't. My side and arm hurt like hell, and the gashes throbbed on the back of my head. Combine that with a hefty load of guilt, and I teetered on the verge of a total meltdown.

I stripped down to my undies, lay down on the soft downy bed, and allowed my body to sink into the oblivion it offered. It didn't matter that the sun would be up soon. I wouldn't. I was going to sleep and then sleep some more. I didn't care what awaited me.

CHAPTER TWENTY-EIGHT

I dreamed of little men in loincloths building dams and offering sacrifices to the gods. (Fortunately, the sacrifices were bunches of fruit and intricate wood carvings. The human kind would have sent me over the edge.) Makaio stood at the top of the Waimea Dam, looking down upon all the smaller workers filling the canyon below. His bare chest was covered in tribal tattoos that emphasized the deep ridges of his muscular torso. A crimson red cloth, with intricate symbols dyed into the fabric, wrapped low around his hips and reached the middle of his powerfully built thighs. He held a spear above his head as he led a fierce chant to the Menehune below.

Pai sat on a throne in the middle of a *Heiau* to the side of the dam. His long, silky hair draped across his broad shoulders, a necklace of boar husks adorning his neck. His thighs were tattooed in a similar fashion to Makaio's chest. The markings linked their bloodline, but his face and chest were also covered with his very own unique tattoos. A solid black band extended across his left eye, giving him the appearance of a masked man.

Very separate in their roles. Pai accepted the sacrifices of the Menehune for the gods. A priest. Makaio led the warriors. A general. Any other time it would have been a good dream. A little different, but… entertaining.

Today, it left me shooting up in bed and gasping for air. Pain pierced my side and stabbed at the back of my eyes. It was just a dream. Just a dream. Just a frickin' nightmare. Covering my eyes from the morning sun coming in the window, I took several breaths and lay back down on the soft, feathered pillow.

Pai's stories had me reviewing my Hawaiian history in my sleep. The Menehune built the dam in Waimea. Until yesterday, the Menehune were just an ancient race to me. Now, I'm a *Guardian* of their race. Whatever.

"Saying guardian like a ghostly howl does not change the fact that you are one." Pai walked into my room with a breakfast tray full of food.

"And if I say, 'nah, nah, nah, nah,' does that mean I can simply ignore being one?" My sarcasm didn't go over well. Luckily for me, Pai was a patient man and overlooked my rudeness. I asked about what was bothering me the most. "How is Makaio today?"

"A few minutes ago he was like you, still asleep. Now that you're awake, we need to talk."

Well, shit, he was going to ruin a perfectly good breakfast with more talk about the Menehune. I looked at the tray lying on the edge of the bed. Eggs, bacon and fruit. No way was I going to let it go to waste. My stomach growled in agreement. I was starving.

We don't have the luxury of time on our hands, Malia. There's a reason we were brought together on this case.

He was doing it again. I could feel it creeping up my legs. When he walked in, my body reacted to the gorgeous man making his way through the door, but I ignored it.

He wasn't letting me ignore it now, so I did the mature thing and pretended I was in control. Pretended parts of me weren't ripening like the fruit on the tray in front of me. Pretended my pulse hadn't quickened and my body hadn't heated. Pretended Pai was a skinny, scrawny computer geek with long greasy hair, thick glasses, a bad complexion and a constant sniffle. That shut down any desire.

Whatever works for you, Baby Doll.

He felt it. Felt my power controlling the drive. It encouraged me to talk to the incredibly shy geek who didn't know how to communicate with women. *We were brought together to catch a murderer. We did it. It's over.*

"Not just the murderer of Peter Johnson. I'm talking about protecting the Menehune. I haven't had a chance to talk to you about the guard that you thought was beheaded the other night."

My fork, filled to the brink with eggs scrambled to perfection, stopped just millimeters before my lips. My mouth stood open, ready to greet the delectable offering. Salivating. Did he really have to bring up something so humiliating? I set my fork back down on the plate, disappointing my mouth, but probably saving my stomach as its growl turned into a groan.

"I'm not making fun of you, Malia. The guards working for me are Menehune. Windy did something to them, both Joe and James Kamakau. He believes she has somehow retrieved the knowledge of an ancient curse. A curse that may not literally cause them to *lose their head*, but it does cause them to lose consciousness."

I didn't need to hang onto the computer geek if he wasn't going to be the one talking to me, so I dumped him. "She probably drugged him."

The tox screen showed nothing in his blood system.

My body electrified with sexual desire. *Computer geek! Come out, come out, wherever you are! Dammit, Pai. Stop jumping back and forth. I'm having a hard enough time dealing with this.*

"I wanted you to remember how quickly and potent the effects can be. Our connection is inexplicable, just as a curse that would cause men to lose consciousness is beyond comprehension — yet both are very real. And an entire race is dependent upon us to figure out what is going on."

I spit out one word in capitulation. "Fine." At least that's what I wanted him to think. I surrendered.

Baby doll, you push a man too far.

The tray was on the floor, swiped off with one quick move as the covers flew from my body. A body now begging to be naked. I'd like to say Pai made the first move, but the truth was, I'm the one responsible for the mess on the floor. I straddled him, pushing him back on the pillows before he could make a move. My mouth crushed his with a force that shocked him. My tongue attacked his while my hands pulled the tie from his ponytail. Once his hair was free, my hands moved to his shirt, wound their way under the crisp cotton material at his neck. His skin was smooth and taut. The ripples of his traps and deltoids drove me insane. I had no time for buttons. I yanked at his shirt, pulling it away from pectoral muscles large enough and defined enough to be worshiped by all women. My hands gloried in the dips and grooves.

I had capitulated completely, and offered myself to him. Just like the Menehune offered sacrifices to him in the *Heiau* of my dream. I served myself up on a royal platter. I didn't care about the consequences.

His hands expertly moved to my ass and gripped the flesh, kneading it, pulling me closer and closer until we seemed to be one and his fingers curved around to touch my core. My knees hugged his hips, the hard length of him pressed against my stomach. Not only did I feel his passion, I experienced it. And he experienced mine.

I couldn't breathe. The rise and fall of his chest stopped. My heart took on another pace. His stuttered. Mine. His. Ours. An entire chorus of tribal drums beating to the gods. The heat so intense our bodies fused like molten lava.

Pai threw me back on the pillow. Finally. This craving would be satisfied. I reached for him, ready to indulge in the passion of the gods. The drug I had avoided captured me, consumed me. I thought he was going to follow, but he didn't.

Pai was across the room, standing at the door, and I was empty handed. His chest heaved, expanding with his recovery. His torn shirt bared an unbelievably sexy chest that was free of tattoos, unlike the image of my dream of him at the Heiau, yet no less desirable. His hair falling loose across his semi-nude torso.

He was fighting it. I could feel it. I needed it. *Don't!*

"Malia. This is wrong. I shouldn't have."

You didn't, I did. My body writhed with unsated desire.

"What about Makaio?"

His words were like ice water in my face. They sobered me. Drove the addiction away like a twelve step program. I pulled the sheet up over my body.

Something that looked a lot like disappointment flashed across his face. I tried to read his thoughts, but his mind was closed like a steel vault. "You need to choose before we can continue, but at least you know how strong a curse can be."

Without another word, Pai walked out of the room, leaving me a believer in ancient curses.

CHAPTER TWENTY-NINE

I was able to clean up the mess from my breakfast tray easily enough and after making sure Pai was no longer in the house, I slipped into Lani's shower. Following the coldest shower possible, I retrieved yet another outfit from Lani's closet.

At this rate, I was going to owe her an entire wardrobe. Especially since I needed to borrow a bathing suit for my surf lessons later that afternoon. It was either that, or go home and break into my boarded up apartment, and then try and get the door fixed before work.

I didn't see that happening. My only option was to borrow the suit and change at the resort.

My head was sore, but not splitting at the seams. My cankle was almost an ankle and my side and forearm gave only slight twinges of pain.

Pai had changed into a buttonless silk t-shirt and was standing at the kitchen counter cutting up more fruit when I brought down the remnants of what had been a beautiful meal.

Wanting to avoid any talk of what had just occurred between us, I got right down to business. "So how do we find out about the curse?"

"We contact Windy."

Of all his responses, I really didn't expect that one. "What for?"

"We find out what she knows. What she did to my guard."

"So you really think it was a *booby trap*?" Finally. He looked at me, a trace of his dimple returning. I really think he felt worse about what had happened between us than I did. I didn't regret it. Hell, no. I just wasn't sure it was morally right if it was an addiction.

"Now you see my dilemma. No regrets. Not between us, Baby Doll."

I returned his smile, feeling a bit of a dimple forming on my face, if not quite my soul. "No regrets."

We ate in companionable silence. I couldn't read his thoughts, but I figured he could still read mine, so I kept them bland. Shared my escape from reality with thoughts of surfing. Riding that imaginary wave relaxed me. I hoped it did the same for him. But something bothered me, and I needed an answer.

"I thought you would have tattoos on your chest."

His fork stopped halfway to his mouth, then he slowly laid it on the table and waited for me to explain.

"I had a dream that you were at a Heiau and your chest and face were covered with tattoos. The sun was rising and ..." I laughed and looked away, realizing how stupid the whole thing sounded. It was just a dream.

"If we were at a Heiau at sunrise, you would see my tattoos."

My eyes met Pai's and he smiled, his dimple confessing and giving me permission to believe my dream, all at once.

"You mean you would have a band across your left eye, and tattoos on your chest?"

He nodded. "That was the reason why I met Peter and Daven before the sun came up. They wanted to meet at the beginning of their day. I couldn't do that without revealing way too much."

It was like a weight lifted off our relationship. That secret he hadn't shared, the lie I knew was lodged between us, drifted into oblivion. Until his smile disappeared.

"I'm afraid my secret played into Daven's plot to kill Peter." Pai's heart was injured, I felt the guilt spreading through his soul. A burden I couldn't allow him to bare.

"Daven would have found the opportunity at another time and another place. Peter's murder is not your fault."

Pai nodded, and I felt his tension ease a bit, but I wasn't quite sure he truly believed he held no responsibility for Peter's death. In time, I hoped he would.

After we finished eating, we hopped into his Jeep and I called John and put him on speaker. He sounded like he'd been up all night. Again.

John apologized to Pai, making me feel a whole lot better about my brother and then told us about his interrogation. Mutt admitted he got involved when Windy introduced him to her boyfriend, MD, who became Mutt's supplier of Special K. Windy's boyfriend worked for Raines, putting up drywall and painting, and hooked Mutt up with a job. But somehow construction graduated to burglaries of Raines' properties.

Mutt didn't know why, he just joined MD on the burglaries to earn money for his dope. When Mutt and MD arrived at *The Garden of the Gods* on the night Peter Johnson was killed, they were supposed to burglarize the construction site again, or so Mutt believed. Then everyone arrived in the middle of the job. To make matters worse, Peter hung around after the meeting. Mutt confessed that Pai left first, confirming Pai's version of the story. Then Raines left, by himself. Which pointed the finger at Windy's lie, and left Peter alone, walking the grounds of his dream.

That's when MD shocked the hell out of Mutt by sneaking up on Peter, and smashing his skull with a ball-peen hammer. When Mutt wanted to run, MD ordered Mutt to help dispose of the body, or go down for Peter's murder. Mutt got the impression the plan never really involved stealing any copper, since they'd taken jet skis that MD had Mutt rent, to the site for the first time. The same jet skis they'd ended up using to dispose of Peter's body at sea.

Before lawyering up, Mutt insisted that Peter never saw it coming. Never felt a thing.

I was relieved to know Peter didn't experience any pain. He didn't deserve to die, but at least his family would know he didn't suffer.

"I'm going to text you a mug shot of a guy. I want you to tell me if you recognize him."

"Okay." My phone beeped almost instantaneously. I looked at the photo.

"Holy Shit!"

Pai jerked the wheel. Kind of like when you're daydreaming and someone comes up behind you. I didn't scare him, just startled an over-reactive jolt out of him.

"Who is it?" My brother and Pai asked in unison.

"That's the guy at the convenience store with Joe. The guy who was going to beat the shit out of him." I looked at Pai. "Remember? I nick-named him Mad Dog.

"It was Mad Dog that killed Peter Johnson… and he was going to kill Misty. Mad Dog was MD."

Pai caught up, his body relaxing now that he was in his comfort zone. In my head. *And MD tried to kill Makaio. When you met Mad Dog, Peter was trying to tell you about him, Malia, but you wouldn't listen. He told you to 'Run!'"*

Okay, that was too deep for me to shovel, but still MD was Mad Dog. The coincidence was pretty freaky.

Pai continued for John's ears, "I didn't see the guy's face last night, otherwise I would have been able to identify him for you. I saw a hole in the side of his head, kicked his gun away and went to my cousin. But what Malia's trying to say, is that we ran into him at Windy's job. He was not a nice individual." Pai's voice showed confidence in my *powers*.

Fate brought Mad Dog and me together, I argued. If I believed anything else, I would have to believe I was a Guardian of the Menehune race. Yeah, I wasn't quite ready to go there yet.

You will, Baby Doll, you will.

Ignoring Pai's onslaught, I started thinking more about what I'd observed Windy doing at LeLe's Convenience Store both times I'd seen her. But the first time, I only watched her actions for a few moments. I'd been watching Joe getting his coffee, walking up to the counter and Windy boob dancing, then Joe stumbling out. The second time I'd gone in, I'd tried to avoid her, but she wouldn't let me.

Whap. It hit me like a two by four right across the forehead. The *other* customer. The woman dragging her very short husband out of the store. He was tipsy.

"There was a woman who dragged her tipsy husband out of the convenience store immediately after he…" I looked at Pai and said for John's benefit, "interacted with Windy. At the time, I

329

thought the woman was irritated because he was looking at another woman wiggle her boobs, but maybe she was protecting him."

Pai was with me all the way this time. John, not so much. "Mal…"

"Maybe she thought Windy was selling him some drugs?" I suggested.

Or the woman knows something I know nothing about, Pai added in my head.

John brought our conversation back to reality. "Short of finding the couple, that theory is dead in the water."

"Did you arrest Windy?" I tried to conceal the hopefulness in my voice, but I knew I failed miserably when Pai's left eyebrow arched.

"No, I've had her in, and questioned her extensively. She claims she didn't know anything about it. Raines threatened to have MD arrested for drugs and murder if she didn't provide Raines with an alibi, but she refused. Then MD threatened to kick her ass if she didn't do it, so she did. She admitted that she never saw Raines or MD the night Peter Johnson was killed. But, because she lied the first time, we're back tracking trying to prove everything."

My entire body tightened. Un-frickin' believable. I could tell by the tone of his voice, John was frustrated. He knew Windy was involved. She'd been in the middle of too much. Yet, she'd also been victimized and the lines were completely blurred.

"What about the other night when she did something to the guard at *The Garden of the Gods*?"

"His tox-screen was negative. She says she went there to 'have a good time.' He can't remember anything after seeing her boobs. He could have gotten too excited and passed out for all we know. I've got her on giving false information, but if she was coerced into her statement..." John was ready to move on, I could tell.

I wouldn't accept that. Couldn't accept that. "But..."

"Listen, Malia, I'm knee deep in this investigation. I shouldn't be talking to you, but you were instrumental in catching Mutt and MD, and I thank you for that. I will let you know when we catch up with Raines. In the meantime, stay safe."

My brother hung up and I turned toward Pai. He already knew what I was going to say.

"You're the only one who can get close enough to Windy to find out about the Menehune Curse. You can drop me off at my apartment on your way. I have two surf lessons this afternoon, but I'll talk to you after that."

"I don't think it's a good idea for us to separate." His voice was unrelenting. He wasn't going to give in without a fight.

I found his reluctance to drop me off endearing. He was worried about my safety, but it was unnecessary.

"Pai, Raines is on the run. He's not about to waste his time with revenge. He's the type to have others do the dirty work for him. Besides, there's no way Windy will talk in front of me."

And I had no doubt Windy would be tripping all over herself to get into Pai's pants. I did not want to see that.

"So you trust me enough to be able to free myself from a *booby trap*?" The tone of his voice was light. Teasing.

"If you know what's good for you…yes." I tried to hide the jealousy rolling off of me like water crashing down the jagged rocks of Wailua Falls. Nevertheless, Pai's sideways glance and barely concealed smile were proof that he knew exactly what I was feeling.

Placing my jealousy aside, Pai and I worked out our plan of attack, and I gave him several locations to look for Windy. The different beaches, her parent's address, her job at the convenience store, and the address of her boyfriend before MD, just in case Windy found herself needing to be consoled.

Pai pulled into the parking lot behind my apartment. Like teenagers on their first date, we sat there wondering if we should kiss goodbye. That awkward feeling engulfed us, threatening to ruin the moment if we waited too long.

Pai leaned over and pulled my head toward him with one hand on the back of my neck. His slow, lingering kiss left no doubt he wanted more. And there was no doubt I wanted more, which produced his dimple as he pulled his lips away and put his forehead against mine.

We stayed there a moment in each other's heads, but in control. I was the first to pull away, amazed that I could.

"A hui hou, Pai."

A hui hou aku, Ki`i pēpē.

Goodbye, Baby Doll. I'd never get tired of hearing that.

CHAPTER THIRTY

Makaio's bike was still in my parking lot. I hadn't noticed it until Pai drove off, then the guilt slammed into my chest.

I wanted to call him. Go see him. Images of him lying on a couch while his *kapuna wahine* doted over him brought a smile to my face. I wasn't sure if it was real, or if my imagination was running away with me, but I did know, he was okay.

The bad news? My feelings continued to bounce back and forth like a beach ball in a football stadium with a crowd consisting of two. Pai and Makaio. Boing, Pai. Boing, Makaio. Boing — I didn't know where the ball would bounce next. I really had no clue. But I think Pai and Makaio were just as confused as I was, so I cut myself some slack.

I grabbed Makaio's helmet (mine being nailed up tightly inside my apartment), and I bypassed the Ducati Streetfighter calling my name. But only because I didn't have the keys. I got on the now friendly orange scooter and headed in the direction of Menehune Pharmacy, the face of a certain young pharmacist popping into my head. Jade knew something about the race of people who were no longer mythical to me. (I wasn't quite convinced of their magical state, but they definitely existed.) And she had a past with Pai, no doubt a member of his harem. (Had they touched, or cheated in the telepathic airways?)

I found Jade in the back of the over-stuffed, aisles assisting an elderly man with his medication. Bending over his cane, he flirted shamelessly with the woman a third his age. And Jade flirted right back; she'd always had a way with men that I envied. After a few minutes, he thanked her and went to pay for his medication, smiling as he passed me. I returned the gesture, but couldn't think of anything to say.

Jade saw me, and the same warm, inviting smile spread across her face. "*Aloha*, Malia."

I gave her a lopsided grin. "*Aloha*, Jade. I wasn't sure if you'd be happy to see me or not. Is there somewhere we can talk privately?" I asked, looking around the store.

"Certainly. There's a consultant room just past the pharmacy desk."

We walked to the glassed-in room talking about her daughter the whole way. Chills went down my spine at the thought of being a parent.

Jade was completely wrapped-up in the real world of adulthood, with a real job and a real husband, who just happened to come from a mythical race.

We entered the enclosure marked *Consulting,* Jade closed the frosted glass door behind us, and we took a seat in the metal chairs with padded seats.

Jade hooked her long black hair behind her ear. "I knew you'd come see me."

Taken aback, I couldn't help but ask, "Why?"

"I figured you'd come back when you wanted more information…about Al…Pai."

I blushed and looked at her sheepishly. "Was I that transparent?"

She smiled that secret smile we shared as teenagers when we had a specific guy one of us couldn't get out of our heads. Funny how applicable that really was. "All women are when it comes to men like Pai. Otherwise you wouldn't be here, would you?"

"Actually, Pai is kind of a secondary reason for me being here." I confessed.

She raised an inquisitive feminine brow. "Oh?"

"This is completely confidential, okay?"

"I understand what confidentiality means, I never told your brother you were sneaking out with me to go to the bars, did I? Or the midnight surfing parties? Or—"

"Okay, sorry. I know you won't say a word." I smiled, realizing just how many times she'd covered my ass during my rule-breaking teen years.

"What can I help you with?" Jade crossed her slim legs and appeared relaxed.

"I'm looking for a drug that wouldn't leave a trace in a person's urine. Something undetectable, extremely fast working, but I don't know how it's ingested."

Jade laughed. "I've been trying to think about that since the other night. To be honest, there is only one thing that could affect Joe like that."

I leaned forward on my chair. "What?"

Jade shook her head. "I can't tell you."

"What? Jade, don't be ridiculous. It's me. You know I won't go blabbering it to the whole world."

"I can't. It will put too many people at risk."

"You should know that Windy has made four men of Menehune descent, including Joe, become ill. The last guy was hospitalized. If you know what's causing this, you have to help me stop her."

Jade's brain hooked on the name of the woman who'd taken advantage of her husband. "Windy was the one who did that to Joe?"

"Yeah, it was Windy."

Jade's lips pursed, no doubt remembering the quarterback who left her for Windy. Yeah, high school had been full of sex drama, thanks to Windy. The floodgates of information opened. "I've noticed an influx of Menehune coming into the pharmacy to buy drug tests, so I started quizzing them about it. Men were coming home, for lack of a better word, intoxicated. But they hadn't ingested any drugs or alcohol. The women in their lives were angry, their routines disrupted, and the men were confused. Periods of consciousness were lost to them, but several of the men remembered seeing a woman's breast right before everything went dark. When I pushed for more information, they were either unable to give it or refused to talk about it anymore. I'm pretty sure that none of the men remembered anything after seeing this woman's breasts."

"Windy," escaped my lips.

It couldn't be that easy. A woman's boobs? Sure, some men can't take their eyes off *any* set of boobs. They prefer to talk to a woman's chest instead of her face, but why wouldn't the Menehune men get drunk from every pair of boobs they saw, if that was the curse? What made Windy's double Ds so special?

"Windy exposed herself and immediately afterwards men became intoxicated. No drugs or alcohol. Just Windy. And her boobs. I know she's the source, I just don't know what she's doing to them." I explained.

Jade folded her arms across her chest. "I need to see her breasts."

If a man had said that to me, I would have scoffed, and been disgusted with his sly attempt to see Windy's double Ds. Coming from Jade, it was kind of funny. Jade didn't think so. Her lips were pressed in a thin, determined line and her eyes sparkled with anger. She didn't see anything humorous about Windy exposing herself to Joe.

"Why do you want to see her breasts?" I asked, not sure I wanted the answer.

"If I see her breasts, I may be able to figure out the cause, which will lead me to the cure." Jade leaned forward, excitement burned in her eyes. It was kind of freaky.

"But what do you hope to find?" I certainly didn't want to look at them.

She grinned, a sly look of a mongoose on the prowl. "Tattoos."

"Excuse me?" The whole thing was getting too much on the hocus pocus side of thinking for me.

Jade's smile softened, knowing her excitement wasn't shared, her shoulders rose and fell in a sign of resignation. "This cannot go beyond these walls." She searched my face.

"I understand." Not really, but hopefully I would soon.

"The Menehune people left Hawai'i because of the Menehune Curse, but it's not so much of a curse as it is a spell, written in *kakau* or tattoo art. According to the legends, a Menehune man can be enslaved for various purposes if exposed to the spell. It sounds as if the spell has been unearthed, but Windy's tattoos may not be placed properly on her body to cast the spell effectively. If I see the tattoos, the men can have wards placed on their body to protect them."

I must have looked skeptical, probably because I was saying 'bullshit' in my head.

Jade tried to convince me. "*Kakau* wasn't just designed to distinguish roles in society and tell family history, it was for protection of health and spiritual strength. It's the art of the gods carefully placed on the body by the *kahuna* to keep our people safe."

Trying to follow what I didn't believe, I asked, "So you think Windy's spell is…misplaced?"

"Yes," Jade unfolded her arms and grabbed my hand. "I need to see her tattoos to protect my husband."

Despite not believing, I completely understood her desire to protect her family, and if she thought a tattoo on her husband would protect him from evil boobs, who was I to argue.

"I have a picture…"

Jade squeezed my hand in anticipation.

I hated to disappoint her. "But I left the camera at Pai's and it doesn't show all of her tattoo."

"We need a picture of the entire tattoo. My mom is a healer in the ancient ways. If there is something unique about Windy's tattoos, she'll know."

I thought about bringing the police into the investigation, but so far, John believed the men just got excited and passed out. Without more information, and a little imagination on everyone's part, I'd be laughed out of the station. Unfortunately for me, the only person I knew who could get us a picture of the tattoos was Pai.

Hua.

I pulled my hand away and squirmed a little in my chair. I couldn't make any promises. "I'll see what I can do."

"Thank you." Jade stood up and smoothed out the front of her lab coat.

I wasn't quite done. "Jade, I...I need to know what happened between you and Pai."

Jade smiled sadly and shook her head. "That's not for me to tell you, Mal."

"But—"

"I'm sorry. Let me know when you have the pictures." She turned and walked out the door.

I left the store numb to my success, and filled with fury about what I had to do. I told myself to get over it as I sat on my scooter and dialed Pai's number. I was immediately sent to voicemail. His smooth radio voice coaxed me to release my edge.

It didn't work. His frickin' phone was turned off. And I hadn't charged my phone the previous night, so I had very little battery left to continue calling him.

I wanted to growl my frustration. He knew I would check in, and yes, part of me was checking up on him with Windy. The other part of me needed to tell him I'd found an invaluable source. And...I needed a picture of Windy's chest.

Again, I wanted to growl. What woman asked a guy she was involved with to take a picture of another woman's boobs?

Yeah, technically we weren't involved, but like my relationship with Makaio, I'd crossed a line with Pai. A line I didn't comprehend and the whole thing was driving me crazy and pissing me off. I left a very short message, my voice deeper and angrier than usual.

"I need pictures of the *booby trap*."

CHAPTER THIRTY-ONE

Everything was wrong. My senses were on fire. My head throbbed so hard, tribal drums couldn't compete with the beat. My heart raced while unreasonable fear snaked through my body. I tried shaking the sense of doom encircling me, but everywhere I looked, I saw tattoos and wondered if they were meant to enslave me to a life of aimless wandering with no direction.

To make matters worse, the Mauna Koa Resort had closed the path to the resort's restrooms so workers could replace it with a new, bigger and better trail to the Big Surf Company tents. The detour took more time than I anticipated, causing me to drive around to the other side of the complex through a large traffic circle and into the parking lot, after I changed my clothes in the hotel.

Rob was in an exceptionally bad mood when I arrived late for my surfing lessons. A busload of tourists had showed up wanting surf lessons on the spot. All the other companies had booked up in advance, and Rob had the opportunity to cash in.

My tardiness cost him a few bills. Big bills.

I tried to make it up to him by working my butt off for the next several hours, which actually helped me focus on something other than the mystical vibes threatening my sanity. Thankfully, we had more customers than we'd seen all last week, possibly the last month. Some of the tourists took a break, and then actually came back for a second lesson. All in all, it was a pretty busy, yet uneventful afternoon teaching honeymooners, some guys looking to get laid by the surfing chick, (I always scoped out a group of babes on the beach before each class and point the players in their direction, whether they scored or not was totally up to them), and a couple of big families who fought, laughed, and competed for the best ride. The best surfer of the day? A little blonde ten-year-old cutie from Wisconsin. The girl had moves.

After putting up the last board in the shed, I felt a little better. Tattoos be damned. And I decided my indecision about the two men in my life wasn't that different than other women my age. I dropped the despair. Dropped the deprecation. Dropped the despera... forget it. I dropped the baggage and decided to go on with life.

I was done bouncing back and forth. Ping...pong...ping...pong. I wasn't desperate. Not about Makaio. Not about Pai. I had kicked ass on the job (I should clarify, surf instructor job). I didn't know what type of crap I was currently working on with Pai, but it was new and different, so who cared.

I clicked the lock on the metal shed and turned around to say good-bye to Rob. I spotted him standing near a picnic table, talking to a tourist dressed in a Hawaiian print t-shirt and shorts, and I smiled. Hopefully tomorrow's schedule was getting busier by the minute.

I closed the distance between us, waving to the competition from *Big Surf* who were leaving for the day, and suddenly heard the desperation in the man's voice as he spoke to Rob.

"I'm your brother. I need your help this time." His emphasis on need reached the desperation level.

Rob spotted me and something flickered in his eyes. He smiled and it was gone. "Mal, I'd like you to meet my brother, Dave."

Rob's brother turned around and it was like seeing double, except Dave had hair on his face and his head. A floral t-shirt hid his back, so I reserved judgment about his need for a shave.

"You're the guy responsible for my days off?" I smiled and reached out to shake his hand. "*Mahalo*."

Dave tentatively took mine with a sweaty palm, and glanced around the area. "No problem."

I looked down and noticed the tattoo on his forearm as I pulled my hand back and discreetly wiped it on my shorts. "Is that the same tattoo Rob has?"

Dave brushed his arm, like maybe he could wipe if off and looked at his brother's red lizard. He laughed.

"At one time, they were the same. Rob's has expanded a little bit."

Rob patted his tummy. "Mine has grown past puberty."

We laughed and I asked, "Did you get them at the same time?"

"Right after high school. We went to a kahuna in Waikiki who insisted mine belonged on my stomach since I was older and wiser." His brother scoffed and Rob's smile grew. "He said Dave's belonged on his arm, he was doomed to be my helping hand." He shrugged his shoulders and his lizard jiggled.

"Can you make your lizard move like Rob's?" I asked Dave.

He lifted his arm and twisted his wrist around in a circular motion. The tail and tongue of Dave's geometric lizard wiggled eerily.

Leave now! Peter returned inside my head.

Distracted, I looked around. The beach had emptied, trash cans were full, sea gulls walked around looking for scraps left behind in the scattered footprints. "That's pretty cool, Daven. I mean…" I met his eyes. "Dave."

The deep brown eyes of the man with brown hair and a goatee searched my face. A red lizard wrapped around his arm. My knees suddenly felt as wobbly as if I'd just finished riding one of the three mile-long waves deep at sea.

"Ah, listen, I gotta get going." I turned toward the lot, vacant now except for two vehicles. My scooter and a red Mustang. I looked back at my boss, who was more than a little bit confused by my behavior. Rob was looking at me as if a coconut had struck me senseless. I wished one had. Then I wouldn't have to worry about Daven Raines being Rob's brother. A brother who *needed* help. A brother who had already hired someone to kill me.

There was no way I was going to stick around with a killer and his brother, even if I had worked for Rob for the past six years. Blood *ohana* was thicker than surf *ohana*.

"See you tomorrow!" I started jogging toward the parking lot, leaving Rob and Daven Raines standing together watching me. My boss looked totally confused, my would-be killer looked totally upset.

I jumped on the scooter, skipping the helmet attached to the rear of the seat, I hit the road, looking behind me the whole time. I didn't see Rob or Daven, but the driver's door to a red Mustang that looked exactly like the john's car I'd seen outside *The Garden of the Gods* with Windy, slammed closed in the parking lot.

Shit, just another confirmation that I was in deep trouble.

346

I cranked the throttle and went around the traffic circle, leaning into the curve. One look at my speedometer sent my heart into palpitations. Thirty-five mph was not exactly a speed that could lose a Mustang. I looked back.

The Mustang was exiting the parking lot. Panicked, I quickly turned off the circle and headed up the coast, hoping to get lost in the condos before he could catch up. I glanced in the side mirror, but didn't see anyone behind me.

I looked down at the speedometer. Thirty-two mph. I cranked the throttle harder and looked down at the speedometer. Thirty mph.

WTH?

I cranked it harder, hurting my hand and stressing the rubber grip on the handle. Twenty-eight mph.

Shit! I looked in the mirror, a red Mustang was making the turn at the circle. The speedometer now read, twenty-six mph.

My heart fell to my toes. The scooter needed to be charged.

I did the only thing I could. I turned into the parking lot of Spouting Horn, praying the vendors were still there.

One car graced the lot. Stand after stand was closed, the metal doors pulled tight and locked. The place was deserted.

Hua.

I drove my scooter in between the small wooden buildings and laid it down. With fumbling fingers, I unlocked the seat and pulled out my phone. Five percent battery left on the screen.

Enough to call the police. I dialed 911 as the mustang pulled into the lot. I ran for the forbidden path blocked by a chain-link fence and a yellow hazard sign stating, '*Keep Out, Danger Beyond This Point.*' I couldn't help but think the danger on this side of the fence was currently higher than hazards I'd face on the rocks.

The operator answered as I topped the fence and scratched my leg on the wire.

"*Hua!*"

I landed on my feet on the other side. Thankful for the barrier, but totally aware it wouldn't stop a man with a gun — just slow down an overweight guy with a knife.

"Ah…what's your emergency?" She asked.

I've been walking down this path my entire life and I still experience the exhilaration of danger, now cranked up by the crazy man following me. Shrubs, immune to the salt of the ocean spray, reached out past the trees. At the edge of the bushes, where the sand was still prevalent, I slipped down the side of the lava shelf to hide.

"I'm being chased by a killer!" I breathed into the phone, making my way down the path to hide behind the rocks closer to the water's edge.

The tide was high, creating spectacular views with the setting sun. Surely, the tourists would begin to show up to watch the display. I couldn't imagine being in a better spot.

I could imagine nicer company, but not a better location.

"Who's chasing you?" She asked.

"It's Daven Raines. The police are looking for him."

I was vaguely aware of the clicking of her keyboard while I slipped on the moss-laden rocks under my feet.

"What's your location?"

"Right now, I'm at Spouting Horn, down on the rocks." I slid and smacked my knee against the rough lava. "Shit."

"Your name?"

"Malia Fern. John Kumu's baby sister." I wasn't sure why I identified myself as his baby sister, maybe something to do with my need for him to hurry up and save me from the big, bad bully on the playground like he used to when we were a kids.

The chain-link fence rattled behind me.

"Can you make it quick—" I looked at the darkened screen. Dead.

Crap.

Beautiful crystal clear pools of water glistened on the rocks. A hauntingly prophetic and painful moan echoed through the caves below as pressure built forcing the water upward. The *puhi* — blowhole — exploded with a powerful stream of water spraying through the air. A visual thing of beauty, the shelf hung out over the ocean with one giant hole in its midst. If you happen to get washed off, or sucked down, the chances of survival were next to nil.

My heart skittered with the sound of a rock tumbling behind me. Rocks don't tumble on their own. Not on this path. They tumble with the fall of someone's feet. I turned around hoping to see a tourist. Praying it wasn't Daven Raines.

The man with the red lizard tattoo stood behind me wielding a knife, but it wasn't Daven Raines. It was my boss, Rob.

My fear was replaced with disbelief. Until a sad smile spread across his face and the fear returned with a vengeance. It was possible for me to escape Daven Raines, but it wasn't possible for me to get away from the man who taught me how to survive on these very rocks. There was no route for me to escape, unless I took the lava shelf that I was too smart to venture on. The shelf where too many uninformed or just plain stupid people died.

"That was your Mustang?" I asked, dumbfounded.

He shrugged and smiled. "Yeah, it's pretty hot, huh?"

"But I've never seen you drive it." I argued.

"It's not exactly like I could take you for a ride in it. You of all people would know I didn't have the money for it."

"But ..." My hands displayed my confusion, waving around in front of me, trying to grasp the meaning of it all. "... why?" I asked.

Rob shrugged again, this time, however, his lizard appeared ready to pounce. "You were just in the wrong place at the wrong time, Mal."

"But I don't understand. You have different last names," I insisted. I had known this man for six years, had worked side-by-side with him. Laughed with him, had my first beer under his supervision, and leaned on him like an older brother who didn't like to yank my chain. He had never shown a mean bone in his body, except maybe when we laughed at our customers behind their backs. But I got just as much joy out of the know-it-all from Utah's dry heaves as Rob had. That didn't make me a killer.

"Rob Aaron is a fictional name I took for business purposes. The double 'A' got us listed first in the phone book, and if tourists wanted to confuse us for a famous surfer's company, who was I to stop them?"

I had to admit, I'd heard Rob use his last name and hint that he was related, but it still caught me off-guard. I really believed Aaron was his last name.

"You don't have to protect your brother," I insisted.

Rob shook his head. "I'm not." His smile increased as he took a step forward and I scooted down the shelf. He laughed. "He actually tried to stop me from coming after you, but when you figured out who he was, I couldn't let you go to the police. Not yet, not until we worked out how to get him out of the mess you created."

Still confused, I asked, "But, why?" That seemed to be the only question my amateur detective brain could spit out.

He laughed again, almost as if he saw humor in my stupidity. It wasn't a laugh I wanted to join. I did anyway, hoping to remind him of what we had together. He immediately stopped and took a step toward me with his stainless steel knife pointed at my chest.

KYM ROBERTS

I countered with a few steps backward toward the shelf. My mouth dried. My laugh disappeared in the hiss of Spouting Horn and the '*oooh's* of a few people who'd arrived at the visitor's center above. Their voices blowing in the breeze. (Now they show up.)

Rob glanced in their direction. "That's far enough, Mal."

"You owe me an answer." I insisted.

"Fine. The truth is *Aaron's Surf Zone* was moving to *The Garden of the Gods*, but then your brother found the *Heiau* and insisted it be preserved, which moved the spa to *our* location on the beach." He pointed the knife at his chest and mine, as if we were a team or something.

"There was no more room for us. Unless the spa went back to its original location, we weren't going anywhere. The only way to ensure *Aaron's Surf Zone* got a new home was for Peter Johnson to be out of the picture. My brother didn't care whether the *Heiau* stayed or went, but he wasn't going to piss off his bank roll either, so he went with Johnson's plan. With Peter Johnson out of the way, Daven would have put us back in, until you insisted on getting in the middle of it." He shook his head as if he just couldn't believe I screwed everything up.

It didn't make any sense. This man could not be a cold-blooded killer. It wasn't possible. "But Daven moved the spa on the plans before Peter even got involved," I reasoned.

Rob stopped, his brow pinching in confusion. "Peter Johnson bumped the *Heiau* to the beach, not Daven."

He didn't know. Rob didn't know his own brother was responsible for *Aaron's Surf Zone* losing its spot at *The Garden of the Gods*. I shook my head, an over-whelming pity filling my gut. Rob had done horrible things for all the wrong reasons. His brother had lied and blamed Peter for taking *Aaron's Surf Zone* out of the plans when he'd been responsible all along.

I told him the truth, knowing it would break his heart, but hopefully stop his desire to kill me. "Kionni told me that Daven changed the plans before Peter even got involved."

Rob's face dropped. It lost all animation, all life. His eyes turned dark, like the last bit of his soul escaped into the depths of the lava tunnels below.

If he wasn't holding a knife, I might have thought he regretted what he was doing, but with the big military blade pointed in my direction, I had no doubt what he was planning. His hand tightened around the handle.

"You're lying."

I put all the conviction I had behind my words, even if I was guessing at part of it. "No, I'm not. I think that's why Dave offered to help us with our schedule and teach some of our classes. He felt guilty about pushing you out of the plans."

Rob's lips thinned, anger rolling off his shoulders. "Apparently loyalty doesn't even extend to *ohana* anymore."

I wanted to scream at him that I'd stood by his side. Through the good and the bad, I'd stayed. He read my thoughts.

"Even you were ready to abandon me. You've taken on new jobs; it was only a matter of time before you left altogether." His voice lost all anger. There was nothing left of the Rob I knew. The shell of a cold, calculating man bent on my destruction stepped in my direction.

"I should have cut your heart out the night you screamed at *The Garden of the Gods*."

My hand rose to my chest. Covered my heart to keep it where it belonged. I tried to speak but the words stalled in my mouth.

Rob was there the night I thought Windy beheaded the guard. The red Mustang with Windy, the car I heard at the gate — it was the same car with Rob behind the wheel?

Stalling for time and trying to keep him talking, I asked, "What were you doing there that night?"

He sneered. The lizard on his stomach move, stalking me. Its bladed tongue slithered out to reach for me, waiting for the perfect moment to strike. I didn't think he'd answer.

Rob 'Aaron' Raines, however, was a cliché. Like all the bad guys in the movies, he wanted to brag. Confess. Blame all his mistakes on everyone else. The perfect crime-gone-bad wasn't his fault.

"I told Windy to distract the guard. We were going to burn the *Heiau* down and get rid of it once and for all. You ruined it."

Rob took a long jump and jabbed at my chest, the knife came desperately close as I sucked in my stomach and did my own backwards leap. I stumbled and almost lost my footing. My misstep created a broad smile across Rob's face.

By now, we were well within view of the people gathering to watch the spectacle of Spouting Horn at sunset. They just needed to look a little to the left.

Please. Look to the left.

I found my voice. Breathless and airy, he strained to hear me over the pounding of the surf. "Why did you try to kill Peter's wife?" I asked in between the crashing waves.

"Apparently, your talk with Mrs. Johnson made her want to take a role in the venture after all. She called my brother immediately after you left, saying she didn't want to sell and they should meet to discuss how to proceed. Again, you messed up my plans and I decided enough was enough. Everyone needed to go, so I called MD and he was going to take care of you and Mrs. Johnson."

"You were the one ordering all of the murders?" Despite it coming from his mouth, I still had a hard time believing it. It wasn't Daven Raines ordering MD to kill people, it had been Rob Raines.

Rob laughed. "You really are a funny girl. I'm going to miss you."

Help wasn't coming. I could feel the surface of the lava change the farther we moved along the shelf. Flatter. Mossier. Wet. We were now in the fatally slippery area.

Hua.

I tried to negotiate. "Rob, you don't have to do this. We can find another place."

"My brother took off running when you headed for the parking lot. Now, I have no doubt that he's going to go to the cops and tell them I stole from his accounts, that I made this mess." He laughed. An evil sound I'd never heard before and I wondered how I could misjudge someone for so long. "I guess I've been blaming the wrong people all along. I should have looked a little closer to home." His eyes lost focus for a moment as he gazed out to the ocean.

I took a tentative step toward the tourists above.

His eyes shifted back. "I can't let you go."

"But there are too many witnesses, you can't get away with this." I insisted, raising my hands in complete surrender.

Rob was no longer laughing, he spit venom and hate toward me. "You were going to leave me, and then your snooping around screwed everything up."

"I was just trying to make some money on the side," I tried to explain, but then I realized how much I sounded like the killer in front of me.

Rob lunged for me and slipped at the same time. The blade struck the backside of my forearm. The arm I'd raised in submission.

Asshole.

I sucked in air and pulled my arm toward my chest, covering the wound with my hand. Blood oozed through my fingers. I couldn't feel the pain, but the liquid warmth was enough warning. Enough to signal I couldn't stay this close to Rob and I needed to make a run for it—across the lava shelf covered with green, slippery moss.

Instantly, I thought about running to the crowd, but then nixed it. The hill would slow me down and he'd catch me from behind. I ran for the blowhole. *Puhi* was the most dangerous spot to go. I hoped Rob wouldn't follow, or would be washed out to sea as waves crashed around us.

He followed and the water tackled my ankles sending my heart rate soaring. The force swept my feet toward shore, wiping them out from beneath me. I slammed into the rock and felt every point of contact. Every spot that I knew would really hurt later…if I survived. I grabbed for anything but only came up with handfuls of loose lava rocks. The receding flow sucked my feet past my body toward the edge of the shelf. The edge of my life.

I saw the end. Felt the waves pulling me over and knew if I ended up under the shelf, I'd never make it out.

Frantic, I looked up, hoping to see…something. Anything. Anyone. One last grasp to end the finality. A grasp for life.

He's here. Peter whispered in my head.

The water disappeared around me. The lava rock bit into my skin. Thankfully, I stopped my wild ride with my feet still on solid ground. I didn't wait for the next wave. Scrambling up, I clawed my way from the edge of my existence. An anxious look toward Rob told me his jog in the park had been almost as difficult as mine. He pulled himself up off the ground and grabbed for his knife that was lodged in the rocks.

I didn't wait for him to catch up. I took off for the lava tube, not sure, where my plan was going from there. One step at a time. One wave at a time. One battle at a time.

Finally, I reached *Puhi*. The ground shook around the hole in the lava shelf and rumbled in anger. Screamed at me for daring to step on sacred ground. I ran past and asked for forgiveness. Water struck my back like a fire hose knocking me down. Face down in a pool of water, the receding force began pulling me toward the lava tube. I sucked in salty liquid as I screamed. Sputtering, I inhaled more.

Once again, I dangled on the rim and the water released its grip. I coughed and hacked. Spewed spit, snot and salt water from my nose and mouth. On my knees, I fought for strength. Felt *Puhi's* anger building beneath me as Rob reached for me from the other side of the hole. He looked almost as bad as I felt.

I crawled away from the lip with Rob stalking me, seeing the pot of gold at the end of his rainbow. He was determined to spill my blood. He lunged and grabbed my hair, pulled my head back for my final breath. I had no weapon this time. This was it.

Puhi bellowed in outrage and struck Rob with such force that he slammed into me. His knife flew through the air. I last saw it bouncing across the shelf, tumbling with the rocks as a wave broke the surface. It was no longer a threat, but Rob and the surf were. We struggled with each other and the back pull of the retreating water. Rob slipped down my body. I kicked at his hands that were clawing my legs.

His grabbing changed. No longer assaultive, but desperately clinging to my legs. I looked over my shoulder and screamed with fear. Rob hung at the precipice of *Puhi*, struggling to stop the suction. I kicked at him, and clawed at the ground, my own desperation reaching a new height, if that was even possible at this point.

Rob went over the edge, his forearm the only thing visible as his hand clasped to my ankle. I was losing. Rob was going and he was taking me with him.

A hand locked onto my elbow. I grasped at it. My fingers wrapping around the muscular forearm, and I looked up into a stranger's eyes. A stranger I knew.

The lizard lost its hold. Disappeared. *Puhi* hissed with satisfaction as Rob disappeared.

You're safe. Peter's voice sounded almost as relieved as I felt.

My savior quickly pulled me to my feet, his lean body manipulating mine with ease as he scooped me up and carried me across the shelf, away from death. Too soon we were approaching the Visitor's Center with people whispering and pointing camera phones in our faces. The entire time, he cradled me in his arms, protecting me from everything and everyone.

Spouting Horn had been the backdrop for my fight against nature. Fight against Rob. Fight against evil. And I'd won. Thanks to *Puhi* and the man who was carrying me.

Phones followed our trek to a bench, where he sat down with me held tightly in his arms. I knew the videos would go viral, but I was too exhausted to care. Sirens blared. Blue and red lights swirled around the parking lot, but all of it was lost to me. It was time to sleep. I looked up in his eyes. His obsidian eyes with flecks of molten lava.

Thank you, Liko.

I think I shocked him. I'm not sure. Everything after that was gone. Gone to the dark mystical place in the recesses of my mind where Peter Johnson was smiling as he watched his wife sing to their baby boy.

CHAPTER THIRTY-TWO

I woke up in the hospital with John, Pai and Makaio pow-wowing on the other side of the room. John looked like he was trying to establish dominance over the other two. Growling. Barking orders. Pai may as well have been pissing all over my room, marking his territory. And Makaio, well, he just looked like dog shit. His face pale, he struggled not to show weakness. The leader of the pack would not back down.

I'm not a conspiracy theorist. But those three? Together? Meant nothing but trouble for me.

Pai turned around and smiled. "*Aloha*, Baby Doll."

Leave it to Pai to read my thoughts. Marking me.

Don't piss on me, Pai.

His smile brightened.

John started snapping orders. "I need to talk to Malia. Alone. This is official police business."

It went on deaf ears. Pai was already a step ahead of him. Somehow, so was Makaio. Pai made it to my left side and Makaio shuffled to my right, both looking down at me, and as usual, I was trapped between the two of them, being pulled in their tug-of-war contest. But this time I was the rope that was about to snap in the middle and hurt the men on both ends.

"Where's Liko?" I asked.

That shut 'em up. They all looked at me expectantly. Finally, John broke the silence. He had the least to lose, and the most to gain.

"Who's Liko?"

"The guy who saved me from being sucked down *Puhi.*"

It was Pai's turn to question my story, citing Hawaiian history like none of the rest of us could. "Liko. As in the guy who led *Mo'o,* the lizard under the lava shelf where the lizard got stuck in Spouting Horn while Liko escaped through the top? The Liko who trapped *Mo'o* forever to hiss and moan in hunger and pain." One brow rose in humor, "That Liko?"

I couldn't help my sarcasm. "You of all people should not question who pulled me out."

"Our grandmother was there." Makaio's voice was soft. Almost defeated. "She said Liko disappeared into the crowd when the ambulance arrived and they put you on a gurney."

He searched my eyes, asking without voicing. He knew there was someone else making this triangle between the three of us even bigger. The rope he pulled with Pai was broken; the ends snapped everyone with the tension. His pain evident, I tried to reach out to him and explain, but I couldn't.

I needed to find Liko.

He nodded his understanding. Accepted what fate had written and left unfinished. For him. For Pai. For Liko. And for me. We had to wait, ride the wave into the curl, through the turbulent tunnel and let the lip spit us out on the other side. Once we were clear of all the dangers and uncertainty, we could throw our hands in the air in triumph.

Pai's smile faded as well. I could sense his confusion. He didn't understand how Makaio had known before him. That was the rope snapping at his end. He accepted fate graciously. His smile still present, just a little less bright.

"Did you find my scooter?" I asked.

John sensed his control returning and jumped on it. Opening the closet, he pulled my purse from the interior. "A uniform found it in the middle of the vendor booths. If you boys will excuse us, I need to talk to Malia."

Makaio nodded and kissed a part of my face not scraped up from my fight with Rob. He left the room without a backward glance, his shoulders a little stiff, but strong.

I turned to Pai. "Did you get the pictures?"

"What pictures?" John didn't like being left in the dark.

363

"This is for our business venture. It has nothing to do with your investigation, John." I looked at Pai, waiting for a response.

I got them.

It was my turn to experience the tightening in my chest. The feeling of betrayal. He reached into his pants pocket and pulled out an SD card. I accepted the card with the pictures of Windy's naked body and curled it in the palm of my hand.

I couldn't hear his apology, I only felt it. Pai wasn't letting me inside his head. No doubt, afraid I would see what happened from his perspective, and since I really didn't want to see it, I appreciated him keeping the wall in place.

He pulled my hand to his mouth and kissed it, and then left without a word.

I leaned back, closed my eyes and relaxed. Let John have the driver's seat he wanted so badly. Somehow, I think he was disappointed that he'd won that easily. He'd always been a sucker for a competition. But he sat down, grabbed my hand and squeezed it before pulling out his recorder to take my statement.

He never got started. The door burst open. My mom, with the rest of the family in tow, spilled into the room, everyone talking at once. Kisses rained on my cheeks, bringing tears to my eyes.

For a moment on that lava rock, I thought I'd never see them again.

My dad clasped my fingers, and I held back the wince of pain. It was too good, just to feel. To be alive.

My two younger brothers, Kionni and Kale were actually grabbing my feet through the blankets. I'm pretty sure Kionni wiped a tear off his cheek, but I wouldn't use it against him.

John received a stern look from the real matriarch, who was in turn supported by my father, when John tried to protest about needing my statement. Police business could wait for family business. There was nothing better than *ohana* to cure the soul.

CHAPTER
THIRTY-THREE

It's been over six weeks since I was released from the hospital. The first time I looked in a mirror, I wanted to cry. I didn't think vanity was an issue for me, but I'd never experienced cuts all over my body, making me look more like a patchwork quilt than an actual person. My injuries were healing, and most of the cuts would mend without any long term scarring. A small cut on the bridge of my nose and the larger one on my arm were the exceptions. Rob's knife attack required twenty-seven stitches in all. It still amazed me that I didn't feel pain when he cut me. But I can assure you, since then I've done plenty of bitching about how much it hurt.

My mom insisted I stay with them when I was released from the hospital. To be honest, there wasn't anywhere else I'd rather be. Kionni and Kale cleaned my apartment and fixed the door. John retrieved my scooter from police headquarters before it went to the impound lot. My brothers are pretty cool, for brothers.

Rob's body was never recovered. At first, I feared he somehow got out alive, and he was out there somewhere watching and waiting for the perfect moment to strike. Then I thought about the lizard and Liko, and I knew there was no way in hell he survived. His body was trapped like *Mo'o* to hiss and moan and complain for eternity.

Daven Raines made a full confession. He suspected his brother was taking funds from his business accounts and tried to straighten him out with a spot for *Aaron's Surf Zone* at *The Garden of Gods*. However, when he continued to steal from him, Daven changed the plans and nixed the booth. He wanted to avoid a confrontation with Rob, so he blamed Peter for the design changes and was relieved when Peter wanted to hire security. He suspected Rob was also stealing from the site and that he was behind most if not all the vandalism they experienced. Like I suspected, Daven started working at *Aaron's Surf Zone* to relieve some of his guilt and help Rob get the business back on track, but Rob continued to squander money he didn't have on fast living and a fancy car. His love for the beach had nothing to do with why he lived in a tent.

When Peter disappeared, Daven lied to Misty because he was afraid his brother had something to do with his partner's disappearance. His worst fears came true.

Daven faced charges for conspiracy to commit murder after the fact. It turned out Daven wasn't the Raines who hired Mutt or MD. That had been Rob Raines, MD's buddy. Both Raines brothers who wore the mark of royalty on their bodies, turned out to be royal assholes. Rob, the bigger of the two.

Jade and Joe came by my parent's house at my request and I gave the SD card to Jade without viewing it. Her mom would study the tattoos and try to find a way to block the affects to protect other Menehune and their children from the Menehune curse. In the meantime, Joe was going to avoid the convenience store where Windy worked.

As hard as he tried, John couldn't get Windy charged. The prosecutor saw her as a victim since MD had threatened her. His real name was Michael Dickens, but he'd always be Mad Dog to me.

Mutt, or if his legal name means anything to you — Cory Bollinger — was charged with aggravated assault and conspiracy to commit murder. I don't know if it will stick, but I plan to see it through. I don't care if he does have an addiction. Something is wrong when you allow your inner demons to control your mind and body.

I haven't seen hide nor hair of Liko since the day he saved my life. That day, my vision of him cleared beyond the haze of dope and cowardice he tried to make everyone see. The man who pretended to be a dope smokin' surfer, too chicken to catch the big waves, was changed forever in my eyes. I know Moa's real name and I know his real character. Liko's out there. I can feel him. It's only a matter of time before our paths cross. The fates have destined it to happen, so it will.

Misty Johnson decided to stay on Kaua'i with her son. She planned to finish the condos and move forward with the dream she created with her husband. I haven't seen or heard Peter since that day at Spouting Horn. I'm pretty sure he's finally at peace.

Pai went back to the Big Island on business. The day I was released from the hospital, I got a text: *'Leaving for the Big Island. Will be in touch soon. A hui hou Ki`i pēpē.'*

I haven't talked to him since he left my hospital room. His kiss still lingers on my hand. I really think his leaving had more to do with Liko and the pictures of Windy, than with work.

When I finally returned to my apartment, I had a new sofa sleeper that had an extra soft mattress and my bright orange bobble head helmet was sitting on my table. A tiara permanently attached to the top with 'Princess' painted on the back. A note lay underneath:

Stay safe, Baby Doll.
You will always be my Princess.
Love, Pai

I cried when I read it and tucked it away in my box of keepsakes, along with my treasured doll from my childhood. Always there, never forgotten.

Pearl and I have made peace. Personally, I think she's found herself another man, which was fine by me. Her insurance company came through with the check for my car. I miss my little MINI Cooper, although it surprises me to say that I enjoy riding the scooter quite a bit. Banking the cash for now, I'm taking my time with my decision on a new vehicle. The orange beast is a chapter of my life. A chapter that's incomplete. With my princess helmet, I get quite a few looks and comments from the tourists. I guess now I'm the spot of humor in their day, instead of vice versa.

Last but not least, Makaio. He's called every day since I was released from the hospital. Most of our conversations are short and sweet. A few have gone on into the wee hours of the night.

Which brings me to today. It's midnight, Makaio's first night back at work. Sitting at my favorite table, I dialed his cell phone. He answered on the second ring. His voice was melodious, and sounding sexy as hell in his attempt to keep the conversation private. "Hey. I was wondering when I'd hear from you."

I could hear the police radio in the background and his new partner singing. Biagio had nothing on Makaio.

"Is he singing a lullaby?"

"Yeah, I was about to fall asleep…"

To wipe any thought of sleep from his mind, my next comment involved the promise of sex.

Nothing keeps a man more awake and alert than the thought of sex. My words did not promise orgasm, my tone did. It all but caressed his naked body.

"I'd like you to *cum* see me. I have *something* for you," I purred.

"Uhhh..." he cleared his throat. "*We'd* love to meet you. *We* were about to stop at Pearl's for a restroom break."

"I guess I better cover my pasties. They're coconut tassels. Do you want to meet me in the men's restroom?"

I could hear the dryness in his throat.

"Ta...Hassle?"

The clearing of his throat made me smile.

"No, it's not a hassle. I'll see you in a few minutes. *A hui hou.*" He didn't wait for me to respond. He just hung up.

A wicked smile spread across my face. Not everything in life was gloom and doom. I actually enjoyed being the instigator of Makaio's discomfort. I gloried in my depravity. Being the tease was fun.

Makaio and Pai had been riding my libido like a zip-line through Waimea Canyon. Non-stop anxiety, anticipation and appetite for more. They built it up higher and higher to the point my body dangled over the precipice for what seemed an eternity, but they never gave me the frickin' ride.

The distance between us the last couple weeks did nothing to stop my body's expectations. My body was ready and primed, and I wobbled on the brink of a sexual nervous breakdown. So yeah, now that Makaio was feeling a little bit of tension…on his *not so short leg*…things were looking up.

Just ask Makaio.

And once again, I find myself sitting in the local pastry shop, waiting for a cop to pee.

Other books available now by Kym Roberts:

Dead Man's Carve

(A Tickled to Death Mystery)

Rilee Dust isn't your typical wood carver, she's young and making a go of it in the small village of Tickle Creek, Oregon. She's also the only one in town who isn't determined to get rid of her strip club neighbor. Everyone else, however, is ready to evict the *Girls, Girls, Girls*.

When a dog adopts her and turns her life upside down, Rilee's not so sure it's a good thing. Especially when he leads her to a moose, a man and a dead body. Because the moose kicked her butt, the man saved her life and the dead body is one of her customers.

Now Rilee's smack dab in the middle of all the small town politics with a killer on the loose who has an ax to grind. And Rilee just may be the next victim to have her name carved in stone.

Handled By Officer

(Women Behind the Badge #1)

Recruit officer Kiley Gibbons has walked in her twin's shadow her entire life—and is the exact opposite of her outgoing, athletic sister. But that's exactly why she's the one woman who caught Officer Walt Raynham's eye.

Officer Raynham is everything Kiley needs, too bad he's wearing the uniform of her boss. But when her friend's death leaves Kiley with two children to raise and a custody battle she just might lose, there's only man strong enough to step in and fill the role of her fiancé, and Kiley's engagement of convenience to Walt could turn into an unstoppable force for happily ever-after...until a killer has another idea that may cost them everything they didn't want.

About the Author

Three career paths resonated for Kym during her early childhood: a detective, an investigative reporter, and...a nun. Being a nun, however, dropped by the wayside when she became aware of boys—they were the spice of life she couldn't deny.

In high school her path was forged when she took her first job at a dry cleaners and met every cop in town, especially the lone female police officer in patrol. From that point on there was no stopping Kym's pursuit of a career in law enforcement—even if she had to duct tape rolls of coins to her waist to meet the weight requirements to be hired.

Kym followed her dream and became a detective that fulfilled her desire to be an investigative reporter, with one extra perk—a badge. Promoted to sergeant Kym spent the majority of her career in SVU. She retired from the job reluctantly when her husband drug her kicking and screaming to another state, but writing continued to call her name, at least in her head.

If you'd like to visit her on the web, she can be found at www.kymroberts.com or on Facebook or Twitter as kymroberts911.

Author's Note

I hope you enjoyed **_Dead On Arrival_**. The fascinating culture and people of Hawai'i inspired the story. Most of Hawaiian history has been passed down from generation to generation through the _lālā ola_ or the 'living branch' in the art of storytelling, dance and art. And although much of it has been lost, Hawai'i's past is as important to its people, as the American Revolution is to most Americans. They have their own language that is beautiful to listen to, and wondrous to learn.

The state's complex history has made Hawai'i a unique and vital part in the variety of cultures we celebrate in The United States. It is important that we respect and preserve the foundation of its ancestry and truly appreciate the _Aloha Spirit_. For more information about the Hawaiian Culture, please visit:

Skin Stories: The Art and Culture of the Polynesian Tattoo

http://www.pbs.org/skinstories/culture/index.html

The Ka'iwakīloumoku Hawaiian Cultural Center

http://kaiwakiloumoku.ksbe.edu/

The Hawaiian Cultural Center

http://hawaiianculturalcenter.org/

The Polynesian Cultural Center

http://polynesianculturalcenter.com/new/?gclid=CO-Dw-eGwr0CFWEV7Aod1GIAng#.UzwkDNGPLIU

*Heiau*s are the ancient shrines or temples of the Hawaiian people and are important to the history of the islands. If you'd like to learn more about them, please visit:

The Property Prof Blog

http://lawprofessors.typepad.com/property/2006/04/pana_oahu_sacre_1.html

Or read:

Jan Becket and Joseph Singer's *Pana O'ahu: Sacred Stones, Sacred Land* (University of Hawaii Press, 1999).

Because the Malia Fern Mystery series is a pure work of fiction, I have taken countless liberties with Hawaiian mythology and locations on Kaua'i throughout the book. If you find part of the paranormal events particularly fascinating, please refer to a more factual account in Martha Beckwith's Hawaiian Mythology. Many of the tourist locations are real; their proximity to other places, however, have been skewed for story purposes.

Also during **D**ead **O**n **A**rrival, I briefly mentioned private investigators serving Temporary Restraining Orders, or TRO's in Chapter Eleven. This is done completely for the purpose of this story. Some states allow private process servers to serve orders of protection. However, in Hawai'i as of 2014, TRO's must be served by the police. For more information about TRO in the state of Hawai'i, please visit:

The Hawai'i State Judiciary

http://www.courts.state.hi.us/self-help/protective_orders/protective_orders.html

Nationwide victims may seek assistance at:
The National Domestic Violence Hotline
http://www.thehotline.org/
or Call The National Domestic Violence
Hotline
1-800-799- SAFE (7233) | 1-800-787-3224
(TTY)
Mahalo,
Kym Roberts